Love's Refining Fire

By Anne McDonald

Love's Refining Fire

By Anne McDonald

This book is set in Artifika and Arapey font.

Love's Refining Fire
Published by AJ Charleson Publishing LLC
Hayden, ID
ajcharlesonpublishing.com

Cover artwork by H. Johanne Flugel.

This is a work of fiction. All of the characters, organizations, and events portrayed in this novel are either products of the author's imagination or are used fictitiously.

ISBN 978-1-7323680-4-0

Scripture quotations taken from
THE HOLY BIBLE, NEW INTERNATIONAL VERSION® NIV®
Copyright © 1973, 1978, 1984 by International Bible Society®
Used by permission. All rights reserved worldwide.

Library of Congress Control Number: 2019952105

2019—Second Edition

To Donna Fletcher Crow
Thanks for sharing your wisdom and encouragement.

To Jason, Jane, Mama Warren, and Becky Wagner
Thank you for believing in me, and helping with the edits.

To Summer and Carol
Thank you for serving as test readers, and for your insistence that I get this book republished.

And

To Johanne Flugel
for the lovely autumn painting
that graces the cover of my book.

Foreword

Love's Refining Fire is a well-developed story of romance, intrigue and inspiration that carries readers from one side of the nation to the other with a full cast of characters. Jennifer Warner is a strong, spunky heroine you'll enjoy rooting for through every step of her harrowing journey as she struggles to protect her daughter, overcome old griefs, and build a new life.

I am honored to accept Anne McDonald's dedication. This first novel sparks the beginning of a career that is sure to bring pleasure to many readers.

An accomplishment to be proud of, Anne. Best wishes with the publication!

Blessings,
Donna Fletcher Crow

Preface

Having lived cross-country on both coasts, I experienced many of the locations mentioned in the book first-hand. I have taken artistic liberties with various names, places and events. Northern Maine will always hold a special place in my heart.

Spirit, the dog in the story, was an actual retired K-9 military dog that I inherited some years back while stationed at Loring Air Force Base. I have incorporated as much of his personality and behavior as possible in this novel. He was indeed half wolf, half husky, and a real gentleman. I don't know that I will ever find another magnificent beastie that will match him.

Anne McDonald

Acknowledgments

The following people assisted me during my initial research for this book. Many thanks to:

Sgt. Dave Cuen, La Habra Police Department, La Habra, California

Deputy Terry Hart, Orange County Sheriff's Department, Orange County, California

Douglas McClure, Fire Investigator (ret.), Bureau of Fire Prevention, Long Beach, California

Heidi Drew, R.N.

Janice Allen, R.N.

Michael P. Kortan, Unit Chief, FBI National Press Office

Special Agent Suzy Balliere, FBI Tucson Office

"But he knows the way that I take; when he has tested me, I will come forth as gold." Job 23:10 NIV

"'For I know the plans I have for you,' declares the LORD, 'plans to prosper you and not to harm you, plans to give you hope and a future.'"
Jeremiah 29:11 NIV

Chapter 1

Exploding thunder shattered Jennifer Warner's already fragile confidence as she left the Long Beach Plaza. She stepped into the cool, wet morning air. Another eruption of thunder made her cringe.

"I don't need this." She glared at the dark sky as she spoke. "I've had enough problems for one day, thank you." The cold autumn cloudburst echoed painful memories of her husband's murder. He never got to meet his own daughter, nor see the new millennium. *If he had kept his promise, he'd still be alive.* "How I hate September!"

Jennifer's shaky hands dug deep into her thin coat pockets seeking warmth. She sidestepped the puddles on the pavement behind the mall and turned the corner. This week had gotten off to a rotten start. She'd left her purse at home, a questionable friend still had her car, and now she had no job.

It irked her that the company had gone ahead with the layoffs. The previous week, they had assured the workers their jobs were secure. Jennifer pulled the pink slip from her pocket and read it again. Her stomach knotted as she thought about job hunting.

She crumpled the slip and shoved it back into her pocket beside her severance check. With only a three-week financial cushion, how could she even afford to take Brianna to Knott's Berry Farm for her third birthday? She bit her lower lip as she mentally calculated the cost of that extravagance.

Jennifer hated to break her promise to Brianna. This was the first year the toddler could appreciate the amusement park rides. Still, jobs weren't easy to come by. She'd have to check the paper's Help Wanted section before heading to the unemployment office.

She crossed the street to the nearest newspaper stand and slipped in some coins. Jennifer pulled on the handle, reached in for a copy of the *Los Angeles Times,* and slipped it into the inner pocket of her coat.

A stiff cold breeze whipped her long auburn curls across her face. Her calf-length black skirt wrapped itself around the tops of her brown leather boots. She quickened her pace as rain pelted the sidewalk.

Jennifer wanted to kick herself for allowing Anton Carducci to borrow her car again. What did he need with her old station wagon when he owned a brand new Porsche? If it had so many mechanical difficulties, the dealership could have provided him with a rental car. Instead, he had borrowed hers and caused some kind of damage. She hoped it wasn't serious.

The more she thought about the situation, the more suspicious she became. Given his recent obsessive behavior, this was likely one more attempt to take control of her life. Well, his shenanigans needed to end. She refused to let anyone control her.

Initially, she had welcomed Anton's friendship this past spring. It had dispelled some of the deep loneliness that had gnawed at her heart since her husband's death three years before.

For the first five months, Anton made her feel special. She had to admit she enjoyed the admiring glances she received when they went to the ballet or out to dinner. He had even agreed to keep their relationship platonic.

But his promises, like his charm, had worn thin. He had become so unpredictable and possessive that he seemed determined to choke the very life out of her. She needed to make a clean break from him.

Raindrops splashed against her face. She clutched her coat around her and scolded herself for not remembering her umbrella. The Metro Blue Line train whizzed by. As she dashed down the street, a familiar awareness tingled up her spine. Doggone it, Anton had another private detective following her again.

Jennifer glanced over her shoulder, but saw only pedestrians jostling to get out of the rain. This was the last straw. When she discovered who he had hired to follow her this time, she'd give Anton something to worry about.

She hurried down the street, hoping to catch the next bus home. Impatience nagged at her as she waited for the traffic light to change. Massive lines of vehicles lumbered by. Her uneasiness remained.

When Jennifer finally stepped out into the street, the squeal of tires and a shout alerted her to danger. Horns blared as she jumped back onto the curb. A wall of water struck her. She glimpsed a blue sedan passing a mere hairbreadth away, careening the wrong way down the one-way street.

Jennifer stumbled backwards against someone and thudded onto the hard concrete. Horror gripped her. Had Anton resorted to attempted murder?

"Are you all right?" The deep masculine voice came from someone sitting beside her on the sidewalk.

Her heart pounded in her ears and her tailbone ached from the fall. Jennifer nodded and finally found her voice. "That was...way too close for me, but...I'm all right." She steadied her emotions and took a quick mental inventory before continuing. "I'm just wet, bruised, and a bit shaken up. I'm sorry I knocked you over. Are you all right?" She looked at the man in the adjoining puddle.

Deep blue eyes met her gaze. His dripping dark hair and well-trimmed beard framed a friendly, rugged face. Water drenched his gray suit, leather shoes, and unbuttoned blue overcoat. "A cold bath isn't my idea of a great way to start the week, but it beats getting hit by a car." He chuckled. "I have to admit, it's my most dramatic welcome to California, yet."

He struggled to his feet and offered his hand to Jennifer. His tall frame towered over her, and he seemed rather pleasant despite the circumstances. "Are you sure you have no injuries?"

"I'm sure," she told him, accepting his assistance. "I'll be fine once I get home." The man's demeanor surprised her. Anton had thrown tantrums for much less. Jennifer tried to rub mud from her waterlogged skirt, but merely smeared it further. Why did she feel like an absolute idiot in front of this man?

"I'm glad you're not hurt, Miss..." Bemusement covered his face. "Is it normal in this state for motorists to drive against traffic and use pedestrians as targets?"

Jennifer's mind replayed the near accident. Fear chilled her very bones, yet she kept her composure. "It hasn't been my experience, but then again, this is California. Anything's possible here." She regretted throwing away her chance to move back to New England.

The man gave her a warm smile. "Somebody's disenchanted with paradise. I sure hope things improve for you soon." His blue eyes scanned the area. "Could you point me in the general direction of the convention center and the Hyatt Regency? I took a walk this morning and lost my bearings."

She nodded and motioned to the end of the street. "Sure. See that large building there? That's the convention center. Behind it and to the right is the Hyatt."

"Thanks. I didn't recognize the center. My only view has been from the hotel." The stranger looked at his watch and grimaced. "I'd better head back to my room and change. I can't give my presentation looking like this."

Jennifer agreed. "You are a mess."

He laughed. "So are you."

Guilt hounded her. "I really am sorry."

"Don't be." The stranger insisted, opening his umbrella as raindrops fell sideways. "It wasn't your fault. Our collision just made my day more memorable. Let's cross together." He wiggled his thick, black eyebrows. "That way we can keep an eye out for crazy drivers and pedestrian hunters."

Jennifer forced a laugh as they crossed the street. A sudden gust of wind turned the man's umbrella inside out as a sheets of rain engulfed them. She yanked her dampened newspaper from her coat and held it over her head. "Do you want half of this?" she offered as he struggled to gain control of his umbrella. "It's better than nothing."

"Let's get inside, somewhere." He grabbed her elbow and guided her into a nearby restaurant. "There's no sense in drowning." He abandoned his dilapidated umbrella just inside the door and relieved her of the sodden paper, tossing it on the floor as well.

Water streamed from their clothes, forming puddles at their feet. "Want some coffee?" He led her to a booth. "I definitely need a cup."

"Sure." He seemed harmless enough. What could a cup of coffee hurt? Jennifer allowed him to take her drenched coat, and then slid into the seat. She watched the rain pound against the window as her thoughts wandered. *Father God, why does everything have to be so hard? When will I finally get a break?*

"Do you want leaded or unleaded?"

The question startled her. "Huh? Oh...leaded. Definitely, leaded."

A harried, middle-aged waitress arrived at the table. The stranger smiled and gave her their order. "By the way," he asked, "is there someplace to hang our coats?"

"I'll get you a chair. That's all we've got." The waitress snagged one from a nearby table, set it beside their booth, and then hurried off.

Three other pedestrians stumbled into the restaurant for shelter. Jennifer glanced at them and shivered in her wet clothes. What was she doing here? If Anton knew that she was with another man, he'd make a public scene.

She visually panned the restaurant for a sign of her shadow. No one seemed remotely interested in her. Yet, her uneasiness remained. Anton had previously hired two rank amateurs, whom she had easily spotted. Had he finally hired a professional? How would she spot him?

Jennifer wound a lock of hair around her finger, a nervous gesture that she had developed as a little girl. Oh, well. If her shadow was here, it'd be too late to dodge him. *I'll have it out with Anton, regardless. Might as well enjoy myself.*

Water dribbled onto her place mat. She used a napkin to dry the ends of her hair. "I wouldn't mind some good towels about now."

"How about a handkerchief or two?" The stranger hung Jennifer's coat on the empty chair backrest. He draped his coat over the seat. Even his gray suit jacket dripped with water.

"Anything would help at this point." To her surprise, he pulled a soggy white handkerchief from his right jacket sleeve.

"This won't be of any use." He reached into his left sleeve tried to pull out a duplicate handkerchief. "Good grief," he groaned. "Seems this one's a bit stuck. Do you mind giving me a hand?"

Jennifer reached up and tugged at the wet handkerchief. To her amazement, it glided out, followed by a long succession of different colored scarves.

"What in the world?" She continued pulling out the sodden scarves.

"There's got to be a dry one in there somewhere." He stared at the scarves, puzzled. "One thing's for sure, I've got to find a way to keep them dry after this."

The stranger helped Jennifer pull on the scarves until a mound of them rested on the corner of the table. With a final tug, two damp white handkerchiefs completed the pile. "These don't seem too bad." He untied them, handed them to Jennifer with a grin. and sat down.

"What are you, a magician?" Jennifer wiped her face with one of the handkerchiefs. Whatever his profession, he had her attention.

He took a furtive look around, and then leaned over, "Don't tell anyone, but I'm really a surgeon," he whispered.

"You're kidding. A surgeon?"

The stranger raised his right hand. "Honest. Magic's my sideline used for cheering up patients. You'd be surprised at how humor helps them heal faster."

"So, what are you here for, a magician's or a medical con—"

"Shhh! Not so loud. You'll blow my cover."

The waitress arrived with their order. As she set down their plates and poured their coffee, she eyed the heap of wet scarves with suspicion.

"They're harmless," the stranger explained. "They couldn't dance right now if they tried."

Jennifer's interest piqued. "Dance?"

He turned toward her. "Yeah, that's part of the act—dancing scarves. I haven't mastered that, yet, but give me time."

The waitress shook her head and laughed. "You'd have to get them dried before they show any signs of life. I'll get a plastic bag for your little friends." She set the coffee and cinnamon rolls on the table and headed back to the counter.

"I also like to try out magic on my colleagues. Helps them loosen up a bit." The stranger took a sip of coffee. "Doctors can get so morbid. I'm eager to try the rabbit trick one of these days, but I can't seem to get the right type of hat. There used to a magic shop at the mall up the street, but it's gone, now."

The waitress returned, handed him a clear plastic bag, and then hurried to the next two tables to pour coffee and take more orders.

"I've got to have the hat before I head back to Maine." He deftly stuffed the scarves into the bag. "You wouldn't know of any good magic stores, would you?"

"Sorry, not my line. There's some kind of magic castle around, but I know little about it. Now, if you asked me where to find the best stuffed animals, I could help you." Jennifer opened another container of cream and poured it into her coffee cup.

He selected a cinnamon roll. "Don't need stuffed animals, but thanks. Maybe I could try the phone book for that magic castle." He glanced at his watch, and then at the pounding rain. "I sure hope this lets up soon. The conference won't wait for my presentation. I'm sure you have plenty to do this morning, too."

Jennifer nodded, inwardly grimacing at the thought of traveling to the unemployment agency. She couldn't do anything about the weather, so she might as well relax.

As they ate, she deliberately steered the conversation away from herself. Jennifer learned the stranger practiced medicine in a small farming community near the Canadian border and that he had come to Long Beach for a medical conference.

He stirred sugar in his third cup of and then gave a slight shake of his head. "Where are my manners? I should introduce myself. I'm Dr. Nathan Pellitier. Perhaps you've heard my name somewhere before?"

Jennifer smiled sweetly. "Sorry, no."

He blinked as if confused by her denial. "Oh, well. No matter." He held up his right hand. "Now, don't tell me your name. I want to try another magic trick. You don't mind, do you? I'm good at this one."

"That depends. What is it?" She cut up another roll and took a bite. At least she wasn't bored.

"I study you for a moment then guess your name."

"This I've got to see."

Nathan held up his hand. "Okay. Now, sit still and don't make any faces at me. This takes deep concentration." He knit his brows together and stared at her, his merry blue eyes scanning her face.

Jennifer found it difficult to keep from laughing.

"Hold still," he scolded. "You'll throw me off if you make faces."

"Can I take another sip of my coffee first?"

He quirked his eyebrows. "Oh, all right. Just don't make me laugh; it'll mess up the trick."

"I'll behave."

"Now, let's see," he mumbled, "Lisa...naw. Mabel...heavens, no. Emerald green eyes...looks Irish so perhaps Shannon...no Gwendolyn... nope, Ashley...hmmm." He closed his eyes and tapped his forefinger against his pursed lips.

She dunked a piece of her roll in her coffee and took a bite. He didn't stand a chance.

"Jennifer!" he said at last, pointing at her. "Jennifer Lynn Warner!"

She nearly choked. Fitful coughs gripped her body. She grabbed for a glass of water. This had to be a set up.

"Are you all right?" He seemed concerned.

Tears streamed down her face as she continued coughing. She nodded and took a few sips of water. Finally, she caught her breath. "How—" Her eyes widened in understanding. How clueless could she be? No wonder she couldn't spot her tail. He sat right across from her.

Jennifer stood and threw the remainder of her water in Nathan's face. "You lout! I can't believe you'd be capable of stooping so low. Did you stage the bit with the car as well? You can tell Anton this is the last straw. If he comes anywhere near me or Brianna again, I'll ensure it's the very last thing he does." She grabbed her coat and dashed into the pouring rain.

Chapter 2

Jennifer ran blindly down the street, raindrops slapping her face. Her drenched coat offered no protection. How could she be so gullible? She'd actually believed his story about being a doctor. Flaming crimson swept across her cheeks. She mentally shook herself, determined to erase Nathan from her memory.

The rain had abated when she entered the bank on Ocean Boulevard, but her anger remained. Jennifer deposited her soggy check, bought another newspaper, and then boarded the next bus home just as the rain started again.

The bus crawled along the flooded streets. Finally, Jennifer disembarked a half a block away from her small duplex. She dashed through the sheets of rain, down the sidewalk to the front entrance, and then up the stairs.

When she opened the apartment door, the smell of hot chocolate chip cookies tickled her nose. Jennifer gave a contented sigh, heartened by her landlady's generosity. Over the past three years, Elyssa Baker had become her friend and surrogate mother.

"Hi, Mom, I'm home," Jennifer quipped, stepping into the tiled entryway. She closed the door and set the damp newspaper on the antique coat rack bench, a gift from her brother.

Elyssa emerged from the kitchen. "You're home awfully early. If you came after your purse, it's on the desk. Oh, before I forget, Margaret stopped by with the Sunday school materials. She appreciates you taking the preschool class while she's out of town."

"I hope she marked the lesson they're on." Jennifer leaned one hand against the wall and removed her boots. "Could you hand me an old newspaper, Mom? I don't want to get mud on the carpet."

The older woman wiped her hands on her bright yellow apron. She grabbed a paper out of the nearby magazine stand and spread it on the floor next to the coat rack. Wisps of graying brown hair escaped the severe knot at the back of Elyssa's head. Her warm brown eyes twinkled with laughter as she surveyed Jennifer's dripping form. "You're a sight to make the eyes sore, Jen. Did you do, walk through every puddle on the sidewalk, or did you wade through the gutters?"

Jennifer's lips curved into a smile. "Actually, a car gave me an unexpected mud bath, and then I got caught in a downpour." She emptied her pockets onto the coat rack seat. Her eyes scanned the room for her toddler. "Where's Brianna?" She peeled off her wet coat.

"In her room, holding a royal tea party for her zoo animals." Elyssa studied Jennifer and cocked an eyebrow. "I'd better get you a towel before you float away." She bustled down the hallway and returned with a large colorful beach towel.

Jennifer noticed the rows of cooling cookies occupying the breakfast bar. "I take it she cleaned out the cookie jar, again."

Elyssa wrapped the towel around Jennifer's shoulders. "It was either that, or give in to her demands for peanuts, honey, and dog food."

"Brianna has quite the imagination, doesn't she?" Jennifer laughed with delight.

Her friend smiled wryly. "And quite an appetite. I opted for the cookies. At least there were only four left. As it is, I've shooed her out of here several times in the last half-hour. Brianna added mountain climber to her game and tried to scale the counter to get the cookies. If I'd let her, she'd down the entire lot." She glanced toward the kitchen. "Speaking of which, the batch in the oven will be ready soon."

Elyssa took Jennifer's coat. "I'll put this right into the washer and come back for the rest of your clothes." She disappeared into the laundry room.

A moment later, a golden-haired toddler raced down the hallway, filmy blue cape and long hair flying behind, toy crown askew. "Mommy, come pway wif me."

Jennifer caught Brianna at arm's length and held her there. Water dripped from her hair and skirt as she knelt. "Mommy's clothes are awfully wet and she needs to get cleaned up first, hon. Do you understand?"

The youngster made a face then nodded. Jennifer gingerly kissed her on the cheek. Brianna cast a wistful eye toward the breakfast bar.

"No more, Brianna," Jennifer told her. "We'll be having lunch soon." She patted the child on the behind and sent her scurrying back to her royal tea party.

Watching her daughter's sweet innocence gave Jennifer a growing sense of satisfaction. Brianna had never experienced the cold emptiness she associated with her own childhood. Jennifer's resolve to ensure her happiness seemed to work so far. *At least my baby knows I love her, and would never abandon her.*

Elyssa returned to the kitchen and set more chocolate chip cookies on the breakfast bar to cool. "So, are you taking an early lunch or something?" She put the empty pan on the stove, turned off the oven, and crossed into the living room.

Jennifer wiped her face with a corner of the towel and stood up. "Actually, I'm unemployed. We got laid off this morning."

The older woman bristled. "Laid off? I thought they told you not to worry about it."

"Well, they announced the store's immediate closure this morning."

Elyssa stood, hands-on-hips. "They filed for bankruptcy last month. You'd think they'd have known then. Were they honest with any of the employees about this whole thing?"

"Why would they?" Jennifer shrugged. "At least we got an extra three-week's pay. That will help for a little while. If things get too lean, I suppose I could dip into some of Danny's insurance money, but that will be my last resort."

Her friend sighed. "What do you plan to do, child?"

Jennifer carefully removed her skirt. "Start job hunting right away. I'll stop by the unemployment office later on this afternoon, if I get my car. I just hope I can find something soon. There could be a decent job listed in the classifieds." She handed the skirt to Elyssa, and then wrapped the towel around her chilled body.

"The job market was tough enough without another company folding. And you've a child to support," Elyssa fumed. She bit her lip and gazed at Jennifer with sad eyes. "I'm not setting a very good example. God's got something in mind for you. We'll just have to trust Him. Get the rest of those wet things off and take a nice hot shower."

Jennifer wiped her face with the back of her hand. "Best idea I've heard all morning." A hot shower sounded inviting. "Did the garage call to say what time my car would be ready? I need it for job hunting."

"No. I got tired of waiting for them, so I called instead. Someone's supposed to drop the car by when they get finished—whenever that is.

The man said it was paid for already. And, no, he wouldn't detail what damage they allegedly fixed." Elyssa rolled the drenched skirt into an old sheet of newspaper then eyed her surrogate daughter with suspicion for a moment. "'Fess up, Jen. What is bothering you?"

Jennifer sighed. "I never could get anything by you, could I?" She pushed back a straggling lock of wet hair. "Anton's having me followed, and I told his goon off this morning."

"Followed?" Elyssa's dark eyes flashed. "What kind of man has a woman followed?"

Jennifer shrugged. "One who needs a brain transplant?"

Elyssa drew her breath. "You need to get rid of him. He's not fit for you to wipe your feet on. How long has this nonsense been going on?"

"About a month," Jennifer seethed over the morning's events. "As far as I'm concerned, Anton's no longer part of my life." She felt smug satisfaction recalling Nathan's shock when the water hit his face. "I hope he takes the message to heart."

Elyssa narrowed her eyebrows. "A month? Do you realize how dangerous that is? Did you tell Mike about this stalking business?"

Jennifer imagined Detective Sergeant Mike Scavone's reaction to her news. She shuddered. He didn't like secrets like this; especially when they involved his former partner's family. "Not yet, but after today, I definitely plan to."

"I'm glad to hear it. That Anton is nothing more than a snake." Elyssa started toward the kitchen, but stopped and turned. "Oh, before I forget, your brother called. He's sending Brianna's birthday present tonight via messenger. He wants you two ready by six o'clock, dressed in your finest."

"I can't imagine what he's up to this time." Jennifer headed to the bathroom. If she wasn't careful, Rob would spoil Brianna. During his Christmas visit, he had allowed his niece the run of the toy store. Jennifer shook her head. While it had been a disaster, at least he bothered with Brianna. *That's more than I can say for my parents.*

Jennifer caught sight of her reflection in the bathroom mirror and laughed. Her carefully set hair had transformed itself into a mass of unruly curls. Mud streaked her face, and smudged mascara created uneven shading beneath her eyes. "No wonder the people on the bus stared at me like that. I must have made some impression."

Her thoughts returned to the winsome stranger and her heart plummeted. She turned on the shower. "Knock it off, Jen," she scolded herself under her breath. "It doesn't matter what Nathan thought of you? *If* that's his name. Only a jerk would work for Anton. He lied to you, remember? When are you going to get it through your head? Men bring nothing but heartache."

She finished undressing and stepped into the hot spray, forcing herself to focus on her daughter's upcoming birthday. She longed to see Brianna's reaction when she experienced the rides at Knott's Berry Farm for the first time. Jennifer let the water massage her shoulders. Soon, it began to soothe away her anger and tension.

If they went tomorrow, at least they wouldn't have to deal with the crazy weekend crowds. That is, if Jennifer had the car back before then. She'd have to cut back on the extras for the party on Saturday, though. Maybe instead of party favors she could have the kids make a craft to take home.

By the time she had toweled off and donned a soft coral sweater and a denim skirt, thoughts of Nathan had vanished. Jennifer bubbled with enthusiasm. The children could decorate their own cupcakes and make sock puppets. She returned to the living room.

Elyssa handed her a large white square box tied with a pink ribbon. "This package just came, Jen."

"It's probably Brianna's gift from Rob." Jennifer set it on the couch for her daughter to open. Brianna abandoned her "Sesame Street" video and eagerly tore the ribbon free and opened the lid. Jennifer lifted out a large brown teddy bear.

"That's strange," she told Elyssa, handing the grinning bear to the ecstatic youngster. "Rob bought her one just like this last Christmas, only this one's heavier."

Brianna smoothed the bear's fur then stopped. "Mommy, Bear-Bear got a owie."

Jennifer picked up the stuffed animal and checked it over. Stuffing poked through the seam in the neck. "Whoever sewed this was a bit careless."

"It's not too bad," Elyssa said, examining the bear. "I can mend this in a thrice. Come on, Brianna, Dr. Grammy needs an assistant." She settled on the couch with a needle and thread.

"Why did that brother of mine want us dressed up to receive a bear?" Jennifer searched the box for a card, but couldn't find one. "Oh well, it's likely another one of his jokes. At least we didn't go to the trouble of getting all dolled up."

While Elyssa and Brianna "operated" on the bear, Jennifer outlined her plan for the trip to Knott's Berry Farm. "Now, Brianna, I can only take you tomorrow if it's not raining and if I get the car back. Do you understand?"

"Yep. We have car," Brianna insisted. "Unca Mike take us."

Jennifer groaned inwardly. "Uncle Mike can't take us. He has to work tomorrow. We have to wait for our car. Do you understand? If we can't go tomorrow, we'll just go later on in the week."

Brianna nodded, still grinning.

Elyssa sighed. "I wish I had a car you could use. I've always relied on the bus since I only go to the hospital and the grocery store on my own." She completed the bear's minor surgery and handed the toy back to Brianna.

Jennifer patted the older woman's shoulder. "You can't provide everything for everyone, hon. We'll have to wait and see what happens in the morning. It's too bad you can't join us."

"I really wish I could." Elyssa put away her sewing supplies. "I've promised to deliver those outfits to the hospital by noon tomorrow, and I have four more to complete before then."

After a quick lunch, Jennifer put Brianna down for a nap. A few minutes later, she grabbed a cup of hot chocolate and joined Elyssa in the living room to watch the midday news. Her friend sat in an armchair, sewing.

"How many of those newborn outfits have you made so far?" Jennifer curled up on the sofa.

Elyssa finished two stitches in a tiny garment and tied off the thread. "Oh, I don't know. I've never kept count." She looked up over the top of her bifocals. "I make them as they're needed, and Lord willing, I'll continue as long as I'm able."

The woman's determination to sew outfits for every baby born at the local hospital amazed Jennifer. Elyssa paid for all the materials herself and lovingly stitched each bit of clothing by hand.

The hospital administrator had stopped by for a visit a few weeks ago. Her attempts to convince Elyssa Baker to accept a special award had fallen flat. "The day I get public recognition," She had balked, "is the day I'll stop sewing." The administrator had reluctantly agreed to let her remain an anonymous donor.

The memory brought a smile to Jennifer's lips. "You're something else, Elyssa."

The older woman quirked her thin eyebrows. "And when you find out what, you'll let me know?"

Jennifer laughed. She picked up the remote and turned on the news channel, hoping to hear something about the store closure. She waited for the commercials to end, and then turned up the volume.

A police barricade flashed on the screen followed by video footage from a robbery. The news anchor described the scene. "Armed and masked jewel thieves continued their nationwide crime spree Sunday by killing two men and stripping an exclusive Long Beach store of over five million dollars' worth of jewels, according to police."

Blood drained from Jennifer's face. This couldn't be happening again. She clenched her fists and choked back her rage. Her eyes remained glued to the newscast.

Her husband's old watch commander faced the camera. "Five men, impersonating SWAT officers, entered the store at about 9 p.m., killed a security guard and a courier, and then pointed automatic weapons at the store owner and his wife," Lieutenant Lee Reynolds said.

A camera panned the inside of the crime scene as the news anchor picked up the story. "According to police, the gunmen handcuffed their hostages to chairs then ransacked the store. After smashing open the glass display cases, the suspects scooped the entire inventory of

diamonds and jewelry into a large briefcase and fled through a back
door. Three unusually large jewels—a sapphire, ruby and an emerald—
are also reported missing."

Tears burned Jennifer's eyes as Danny's photo flashed on the
screen. "The jewel thieves are lead suspects in the murder of Daniel
Warner, a Long Beach police officer who was shot to death after
responding to a similar robbery call three years ago tomorrow. The
suspects allegedly fired on Warner and his partner as their squad car
pulled up in back of the Mills Jewel Boutique on Somerset."

The camera locked on the news anchor. "This string of robberies,
spanning five years and stretching from New York to Los Angeles, has
baffled police and the FBI. Law enforcement has no solid leads.

"According to witnesses, all but one gunman are of medium build
and height and were last seen wearing black flight suits, stocking caps
and combat boots. The fifth gunman is slightly taller than the rest and
has a stocky build. Anyone with information regarding—"

Jennifer shut off the television. Her nails bit into the soft flesh of
her palms. Sorrow and rage washed over her in overwhelming waves.
Her anguish over Danny's brutal death had slowly diminished over the
past three years. Now it flamed again. She dropped the remote and
hugged her knees.

Chapter 3

Danny's murder had amounted to a cold and calculated game against the police. His killers had even stripped him of his wallet and gun. They hadn't touched Mike Scavone, however—too much blood, the police had speculated—too much of a chance to leave prints behind.

Jennifer blinked back the tears threatening to fall. Anger dripped from her voice. "It's not fair. Danny's dead and his killers keep slipping past police. Where's the justice in all of this? Why isn't God doing anything about it?"

Elyssa moved to the couch and put her arm around Jennifer's shoulder. "He is doing something, Jen. We can't see where every puzzle piece fits," she said gently. "As hard as it seems right now, we have to trust Him."

Nagging questions pricked Jennifer's heart. "I don't know how, Elyssa. How can I trust God when He—" Jennifer broke off and bit her lower lip. She knew better than talk this way.

"Go ahead and say it, child," Elyssa urged. "It won't put God off His throne to hear your doubts. He knows them anyway. You're wondering where He was when Danny died—why He didn't protect him."

Jennifer looked up, her eyes glistening with pain. "It feels like God abandoned us when we needed Him the most." She gestured with her hands in frustration. "I guess I could let go of this if I could just understand. What's the purpose in any of this? Where's the justice? Why Danny?"

"I could give you some pat answers, child, but they're not what you're looking for. You're needing something much deeper—something that only God can give you."

Tears etched paths down Jennifer's cheeks. How she wished she could turn back the hands of time. She got off the couch and took Danny's photograph from its hiding place in the top drawer of the end table. "I should have made him keep his promise to take the day off, Elyssa. It was our second anniversary, and he promised to take me to San Diego."

She sat on the corner of the coffee table and gazed at Danny's smiling face. She hated to admit she still felt angry with him, and with herself. "Why didn't I speak up? If I had, he'd still be alive."

Elyssa put down her sewing and moved closer. "Beating yourself with guilt won't change anything, child. You couldn't have known what would happen that day. None of us could."

Jennifer's anger surged. "But God knew. He's supposed to be loving. This seems more like an act of cruelty." She hugged the picture to herself and stared out the window. "I never even got a chance to tell my husband goodbye."

"It was an act of cruelty, Jen, but not on God's part. A man decided to pull the trigger, not God."

Jennifer stiffened. Raw anger spilled into her voice. "God could have stopped him, but no. Danny's dead, Brianna and I are alone, and Mike lives with amnesia and night terrors." Her voice dropped to a whisper. "It's like God doesn't even care."

Elyssa reached over and touched Jennifer's arm. "The suffering in the world is a result of man's sin, not because of God's neglect," she admonished. "For God to wipe it all out, He would have to take away our free will. We'd be no more than puppets. Since God allows us to make our own choices, often innocent people—like Danny, you, Brianna, and Mike—get hurt."

Jennifer buried her head in her hands. She knew Elyssa was right, but facts wouldn't erase her pain. Images of that horrible night flashed before her—the desperate ride to the hospital in the pounding rain; Tina Scavone's stricken face; the word of Danny's death; the ripping pain inside her swollen stomach.

Her mind skipped forward a few days later to Brianna's perilous birth and the premature infant's battle to live. For two months she had watched her daughter struggle for life in the neonatal unit. For two months she wondered if death would rob her of yet another loved one.

Heart-wrenching sobs convulsed Jennifer's body. Elyssa sat beside her and stroked her hair. "Let it out, Jen. It's been a long time coming."

The solemn ticking of the grandfather clock in the corner measured the passing minutes.

Jennifer finally looked up, her eyes swollen. She reached over for a tissue and wiped her nose. "I couldn't even go to Danny's funeral. The doctor said I...I could lose Brianna. I had to hold onto that part of him, Elyssa." She rocked herself back and forth. "Why did he have to leave me? I want him back."

"I know, Jen. The pain can be so overwhelming."

Jennifer searched her friend's face. "Were you angry at God when Roger died?"

Elyssa nodded. "Yes, at first. For months, I screamed and raged at Him, demanding an answer. Roger was a good cop, so why did it have to happen to him?" Her gentle voice cracked with emotion. "I cried myself to sleep every night—hoping that I'd awaken from this nightmare; that I'd reach over and Roger would be beside me. Eventually, I had to accept the fact that he was gone and nothing would bring him back."

"But how did you resolve your anger with God?"

Elyssa remained silent for a few moments. Her eyes seemed to gaze into the past. "When I stopped throwing my emotions around, I could finally listen. You see, while I questioned God, I never wanted His answer. I only wanted Him to bring my Roger back to me."

Jennifer's throat tightened again as she recognized her own rebellion. She didn't want God's answers; she wanted her husband. Danny's death had left a gaping hole in Jennifer's life. At first she had thought her newborn daughter would help dispel the emptiness. She soon realized that Brianna could never fill his place in her heart.

"I miss him so much."

Her friend hugged her. "I know, child. It's hard to let go of someone we love. It helped me to know that my husband knew the Lord and went to be with Him. I know that I'll see him again. I didn't have that assurance with Roy, the son I lost in Vietnam. Roger and I didn't become Christians until five years later. While that grief has remained with me through the years, I can't let it hold me back. It's my job to get on with life and fulfill God's purpose for me."

Jennifer chewed her lower lip. "I haven't really thought about seeing Danny in the next life," she admitted. "I know I will since he had become a Christian a few weeks before he was..." She choked back tears. "It just seems senseless that God would let one of His new children die like that."

"God cared enough to make sure Danny was ready to face eternity," Elyssa reminded her. "Of all the people in this police department, God gave him Mike Scavone as a partner."

Jennifer looked at Danny's picture and smiled weakly. "What a team. Those two would have some real go 'rounds about Christianity. Danny was always researching a new argument for Mike. One night when the Scavones were over for dinner, Danny hashed it out with him. They weren't angry or anything; they just enjoyed debating facts."

Elyssa laughed softly. "Mike called me almost every night to go over Danny's newest argument. The exchanges between them definitely stretched his faith during that time. When Danny finally accepted Christ, I thought Mike would sprout wings."

Jennifer's smile broadened. "I remember that night. Danny came home so happy, like someone had lifted a huge weight off of him. Mike and Tina came over with a birthday cake. That was some celebration. Danny had so many plans and dreams that he wanted to get started on right away." She brushed back a tear. "It just hurts so much to know that he saw none of those dreams fulfilled."

"I know, Jen. But we must trust that God knows what He is doing. After all, He is the Creator. Who would better know how to direct each aspect our lives?"

Jennifer looked at Danny's picture and held back the flood of emotion threatening to burst forth again. "I want so much to trust God like that. It's just so hard sometimes."

"Do you remember the beautiful Pacific seascape you gave Rob last Christmas?"

What did the painting have to do with their conversation? Jennifer humored her friend anyway. "If my memory serves me well, you were a bit antsy about that one."

Elyssa nodded. "What was the very first thing you did to that crisp, white canvas?"

"I painted the entire thing black."

"And at that moment I thought you were stark-raving mad. I was convinced you had destroyed the painting before you had even started." Elyssa shrugged. "From my viewpoint then, you carelessly smeared black oil paint all over the canvas. You then abandoned it and started an entirely different painting."

Jennifer sighed. "As I explained to you then, I had to use a black background to make the subtle colors of the waves stand out. I set the canvas aside so that the paint could dry."

"Ah, but to my untrained eye, it seemed that you had no real use for the black canvas. Then, when you began to work on it, the dark colors you chose made no sense to me. Of course, I understand it all, now, since you completed the painting. Before then it seemed only chaos."

A chuckle escaped Jennifer's lips. "Individual brush strokes make little sense to anyone but the painter. I see in my mind's eye the finished work. I know the exact background, lighting and shading I need to bring out the best of each painting."

"Exactly." Elyssa's brown eyes seemed to twinkle in delight. "God is the Master Painter, and each Christian is a living canvas. God alone knows what background, trials, and blessings are necessary to bring out the best in each masterpiece. He alone determines when each painting is complete. Often, it's against the dark night of the soul that the subtle work of the Holy Spirit shows up best."

Jennifer thought about the painstaking care she put into each of her paintings and sketches. She had to admit that her most eye-catching oil paintings incorporated dark, somber backgrounds.

She pondered Elyssa's words. *It's true. I can't see what God is doing. The colors seem too dark and His brush strokes make no sense.* She looked up at her friend. "You said that you struggled with Roger's death until you finally listened to what God had to say. What did He tell you?"

Elyssa smiled gently. "He reminded me about Job in the Bible. The man lost his children and everything he owned. He found himself left with only a battered body and a sharp-tongued wife who urged him to curse God and die. He chose to trust God even though, in this life, he never knew why God let him go through so much."

The older woman quickly glanced at her watch then stood. "I've got to get those other outfits cut out. Look up the book of Job, Jen. You'll find that you're not the only one with questions. I'll be downstairs if you need to talk more. Otherwise, I'll see you around four or so to help start dinner."

After Elyssa left, Jennifer dug out her Bible, plopped down on the couch, and began reading the story her friend had mentioned. Throughout the afternoon, she read the scriptures in snatches as she tended to Brianna and the housework. When she had finished reading the last few verses, conviction gripped her heart.

"I'm sorry for doubting You, God," she prayed. "I still have a lot of doubts and fears, but I ask You to cover them with the healing balm of Your love. Help me get through this."

Once again, she picked up Danny's picture and outlined his face and blonde hair with her finger. Even now she could hear his infectious laughter and see his smile. *I've got to hold onto the good memories, Danny. I want Brianna to know all about her daddy.*

The clanking of the mail slot disrupted Jennifer's thoughts. She put Danny's picture on the coffee table, glad she now had the freedom to display things where she wished without fearing any of Anton's mean-spirited criticisms.

She glanced down the hallway toward Brianna's room to check up on the youngster. Brianna sat on her bed, teaching songs to her large entourage of stuffed animals friends.

Jennifer smiled, scooped the mail up off the floor, and sank onto the couch. She pushed aside the advertising circulars that made up the bulk of the pile. "Junk mail should be outlawed!" She dumped the offending papers into the nearby recycle bin. Anything bearing the word "Resident" had the tendency to set her teeth on edge.

A letter from her brother Rob Tyler, a successful architect on the East Coast, caught her eye. Jennifer eagerly tore open the envelope. She hadn't seen him since Christmas and he hadn't written for the past three months. Maybe he would explain his earlier prank.

> *Dear Jen,*
>
> *Hi, kiddo! Sorry it's taken me so long to write. I sure do miss my favorite (and only) sister. I finally completed that massive job in Boston. Since then, I have been wading in paint, wallpaper and spackling—you guessed it, I've been renovating that old place in New Sweden, Maine, that I told you about. I'm happy to report that, with the help of some good friends, I have created a masterpiece!*
>
> *I do have a bit of a problem, however. I have discovered that I can't stand living by myself. Do you*

think I could talk you into moving up here? I know you said you were tired of the big city and I thought you might be interested in living in a nice, quiet farming community.

The countryside is real pretty, and it's a great place to raise Brianna. You won't have to find a job if you don't want to. My work pays more than enough to take care of us all.

If you get restless, though, there's a gallery in nearby Caribou that you can show your amazing sketches and paintings in.

I wish you would come. There's even an elementary school down the road from here—for when Brianna gets old enough for school. Anyhow I've been incredibly lonely, Jen, and I could really use your lively spirit and my active niece to keep me company. Face it; I need you.

At the very least, come up for a visit to see if you can tolerate your fun-loving and lonely brother. Here's my new address and phone number.

Waiting eagerly for your reply.

Love, Rob

P.S. I meant it when I said you're only allowed to call collect! I'll hang up on you otherwise.

Jennifer chuckled at her brother's threat, and then re-read the last two paragraphs of the letter. Although Rob was four years older than she, they were very close. After all, he was her only sibling and neither of them knew where their parents were. Not that Jennifer cared to find them; her heart had closed to them long ago.

She got up and walked over to her desk. Jennifer tucked the letter into her black leather purse for safekeeping. "I wish we could visit, Rob, but money's too tight right now. Maybe when this whole mess clears up, we'll be able to go."

Jennifer refused to consider her brother's offer to let her and Brianna live with him. *I've got to make it on my own.* The intense pain associated with her father's disappearance and later with Danny's death, remained. She couldn't get dependent on a man ever again. Something always happened. *I'd just set myself up for another fall, and I couldn't survive it.*

The rest of the afternoon slipped by with no word from the garage. Jennifer contemplated taking the bus to do her errands, but the sky did not clear until four. Her frustration mounted as she realized she had no way to get to the unemployment office on time.

At six o'clock the doorbell interrupted the family's dinner preparations. "Stay right there, honey," Jennifer told Brianna, who sat on the couch telling a bedtime story to her new bear. "That must be about the car."

Jennifer opened the door. "It's about time you..." Her eyes widened in surprise. Her puddle partner of the morning stood smiling in her doorway, smartly dressed in a black tuxedo.

"Hi, Jennifer. I hope you're not planning to hit me with any more water. I have to return this tux in good shape." Puzzlement filled Nathan's face as he surveyed her casual clothes. "Oh, you're not dressed to go out. Didn't Rob tell you I'd be coming? He said he'd call and tell you to be ready by six."

She crossed her arms. "What are you doing here?" she demanded. "I told you what I thought this morning. Is Anton paying you triple-time for your trouble?"

"Who's Anton? Rob's the one who sent me."

Jennifer narrowed her gaze. "What does he have to do with this?"

"I'm the messenger that's supposed to take you and Brianna out to dinner. Your brother didn't call, did he?" Nathan slapped his right hand to his forehead. "I've never met anyone more absent-minded. How he's made it as an architect, I'll never know."

"Rob left a message, but I thought..." She stopped herself. "How do I know that Rob really sent you?"

He smirked. "Call him. He'll vouch for me, honest."

"I will. You stay right there." Jennifer closed the door in his face.

"Who is it?" Elyssa asked from the kitchen.

Jennifer removed Rob's letter from her purse. "Anton's goon with some outrageous story."

"You're calling the police, right?"

"I need to settle something, first."

Elyssa walked to the front door and peered through the peephole. "Nice-looking young man. He doesn't look like the criminal type."

"Since when do looks have to do with anything?"

The older woman chuckled and stepped back from the door.

Jennifer looked up her brother's new number and dialed the phone. "Collect call from Jennifer. Thank you." She felt relieved when she heard Rob's voice on the line.

"Sure, I'll accept charges." Her brother's warm baritone greeted her. "Hey, little sister, it's about time you called."

She sighed. "Rob, did you send someone here to take Brianna and me out to dinner?"

He seemed puzzled. "Yeah. Didn't you get my message? I called."

She twisted the phone cord around her finger. Her stomach knotted. "Your message was way too vague. Tell me, what does this person look like?"

"Whoops, sorry. Let's see..."

Jennifer heard the sounds of rustling in the background. Her brother's poor memory was legendary when it came to anything but his architectural projects. *He's probably looking for a picture.*

"Uh...uh...oh yeah." he stammered "Nathan's about six-three, dark brown hair, umm...a beard, mustache...dark blue eyes, and uh...he grins a lot. He's also supposed to be wearing a tuxedo. Has he shown up yet?"

Her cheeks began to burn. "Is this Nathan person a doctor by some chance that doubles as a magician?"

Cheerfulness rang in Rob's voice. "So, he is there. Great! He's my best friend, so you can trust him. I want photos of all of you. Have a good time at dinner. Call me after you've read my letter. Got to run. My dinner's about to burn."

"But, Rob?" Jennifer stared in horror at the dead telephone. *Oh, no, what have I done?*

Chapter 4

Jennifer wished the floor would just open and swallow her. She hung up the receiver and willed herself to open the door. "I am so sorry, Nathan." She ushered him into the living room. "Believe me, I had no idea."

"Obviously." His gaze traveled between Elyssa and Jennifer. "Is this a bad time? I seem to have come in the middle of something."

Jennifer's face burned in humiliation. She motioned Nathan to the couch. "Oh... it's all right... really. Please sit down. This is my surrogate mom, Elyssa. Mom, this is Nathan Pellitier—Rob's messenger."

"Me wikes you." Brianna immediately crawled into Nathan's lap and offered him her new bear.

Jennifer stared at her daughter in disbelief. What had gotten into her? She never warmed up to strangers.

Elyssa snickered and went back to the kitchen.

Dr. Pellitier cuddled Brianna close. "I like you, too, kitten. You must be Brianna. Your Uncle Rob told me all about you. Who's this big guy?"

"Bear-Bear. Me wikes him, too." Brianna smiled as Nathan admired her new stuffed friend.

Jennifer sank into a nearby chair and contemplated the man who had so easily won over her daughter. Ignoring Elyssa's gloating smile, she took a deep breath and gathered her courage. "You knew who I was from the beginning, so why weren't you up front with me?"

Nathan looked up. "I tried to tell you in the coffee shop, but I guess my delivery needed some work."

Shame burned her cheeks as Jennifer recalled her rash behavior. "I thought you were someone else and didn't give you a chance to explain. I'm so sorry."

He waved off her apology. "I can't blame you for feeling threatened. Don't worry about it."

Jennifer couldn't forgive herself that easily. She withdrew into her own morbid thoughts.

Elyssa leaned over the breakfast bar. "Nathan, humor an old woman. How in the world did you know you were talking to Jennifer earlier today?"

Nathan shrugged. "It was hard not to. Rob has the walls of the house plastered with pictures of her and Brianna." He turned and gave the child a warm smile. "I must say, though, it's a vast improvement over the wallpaper."

Jennifer's curiosity slipped out. "Oh, so you've seen his new house?"

He cocked an eyebrow and opened his mouth to speak, but seemed to hesitate for a moment. "Yeah. I even helped fix it up a bit. I had no say in some of the decor, though. Well, would you three ladies care to join me for a fancy birthday dinner?"

Jennifer couldn't believe her ears. "You still want to take us out to dinner after the way I acted?"

"It's all on me. I should have told you who I was from the beginning rather than teasing you. Besides, I'd hate to waste the use of a good tuxedo." His blue eyes twinkled with merriment. "Perhaps Bear-Bear would like to come along with us."

Brianna nodded and grinned. Confusion niggled at Jennifer. What was it with this man? The child did not open up to strangers like this.

Elyssa stepped into the living room. "You young people go on without me. I've got plans for tonight." She turned toward Jennifer. "I'll get Brianna dressed while you're getting ready."

Jennifer looked toward the kitchen. "But we started..."

Her friend patted her shoulder. "I'll take care of the kitchen, dear. Go and have a good time."

Resigned, Jennifer turned toward Nathan. "Could you give us about forty-five minutes?"

"Sure, no problem. I'll just call the restaurant and change our reservations. May I use your phone?"

Jennifer nodded and led Elyssa and Brianna to the child's room. She pulled a bright pink dress from Brianna's closet. "Here's her birthday dress, and her slip." She laid the items on the bed as she spoke. "Oh, she won't go anywhere without wearing her lacy tights..." Jennifer bit her lip as she scanned the room. "Now, where did she put those shoes?"

She knelt on the floor and looked under Brianna's bed. *The one time you need those shoes in a hurry they're nowhere to be found.* "Let's see, she was playing fairy princess yesterday."

Elyssa laughed. "Quit stalling and go get yourself dressed. If I need help, I'll ask Nathan. I knew that young man couldn't possibly be a hardened criminal."

Jennifer rolled her eyes, and then hurried to her own room. She rummaged through her closet for something suitable to wear. Why had Rob put her in such an awkward position? She berated herself for being so stupid. How was she supposed to know who Nathan was? Her brother could have at least given some specifics to Elyssa, for heaven's sake. *I could have also called him earlier to clarify the message.*

She finally slipped into a tea-length emerald green silk dress that accentuated her slender figure. Her hands shook as she touched up her makeup and brushed her hair. Nathan likely thought she was out of her mind. She'd never live this down. Elyssa had to change her mind and come with them.

Jennifer finished dressing in record time and headed to Brianna's room. "How are things going in here?"

Elyssa ran a brush through Brianna's long golden curls. "Almost ready. Nathan is helping us look for the elusive shoes. There you go." She hugged the child, and then set the brush on the dresser. "I'm going to take care of the kitchen, now."

Nathan looked up from buckling a black patent leather shoe on Brianna's right foot. "One down and one to go."

Jennifer laid her purse on the bed. "Where was that one?"

"Her other bear was wearing it." He motioned toward Brianna's mound of stuffed animals. "Say, is she collecting brown bears or something? These two could almost be twins."

The floor of Brianna's closet revealed no sign of the missing shoe. "I really can't say what's going on. The new one came today for her birthday. Rob likely forgot that he gave her the other one at Christmas."

Perplexion crossed Nathan's face. "Rob said nothing about sending her a bear. I wonder—"

Jennifer scoffed. "As you have most likely learned, my brother's forgetfulness is legendary." She stood and surveyed the room. "Did you check her toy box?"

"Huh? Oh, no. I was so thrilled at locating the one shoe that I figured I'd get it on her before it disappeared."

"Good choice." Jennifer opened the lid of the multi-colored wooden chest and pushed the toys to one side. "Ah, ha! The missing shoe!"

"Fabulous." Nathan took the shoe and gently slid it onto Brianna's other foot. "Your magical slipper, princess."

"Fank you." Brianna slid from the bed. She grabbed her new bear. "Bear-Bear come wif us."

As they entered the living room, Jennifer tried to change Elyssa's mind. "Are you sure you won't join us, Mom?"

Her friend waved her off. "I've got a lot of sewing to do before tomorrow. *Really.* Now go and have a good time."

Despite her misgivings, Jennifer accepted defeat. "Okay, Brianna, it's time to go." She grabbed two light coats from the hall closet and picked up her purse.

"Cape, Mommy," Brianna insisted, running back into her bedroom.

Jennifer set the coats and her purse on the couch then followed after her daughter. The toddler opened the bottom drawer of her dresser. She pulled out a large bright blue rectangle of filmy cloth and a toy crown.

With patient hands, Jennifer pinned the cape to Brianna's dress, and placed the toy silver crown on her head. Then, she herded the youngster toward the front door. "We're ready now," she told Nathan. "I'm sorry we've kept you so late."

Nathan smiled at her. "Don't worry about the time. This whole thing's obviously taken you off guard. Besides, it's not seven yet, so don't worry about it. Let's just enjoy ourselves."

Elyssa retrieved Brianna's car seat and day bag from the hall closet and handed them to Nathan. "Don't forget these!" She gave Jennifer the coats and her purse."

Jennifer hugged her. "Thanks, Mom. Have a good night. We'll bring you home some c-a-k-e."

Nathan held the front door open for Jennifer and Brianna.

"Bye, bye, Gwammy," Brianna shouted from the porch

Elyssa waved and blew kisses to the youngster.

Bouquets of balloons decorated the colorful lobby of Funny Bones' Attic. Nathan carried Bear-Bear and the day bag while Jennifer led Brianna by the hand. Mouth-watering aromas wafted from the kitchen, reminding Jennifer just how long it had been since lunch.

A woman dressed as Miss Muffet greeted them from behind the counter. "Good evening, welcome to Funny Bones'. Do you have a reservation?"

"Pellitier, party of three," Nathan told her.

Brianna quietly danced back and forth in place, swirling her cape around her.

Miss Muffet ran her finger down her book. "Here we are." She peered over the countertop at Brianna and smiled. "Oh my goodness, we've got a real princess visiting tonight. We must get the best table in the house for her." She led them toward the dining area.

A brightly clad circus clown tumbled by, shrieking with laughter. Brianna pointed to the colorful figure and squealed with delight.

"That's Funny Bones himself," Miss Muffet explained. "You'll have to excuse him. He ate too many jellybeans again. Do you want a highchair or a booster chair for the young lady?"

"I think a booster chair would be best tonight," Jennifer answered. "Highchairs are for *babies*."

"I understand. We have an independent young lady here, don't we?" As Miss Muffet showed them to their table, she picked up a green booster chair.

Various storybook characters moved about the restaurant, carrying food and talking to diners. Brianna craned her neck, trying to take in everything at once.

Miss Muffet stopped beside a booth. "Here's your table. Your waiter is Davy Crockett. Enjoy yourselves."

Jennifer scanned the room. An ice-filled claw-foot bathtub in the center of the room served as a salad bar. A hodge-podge collection of chandeliers hung from the high ceiling. Various antiques adorned the walls and wooden ceiling beams. "How did you ever find out about this place?" she asked Nathan as they sat down. "I never knew it existed."

Nathan placed Bear-Bear next to Brianna. "Some colleagues took me here for my birthday two years ago during our last medical conference. I've been wanting to come back ever since. When Rob asked me to take you and Brianna out to celebrate her birthday, I knew this would be the perfect place."

"Well, they have a very unique way of decorating." Jennifer's eyes scanned the various interesting items. "I've never seen such a collection of antiques before."

"It does kinda look like someone's attic, huh?"

A young man, dressed in pioneer clothing and a fake beaver-skin cap, sauntered up to their table. "Hey, what's this?" he growled in a heavy southern accent. "Who let this bear in my section?"

"Bear-Bear mine!" Brianna hugged her bear and glowered back.

The waiter doffed his cap and bowed in Brianna's direction. "Ooo, excuuuse me, miss. I didn't see you there at first," he drawled. "I thought that there bear had wandered in by himself."

The child refused to smile.

He turned to address Nathan and Jennifer. "Hello, I'm Davy Crocket. My mama always told me I had no tact. Now I believe her."

Jennifer laughed. "She'll get over it, eventually. Just treat her friend with kindness."

"Yes, ma'am!" Davy set menus in front of Nathan and Jennifer, and then handed a paper place mat with drawings on it to Brianna. "I'd better go get another table setting and a booster chair for Sir Bear-Bear. I wouldn't want to insult the princess any further."

"You'll want to bring two more b-i-g m-e-n-u-s, too," Jennifer told him. The young man smiled, bowed again, then left.

Jennifer got a package of crayons out of the day bag and helped her daughter connect the dots on the place mat. A few moments later, the waiter returned as promised.

"Here we go, ma'am." The waiter gave Brianna the large glossy menu and set the other, along with the table setting in front of the stuffed bear. "I think perhaps one of you should help Sir Bear-Bear into this. I thought I heard him growl at me."

Davy handed the booster chair to Nathan and stepped back from the table in mock fear. "In the meanwhile, can I get you folks something to drink?"

Nathan set the bear on the chair and patted its head affectionately. "Jennifer, how about a virgin banana-berry daiquiri?"

"That sounds good. I can share a little of mine with Brianna." Jennifer looked up at the waiter. "Could you also bring a small glass of milk with the meal?"

"Sure. Two banana-berries and one milk. I'll be right back."

Brianna sat up tall and proudly held her big menu upside down. Nathan glanced at Brianna and smiled, then turned back to Jennifer. "How would you like to handle the ordering?"

"You can ask her what she wants. It'll be s-p-a-g-h-e-t-t-i and c-a-k-e. Wait and see."

He smirked. "You're kidding, right?"

"Nope. Experience." Jennifer took a package of crackers from the day bag and handed one to her daughter.

Nathan addressed Brianna. "Well, fair princess, what do you think? Have you found something you'd like?"

"Sketti, pwease," she answered in muffled voice from behind the huge menu.

"Impressive. And what about Bear-Bear? Do you think he'd like some honey and berries?"

After a whispered conference with the stuffed toy, Brianna peered around the edge of the menu. "Cake, pwease."

Dr. Pellitier raised his eyebrows and looked at Jennifer. "Spaghetti and cake? I think we can manage that."

Jennifer struggled to stifle a peal of laughter.

"And what about you, Jennifer? Have you decided yet?"

She scanned the menu again. "I wish I could. Everything looks so good, I just can't decide."

"I'll make it easy on you. How about sharing the Grand Medley with me? It's got smoked chicken, barbecued baby back ribs, grilled scallops and shrimp scampi, and it comes with salad bar, vegetables, and choice of potato or hot cornbread."

Jennifer sighed happily. "My mouth is watering already." She handed him the rest of the menus.

Davy Crockett returned a few moments later with their drinks. "Are you folks ready to order, now?"

"Sure." Nathan said. "Spaghetti for the birthday princess, cake for Sir Bear-Bear, and we'll have the Grand Medley."

The waiter scribbled down their order. "Anything else?" he asked after reading back what he had written.

Jennifer looked up from coloring. "Could we also get a small plate of fries right away? She's pretty hungry."

"Absolutely. In the meanwhile, help yourselves to the salad bar."

Nathan and Jennifer took turns watching Brianna while the other got salad. "What an idea for recycling a bathtub," Jennifer said, returning to the table. "This place is incredible."

The evening passed quickly. While Jennifer enjoyed her meal, she felt discontented. She couldn't help but notice the change in Nathan's attitude toward her. This morning he had been so open and friendly— now, he seemed somewhat distant and spent the majority of his time talking to Brianna.

Who could blame him after the way she had acted? *I'm surprised he followed through with the dinner.* If only she could rewind time and start over.

Brianna's happy voice broke into Jennifer's reverie. She listened as her daughter and Nathan discussed the merits of Mister Rogers'

Neighborhood and imitated Brianna's favorite Sesame Street character, Cookie Monster. Brianna sure was talkative tonight.

"Mommy takin' me to Bewwy Farm 'morrow," Brianna told Nathan toward the end of the meal. "You come too."

Jennifer supressed her frustration. *Brianna still doesn't understand about the car.* "Honey, we can only go if Mommy's car is fixed, remember?"

"Nafan has car," Brianna said, matter-of-factly. "He take us."

"Honey, he has to be somewhere else tomorrow."

Nathan put down his fork. "Actually, tomorrow is the only day I don't have to be at the conference. I've never had the chance to see Knott's Berry Farm before. I'd really like to go."

Jennifer groaned inwardly. *Why did Brianna have to do this? Now I have to find the money for Nathan's admission fee.* She smiled as gracefully as she could. "It would be nice to have you join us, Nathan."

"I'll go only on one condition—that it's my treat." Nathan leaned back in his chair.

Jennifer's smile vanished. "I can't let you do that, especially after everything you've done."

He raised his hand as if to breach any argument. "The dinner's on Rob, tomorrow will be on me. No arguments."

Before Jennifer could reply, Davy Crockett and several of the other characters arrived at the table singing "Happy Birthday." Davy set a miniature chocolate birthday cake in front of Brianna and took a picture of her blowing out the candle. Moments later, he slipped the picture into a bubble snow globe and handed it to Jennifer. "Hope you have a real good evening."

Nathan took a disposable camera from his pocket and handed it to Davy Crockett. "Could you take a few more pictures for us, please? I promised Rob that I'd get some for him."

"Certainly. Smile everyone."

Brianna hugged Bear-Bear and gave the camera her cheesiest grin.

Davy Crockett returned the camera to Nathan then left.

Jennifer helped Brianna cut the cake into four small pieces. "Maybe we should let Bear-Bear share your piece, so we can give this one to Grammy in the morning."

"Okay, Mommy. Me give it to her."

"If it's not too late when we get home." After they had eaten the rest of the cake, Jennifer put Elyssa's piece in a small, round take-out container and slipped it into her purse. By the time they got settled in Nathan's car, Brianna nodded sleepily.

Chapter 5

Half an hour later, Nathan pulled up in front of the apartment building. "Why don't you let me carry her up? You can get the seat."

"Thanks. That would be a big help." Jennifer watched him gently pick up Brianna. *He'd make a great father.*

She removed the car seat and day bag, locked, and then shut the car door. She quickly looked up and down the street for her tan and brown station wagon, but couldn't find it. *I'll never loan Anton anything again.*

Jennifer crossed the street with Nathan. "Brianna will have to give Elyssa her piece of cake tomorrow. She won't wake up anytime soon."

She led the way up the stairs and unlocked the door. Dr. Pellitiern carried Brianna to her room, and then helped Jennifer get the sleeping child ready for bed.

"Thanks so much for your help," Jennifer said as Nathan followed her into the living room a few minutes later.

He shrugged slightly, flashing her a warm smile. "No problem. What time shall I pick you up in the morning?"

"Are you sure you want to do this?" While she hoped he'd back out of the trip, part of her wanted him to go.

"I'm sure. This will be my only chance to go and amusement parks are no fun alone." Nathan frowned. "Am I barging in?"

A surge of panic brewed inside Jennifer. "No, not at all. I just didn't want you to feel obligated because Brianna put you on the spot."

"Believe me, I don't feel obligated." His smile returned. "In fact, I'm honored she wants to include me. So, what time does the park open in the morning?"

She smiled back, relieved. "I think it's around ten."

"Why don't I pick you up at around eight-thirty and we can go out for breakfast. I've heard Mrs. Knott's Restaurant has great food."

Jennifer knew that for a fact. "It does. You have to try their homemade biscuits."

"Sounds good. I'll see you at eight-thirty, then. Goodnight."

"Goodnight, and thanks for the lovely evening."

When Nathan had gone, Jennifer reflected on the pleasant outing. How refreshing her brother's friend had seemed. Too bad Anton couldn't be like that.

Anton Carducci arrived fifteen minutes after Nathan's departure. "Where were you?" He pushed his way past her. "I've been trying to call for the past three hours."

"Brianna and I went out for a birthday dinner." Jennifer closed the door. What gave the man the idea he owned her?

Anton went to the kitchen and started making a pot of coffee. "Why didn't you say anything to me about it? I may have wanted to go."

She hadn't done any favors by ignoring his presumptuous behavior for so long. This needed to end. "Dinner was a special gift from her uncle and...you weren't invited." Jennifer wanted to confront Anton head on, but felt a check in her spirit. *God, something's really off tonight, but I'm not sure what it is. Help me know what to say.*

"Your brother's here, now?" Anton spooned coffee into the filter.

Jennifer's mind raced. She couldn't tell Anton about Nathan, but she couldn't lie, either. "No, he...just made the arrangements."

Anton poured water into the coffee maker. "I don't see why I couldn't have gone. I could pay for my own meal. He didn't have to know anything about it."

"He meant this time to be special for just Brianna and me." She watched his face. Would he pursue this further? The smell of brewing coffee filled the apartment.

Anton threw some keys on the coffee table and sat on the couch. "There are your car keys. I parked it on the street."

Relief flooded through Jennifer. *Thanks, Lord; he's dropped the subject.* She quickly pocketed her keys and shifted focus to her car. "I had hoped to get the car back earlier today. I needed it this afternoon."

"For what?"

Resentment brewed within her. *Get a life, Anton. I don't have to report to you.* She refused to tell him about the layoff. Anger laced her voice. "I have a birthday party coming up on Saturday and need to get my shopping done."

He snarled in disgust. "Where do I even fit in your life. If you're not off to some church thing, you're spending time with your daughter. Are you avoiding me, or are you dating someone else?"

"Keep your voice down. I'm not dating anyone, not even you. *Remember?* I have absolutely no room in my life for romance." Jennifer went down the hall to check on Brianna. While the child tended to sleep heavily, she detested Anton so much that she seemed to listen for his voice.

Satisfied that her daughter still slept, Jennifer gently closed the bedroom door. She wished Anton would vanish from her life— permanently. *I'm tired of dealing with his tantrums.* She took a moment to bring her own anger under control before returning to the living room. "Anton, my life does not revolve around you."

He launched himself off the couch and poured a cup of coffee. "I didn't realize when I started seeing you, that I'd end up competing with your religion and your daughter."

Jennifer stared at his back. "No one has asked you to compete, Anton," she answered, her voice even and controlled. "As a *friend,* you need to understand that Brianna and my personal relationship with God are highest priority."

Anton's face turned sulky. "What do you have against me, anyway? Aren't I good enough for you?"

She took a deep breath to calm the butterflies in her stomach. "I have nothing against you personally, Anton. Friendship is all I have room for in my heart. My daughter needs me and I must straighten out the most vital area of my life—my personal relationship with God."

"It's obvious that you're shutting me out," he spat, whirling to face her. His dark eyes flashed in anger. "Why couldn't that meddling cousin of yours leave well enough alone? You were happy enough with me before she showed up."

"Michelle has nothing to do with this." Jennifer hardly recognized this vicious man in front of her. His explosive temper frightened her. "I said nothing before because I didn't think you'd understand."

She groped for the right words. "I haven't been happy in years. I turned my back on God after my husband's murder. I blamed Him for what happened. I didn't see any sense in serving Someone who couldn't keep tragedy from my life. So, I started looking elsewhere for ways to ease my pain."

She paused and waited for his reaction. Anton's face turned stony. Jennifer took another breath. "When I met you this past spring, I honestly thought you could help make the pain and emptiness in my heart go away, but you couldn't. I understand now that's something only God can do. Anything else is only a temporary diversion."

Anton sneered. "I'm a temporary diversion? That's just great! Here I thought the woman I chose to marry was content to be a part of my world—to share my life and my dreams. Now I find out you were merely using me?!"

Color drained from her face. Chose to marry? She sank into the easy chair and bit her lower lip. "Anton, I made it quite clear from the outset that we would never be more than friends. If I've said or done anything to make you think I felt any differently, I'm sorry."

"As if that would absolve you." Anton leaned against the kitchen counter and narrowed his eyes. His voice held a caustic tinge. "I've invested a lot into you. If you think you can just apologize and hide behind a fairy tale, think again."

Panic gripped her. *I must stay calm.* Jennifer forced herself to breathe. Her eyes wandered to the phone behind Anton. If only Mike would call, she could get a message to him to come over. The device remained silent. *God, what have I gotten myself into?* How could she set Anton straight without him going off the deep end?

She weighed her words carefully. "Anton, I never said I'd be anything more than a friend to you. And I never wanted you to spend money on me. We've had enough arguments on that subject. But each time you insisted that I was insulting you not to accept your hospitality. Tell me how much I owe you and I'll pay you back every cent."

Anton growled savagely. "Forget your blasted money. I want you!"

Fear rose with a bitter taste in Jennifer's mouth. "I'm not in love with you, Anton." She spoke softly, hoping to diffuse his anger. "My heart is completely locked away, and will never open again. Not for anyone. Since you can't accept that, it would be best if we stopped seeing each other."

Anton smashed the coffee mug against the kitchen wall, splattering its contents over the wallpaper and floor. "That's what you think!" Rage marred his handsome Latin face. He cursed, clenched his fists, and glared at her. "You're not telling me what to do. I call the shots here and don't you forget it."

Jennifer tried to stop her hands from shaking. Her heart pounded and her mouth felt dry as she tried to hold onto her fleeting courage. *Don't lose it now, Jen. You've got to stay in control.* "Anton, I can never be what you want me to be. We need to go our separate ways."

Anton knocked the entire coffee maker onto the floor, shattering glass across the kitchen. "You're not going anywhere." He lunged toward her, grabbed her right arm, and yanked her from the chair. His fingers dug deep into her tender flesh.

"Let go, you're hurting me," Jennifer pleaded. She thought she sensed a streak of insanity in his eyes. Fear traced its icy finger up her spine. *He's crazy. Oh, God, what am I going to do?*

A bitter laugh escaped Anton's lips. He tightened his grip and lowered his voice to a near whisper. "I've got news for you, *mi cara*. I can hurt you even more than this. Don't get any ideas about walking out. You'll leave when I tire of you and not before. Is that clear?"

Jennifer bit her lower lip and nodded mutely. Fighting with him now would be dangerous. She had to go along with him until after he left.

"Good. I'd hate to see anything happen to your precious little daughter." Anton pushed Jennifer away. "I'll be out of town for a week or so on business. You'd better drop the religious garbage by the time I get back, because I refuse to tolerate it any longer." Anton stormed out of the apartment, slamming the door behind him.

Churning emotions pummeled her as she locked the door, fearing he would change his mind and come back. *Praise God he doesn't have a key.* Jennifer rubbed her bruised arm. The finger marks on her skin began to darken. What had she gotten herself into?

Jennifer wound a lock of hair around her finger. *God, what am I going to do?* She leaned against the door, numb with heartache and fear. Anton threatened to harm Brianna if she didn't comply with his wishes. Every article she had ever read about obsessive men crowded into her mind. Their lives were in danger here, but what could she do? There seemed to be no easy answer. Where could they go? How could they get away?

Jennifer forced herself to clean up the mess in the kitchen. What a horrific day! Her shaking hands grabbed the broom and swept the glass shards into the dustpan. She dumped them into the trash then she began to mop up the coffee.

She dialed Mike's number, but when she got a busy signal she abandoned the idea. *You can't go running to him every time something goes wrong,.* Besides, she doubted the police could even stop Anton. *You got into this; you get out of it. Figure things out for yourself.* Jennifer sagged against the kitchen counter as terror chilled her soul.

God, You said You'd take care of me. Where are You now? Will You be like my dad and disappear when I need You most? How do I get out of this mess? She and Brianna needed to disappear, but where?

Immediately, Rob's letter came to mind. God really did care. He had everything planned out already. She made some quick calculations. *A week? Yes, I think I can pull it off.*

Chapter 6

Though Jennifer went to bed confident in her escape plans, the next morning found her wrestling with moving details. How could she get everything to Rob's without Anton being able to trace them?

She quickly dressed in a light cotton skirt and a lavender t-shirt. As Jennifer opened her bedroom drapes, sunshine spilled onto the powder blue carpet. She washed her face, brushed her auburn locks, and then debated whether to wear makeup. Vanity won out. *I'm not going public without makeup.* She reached for her makeup kit and noticed the ugly bruises on her right arm. The horror of Anton's actions gripped her yet again. She immediately exchanged the t-shirt for a pale blue long-sleeved cotton blouse.

Jennifer's mind shifted back to the upcoming move. How could she get this stuff out of here? A moving company would have to keep records. *I could rent a truck.* She stepped into her penny loafers. *Maybe I'd better talk to Mike about this, after all.*

She pushed her troubling thoughts aside and headed for Brianna's room. She dressed her daughter in flowered cotton overalls and a pink short-sleeved shirt. The child squirmed as Jennifer slathered sunscreen on her exposed skin.

Minutes later, the youngster danced merrily around the apartment in excitement. Jennifer filled a small canvas bag with little necessities for the day, including an extra set of clothes for Brianna. *Just because she's finally potty trained doesn't mean she won't have an accident.*

Jennifer tucked her camera, a few of rolls of film, and a small first aid kit into the large side pockets.

A small knot crept into her stomach. *Nathan will be here in less than an hour.* She took an anxious survey of the street through the front and side windows. *No sign of Anton.* Had he told the truth about being gone? What if he had lied?

A sense of urgency tugged at her. She made sure Rob's letter was in her purse. Brianna's eager face kept her from calling off the trip so she could start packing. *I can't disappoint her like that.*

"Bear-Bear, too, Mommy," Brianna insisted, pushing the large stuffed animal into her hands.

The large brown teddy bear had no hope of fitting in the small canvas bag. Jennifer sighed. "I'll need to get the big bag, honey." Moments later, she had transferred the bear and the contents of the smaller bag into the roomier day bag.

On sudden impulse, she also stuck in her purse. She set down the large canvas bag then retrieved Brianna's car seat and striped foldable stroller from the hall closet.

Problems continued to recite themselves in Jennifer's mind as she stacked all three items beside the door. How would she break the move to Elyssa? She'd expect a thirty-day notice and Jennifer couldn't give her that. She twisted a lock of hair around her finger.

She could give her friend an extra month's rent. That way, Elyssa wouldn't be out the money, and would have more time to find a new tenant. She chewed her lower lip while pondering her decision. No, she couldn't give up that much money. *It'll take a huge bite out of my moving funds, and I'd just end up stuck here.*

Jennifer poured a small cup of milk for Brianna to tide the child over until breakfast. Craving coffee, she reached for the carafe, and then stopped herself. Her stomach churned as she remembered Anton's fury and the sound of shattering glass. She shivered in fear. What if Brianna had awakened and gotten in his way? "I've got to talk to Mike."

She glanced up at the clock. Maybe he hadn't left home yet. At least she could a leave a message with Tina. Her trembling fingers dialed the Scavone's number. After three rings, Tina answered, sounding rather groggy.

"Hi, Tina, it's Jennifer. I hope I didn't wake you up."

Tina yawned. "No, I never went to sleep. Mike had a horribly rough night. I can talk, if you don't mind me fueling up."

Jennifer heard a spoon click against glass. She smiled, picturing Tina's worn coffee mug. "Go ahead. Mike had another night terror?"

"Yeah, triggered by the news coverage of the recent jewel store robbery. His screaming curled my hair this time. Mike's so frustrated about the amnesia he can't stand himself. He said this time he could see one of the faces in his dream, but when he woke up, he couldn't remember it."

Jennifer's heart ached for her friends. While Mike's night terrors had lessened somewhat over the years, they still haunted him. He had insisted that nothing short of catching the killers would erase them. "I'm so sorry, Tina. The anniversary of the attack probably didn't help much, either. Is he doing all right today?"

"We'll get through this." Tina sighed. "He left early this morning, determined to convince his supervisor to let him work on the case.

Mike thinks it'll somehow help him get his memory back. But enough about us. How are you doing?"

Jennifer winced. It seemed self-centered to bring up her troubles. Still, she needed to protect Brianna. "All right, I guess. I got pretty depressed yesterday after seeing the news. It's hard to know that Danny's killers are still dodging the police. I'm hoping they'll slip up somehow and get caught." She paused a moment, then continued. "I was hoping to catch Mike before he left this morning. I need to pick his brilliant brain."

"Is there anything I can do to help?"

Shame nearly kept Jennifer from revealing Anton's threats. *What will she think of me?* She caught her lower lip between her teeth. She couldn't let her pride endanger her daughter. She'd start easing into it and see how Tina reacted. "Well," she said, finally. "I got laid off yesterday and have to move. I have a lot of details to juggle and I'm feeling overwhelmed."

"Moving?" Tina's voice took on a note of concern. "Where? Why don't you just take that job with the police department? It's still open. After all, you're a natural."

Jennifer watched Brianna try to fit two more of her stuffed animals into the day bag. "Hold on, Tina." She put her hand over the receiver. "Brianna, only one of your animals can go today. Do you want your new bear, or one of those?"

Brianna looked at her stuffed animals and sighed. "Bear-bear." She took her other animals back into her room and shut the door.

Jennifer turned her attention back to the phone. "Sorry about that. I know the P.D. job pays well, but police drawings aren't my forte. I can only draw what I've seen. No. My brother invited Brianna and me to move in with him. I think it would be a good change for us."

Sarcasm oozed over the phone line. "Miss Independence moving in with her brother? There's something more, isn't there, Jen?"

"I guess I'd better be up front." Jennifer grimaced. "I tried to end my friendship with Anton last night. He threatened to harm Brianna and me. He said he'll be gone for a week or two. So, I must disappear before he returns."

"What threats?"

Jennifer quickly filled her in on the details before Brianna could come back and overhear.

Alarm sounded in her friend's voice. "Have you reported him to the police, yet?"

Good ol' practical Tina. Jennifer rolled her eyes. "What good would it do? The cops can't touch him unless he does something major. Even then, he'd be out on bail within an hour of being arrested."

"You could get a protection order." Tina meant well, but she didn't understand.

Jennifer forced her voice to remain cordial. "A piece of paper won't stop him. Things are crazier than you know and we're not safe here."

"Listen, let me get a message to Mike." her friend offered. "I'll have him stop by your place as soon as he has a chance."

Jennifer looked at the clock. "I'll be gone all day. I promised to take Brianna to Knott's Berry Farm and we won't be back until about five. Could he call or stop by then?"

"I'll have him stop by," Tina promised. "You hang in there, kiddo. If Anton shows up again, don't open the door. Just dial 9-1-1 and keep the door locked."

Fear brushed her spine. "I'll keep that in mind. I'm hoping he was telling the truth about going out of town. I'll talk to you later." Jennifer hung up, relieved that Tina hadn't judged her for her mistakes. She then made a quick call to Elyssa. "Your cake is in the 'fridge. We'll see you tonight."

After she hung up, Jennifer peered out the window for any sign of Nathan. *Calm down, he's got ten minutes, yet.* She decided it would be best to take her car today, in case Anton was still around. She couldn't risk his taking her station wagon again, especially since she needed it for her move. She prayed Nathan wouldn't press for an explanation.

She went through the apartment, gathering up trash. The doorbell rang as she tied off the white plastic bag. Brianna ran to the door.

"Hold on, Brianna." Jennifer looked through the peephole. Her pulse quickened when she recognized Nathan's friendly face. She opened the door and ushered him inside. He looked relaxed in faded blue jeans, a light green cotton t-shirt and battered tennis shoes.

"Everybody ready to go?" He scooped Brianna up into a hug. "I had to park almost two blocks away, so I hope you don't mind a short walk." His blue eyes scanned the room. "Where's Sir Bear-Bear?"

Jennifer picked up the large canvas bag and the trash. "He's in the day bag. Couldn't go anywhere without the newest member of the family, now could we?"

"That looks heavy, let me get that." Nathan slung the day bag over his right shoulder and reached for the striped foldable stroller. "You almost have to pack up the whole house to go on outings with youngsters, huh?"

Jennifer laughed. "It sure seems that way sometimes. I carry more now than when Brianna was smaller." She picked up the car seat. "I think I've got everything." She opened the door. "If you don't mind too much, I'd rather take my car."

Nathan shrugged. "That's all right with me. You know the way to Knott's. I'd have needed navigational help. This way I can just sit back and enjoy the company." He let Brianna clasp his free hand. "The rental car should be all right where it is."

Jennifer locked the door then followed Nathan and Brianna down the stairs. "Let me get rid of the trash."

She set the car seat on the sidewalk, walked to the dumpster at the back of the duplex, and tossed in the bag. Rejoining Nathan and Brianna, she grabbed the car seat and led the way to her car.

Two hours later, they had polished off breakfast at Mrs. Knott's Chicken Dinner Restaurant and headed on their way to the park's many attractions.

Jennifer smoothed an extra layer of sunscreen on Brianna's arms and face. "All right, let's go through the rules, first." She placed a purple beach hat on her daughter's head. "You can walk as long as you hold onto the stroller, Mommy's hand, or Nathan's hand. Do not go with anyone else, understand?"

"Okay." Brianna grinned and grabbed onto Nathan's hand.

Jennifer nodded her approval. She strapped Sir Bear-Bear in the stroller. "Good. Now, if you get too tired to walk, you must ride in your stroller. We will not carry you."

Brianna continued grinning. "Okay."

"All right. Last rule." Jennifer knelt and placed the day bag on the cloth shelf under the stroller. "You can have only one birthday goody today and it must cost under twenty dollars."

"One goody!" Brianna's grin broadened to a toothy smile.

Nathan seemed puzzled. "How will she know what's under twenty? She's rather young."

"She's quite brilliant," Jennifer confessed. "Elyssa and I've been teaching her how to count up to twenty." She lowered her voice. "Brianna will most likely spend most of her time in Camp Snoopy. So if you're inclined to go on the more daring rides, you'll have to wander off on your own."

"What? And miss sharing this time with you two?" Nathan shook his head. "No way. We're in this together. Let's go."

Jennifer eyed him warily for a moment. What was he after? Men didn't spend time with kids or their mothers unless they wanted something. She remembered how Anton had tried to win Brianna over during their first meeting, but the child proved unmovable and the two declared open war.

We'll see just what Nathan's made of, she told herself. Could he survive a whole day with Brianna without losing his cool?

"Okay, folks. First stop: Camp Snoopy. Herbie is waiting."

Brianna pulled Nathan along in her rush to get to the petting zoo. "Come see tuttle," she insisted.

Jennifer pushed the stroller with her daughter's fuzzy friend inside. The front left wheel kept sticking, making maneuvering difficult. *I'd better oil that when we get home.*

When they entered the petting zoo, Jennifer wrinkled her nose at the acrid scent of animal waste mixed with dust. Noisy children waited for their turn at the pony rides. Barbados sheep stuck their heads through the fence to take food from the hands of visitors. Goats roamed freely throughout the zoo.

Jennifer followed Brianna and Nathan over to a large pen. Inside, Herbie, a giant Galapagos Tortoise, sunned himself.

Brianna's excitement was uncontainable. "See? Tuttle my fwiend," she told Nathan before dragging him away to see the sheep.

For the next forty-five minutes the trio fed, petted, and gazed at the various animals. Jennifer and Nathan took turns photographing the events. Jennifer laughed as the goats and sheep nuzzled her hands with their warm, moist mouths.

One goat developed a taste for Nathan's jeans and followed him throughout the petting zoo, much to Brianna's delight.

When Brianna took her turn on the pony ride, Jennifer and Nathan stood along the fence and cheered her on. Later, Brianna led them to the cages at the very back of the zoo. Soft rabbits peered out of the mesh screens.

A blonde-haired woman in blue jeans and a red cotton shirt opened the various cages and filled containers with water and food pellets.

"Me wants bunny, Mommy," Brianna announced, pointing to a small, black lop-eared creature.

"You can't, hon," Jennifer explained. "They're not for sale."

Nathan fingered a tag attached to one of the cages. "Actually, this one is. Here's the sign."

Jennifer rolled her eyes and shook her head in frustration. She wished she had thought to ban live creatures from Brianna's wish list.

Nathan grimaced. "Whoops, sorry. That wasn't very helpful."

No kidding. She drew her breath. "We must find out how much he costs, Brianna."

The caretaker approached them. "My name is Judy. May I help you?"

Jennifer pointed to the rabbit. "Yes, how much is the floppy-eared bunny?" She hoped the price would be too high. Brianna wouldn't understand the extra costs that would come with adopting a pet.

"She's fifteen dollars. We also have other rabbits at twenty each."

Jennifer's heart sank. She regretted teaching Brianna her numbers so early. Now, how did she get out of this? "Why is she cheaper than the others? Is there something wrong with her?"

Judy opened the cage and lifted the rabbit out. "She's an orphan and the runt of the litter. Other than that, she's healthy, curious, active, and quite friendly."

She held the rabbit so that Brianna could pet her. "Rabbits make great house pets if you bunny-proof your electrical cords. You can train them to use a kitty box and they make very little noise. You won't need to keep them caged, except for when you first get them acquainted with your home. Also, they're cheaper to feed and easier to care for than other house pets."

"Me wants bunny, Mommy." Brianna insisted. She kissed the rabbit's ebony head. "My goody."

Jennifer shrugged and looked at Nathan. "I gave her my word. I have no idea how we can take her," she whispered. "I don't have a cage, and...well...Rob invited us to live with him in Maine. How can I possibly get a rabbit to Maine safely?"

Nathan raised his eyebrows and whispered back, "You're taking Rob's offer?" He grinned. "That's great! We...uh, there's plenty of room at the house for a rabbit. In fact, since I got you into this, I'll even take care of the cage, food and the transportation for our furry little friend."

Jennifer felt puzzled by Nathan's enthusiasm, but appreciated his generous offer. *At least he's man enough to take responsibility for his part of this problem.* Still, there had to be a way out.

She thought for a moment. Her daughter might lose interest by day's end. "Tell you what, Brianna. We'll ask this lady to keep the bunny until we get ready to go home. If you *still* want her then, we'll buy her and take her home with us."

Tears welled up in Brianna's big blue eyes. "Me wants bunny, Mommy. You pwomised. My goody."

The child's insistence surprised Jennifer. It wasn't often Brianna really wanted something. She resigned herself to the purchase and made out a check.

Brianna begged to take the bunny on the rides with her, but Nathan talked her out of it. Soon, they left the petting zoo with the adoption papers and a firm promise to pick up "Bunny" at the end of the day.

A balloon-popping contest soon caught Brianna's attention. She giggled as she joined other youngsters in sitting on the elusive balloons. When Snoopy showed up to pose with the children, Jennifer took a picture of Brianna with the star.

After a quick stop to the bathroom, Brianna started a tour of the kiddie rides. She ended the rounds with Snoopy's Animal Show and another stop at the petting zoo to check on "Bunny."

Nathan suggested finding a place to eat lunch.

Jennifer agreed and strapped Brianna into her stroller and placed Bear-Bear on her lap. "You must hold him tightly so he doesn't fall out," she told her daughter.

Nathan scanned the park's map. "Ah, here we go," he said, looking up. "How about the barbecue? That way we can see the dinosaurs and catch the train after lunch?"

Jennifer stood. "Sounds good to me. Which way?" She maneuvered the stroller and followed him toward the center of the park, hoping to find some shade. The sun beat relentlessly on the pavement. She licked her parched lips and longed for an ice-cold soda.

They passed the Wagon Camp. Along the way, Nathan pointed out the landmarks and made hilarious remarks about each. Jennifer's stomach hurt from laughing.

The front left stroller wheel caught again. Jennifer struggled with it. When it didn't move, she backed up the stroller and pushed harder. Without warning, the stroller tipped over and a wheel rolled away. Brianna shrieked as she hit the pavement, still strapped into the seat. Bear-Bear flew into the dirt.

Jennifer knelt down and quickly released her daughter from the seat. She picked up the crying child and cuddled her. Bloody scrapes marked Brianna's elbows, and tears stained her cheeks.

Nathan checked the youngster over. "She seems to only have minor injuries, but those scrapes sure look nasty. Why don't you go ahead and clean her up? I'll put this stroller back in the car and rent one for the rest of the day."

Jennifer didn't want to argue. She took her keys from the day bag and handed them to Nathan. He pocketed them, picked up Sir Bear-Bear, and brushed the toy off. "It looks like he needs a few hugs," he told Brianna. "Can you help him?"

Brianna hiccuped and reached for her stuffed animal. The child hugged him close and leaned against her mother.

Jennifer felt warmed by Nathan's gentleness with Brianna. She watched as he rounded up the stray wheel, unhooked the day bag and picked up the broken stroller.

"Do you need any bandages?" he asked.

Jennifer took the bag. "Thanks, but I packed a first aid kit. I'll take her to the bathroom and we'll meet you back here in a little while."

Nathan nodded then headed for the park entrance.

Twenty-five minutes later, Nathan parked a rented double stroller in front of them. Jennifer's heart fluttered. *Uh oh, he's starting to get to me. I'd better be careful.*

"Have you been waiting long?" Concern marked his face.

Jennifer's knees felt weak. *So, he's being nice to us. You don't have to fall for him.* She took a deep breath and steadied herself. "We just got here ourselves."

"Good. I hope you three are hungry, because I'm starved." Nathan helped arrange Brianna and her beloved Bear-Bear in the rental stroller. "Well, let's go."

The savory smell of barbecued chicken and chili made Jennifer's mouth water. Few people stood in line, so they moved through quickly.

"I'll take the trays if you'll take the bag and the stroller," Nathan offered. "That way you can get Brianna settled at a table."

Jennifer nodded and went ahead of him, giving her and Brianna's order to the young man behind the counter. Minutes later, she led the way to the table. Nathan carried two trays of succulent chicken, salads, beans, cheese toast and soft drinks.

Before they reached the table, a heavy-set man dashed directly in front of Jennifer. When she stopped to let him by, Nathan plowed into her back, knocking trays of food onto his chest. Jennifer stifled a scream. Barbecue sauce clung to the doctor's shirt and soda covered the front of his blue jeans. The containers of chili and salad had burst open on his shoes.

She wanted to crawl under the nearest table. "I am so sorry."

He seemed a bit dazed as he peered down at his soiled clothing. Jennifer's muscles tightened in fear. Would he explode in anger?

To her surprise, Dr. Pellitier threw his head back and roared with laughter. "I've heard of getting into food, but this is ridiculous."

Jennifer quickly parked the stroller beside the nearest table and grabbed the box of baby wipes from the day bag. "Here, this might keep the sauce from staining your clothes."

He stepped aside, took the baby wipes and scrubbed at the sauce. A worker hurried over to help clean up the mess.

Jennifer relaxed and studied Nathan with amazement. What made this man tick? Didn't anything bother him?

Nathan looked over at her. "Don't worry, Jen. This is an old shirt." He looked around, mischief twinkling in his blue eyes. "I just hope I don't run into any of my colleagues, because I'll have a hard time explaining why my jeans are wet."

Another worker replaced their food. They sat at a canopied table and enjoyed the fare. A couple of tourists strolled by, drenched to the skin. Nathan touched Jennifer's arm and pointed them out. "I could use a shower like that, right now. Where do you suppose they got soaked?"

Jennifer chuckled. "That's easy. They must have gone on Big Foot Rapids. I can lead you over there after we eat."

"Would you?" Nathan beamed. "That would be great."

After lunch, Jennifer and Brianna settled themselves at the entrance to Big Foot Rapids.

Nathan stuffed his wallet and wristwatch in the side pocket of the day bag. "I hope you don't mind holding onto these for me. I just don't want them to get wet." He grinned. "Would you happen to have any soap in that handy bag of yours?"

"Nope." Jennifer shook her head. "They wouldn't let you use it on the ride anyhow."

He shrugged. "It didn't hurt to ask. Well, I'm off to adventure." After giving them a mock salute, he dashed up the wooden walkway, and stood at the end of the line. Soon, he disappeared from view.

Fifteen minutes later, Nathan emerged from the ride, thoroughly soaked. Brianna presented him with a towel that she and Jennifer had purchased at a nearby booth. The youngster giggled. "You wook funny."

The doctor leaned toward them and shook the water off of his hair and beard. Brianna squealed and hid behind her mother. Nathan grinned. "Boy, what a great way to cool off." He towel-dried his dark hair. "Thanks for the towel. Where to now?"

"We should wait on the active rides a while longer. Brianna gets motion sickness right after eating." Jennifer unfolded the map. "We could find something tame. Since we're by the Kingdom of the Dinosaurs, why don't we go there?"

Nathan peered over her shoulder. "Where else do we want to go to? Should we come up with a schedule or something?"

After a brief conference, they hit the dinosaur attraction, the dolphin show, the mine ride, then headed for the train depot.

Nathan parked the stroller inside the small wooden building. "Okay, Kitten, let's get the rest of our baggage and board the train." He set Brianna on the floor.

To Jennifer's trained eye the toddler looked too warm. "Are you feeling all right, honey?"

Brianna nodded. "Me want to go on twain."

She'd have to take the child's word for it. "All right. Let's go."

The toddler held onto Nathan with one hand and clutched Bear-Bear with the other. Jennifer carried the day bag.

Once on board the train, Brianna crawled onto Nathan's lap and peered out the window. Jennifer settled beside them. "She's never been on any of these rides before," she told him. "Last time we came, Camp Snoopy wore her out before we could head this way."

The old-fashioned train started forward with a sudden lurch and soon settled into the soothing rhythm of the rails.

Nathan smiled down at Brianna. "Well, what do you think? Do you like trains?"

Brianna looked around, her blue eyes round with wonder. "Twain makes funny noises."

A loud commotion erupted at the back of the car. Two bandits ran down the aisle, brandishing guns. Brianna's screams pierced Jennifer's eardrums. As the men hurried into the next car, she tried to comfort the youngster. "Honey, it's only pretend."

Brianna's face had turned chalky white, and she trembled as she clung to Nathan. The child buried her face in his chest and promptly threw up.

Jennifer felt she would die of embarrassment. *Poor Nathan. He'll probably be glad when this day is over and he can escape us.* She reached into the day bag and brought out the container of baby wipes

Nathan shifted Brianna to his clean right shoulder and rocked her soothingly. "The bad men are gone, Kitten. I'll protect you."

Tears sprang to Jennifer's eyes. How could a complete stranger be so loving like this? Nathan's compassion chipped away at her defenses. Her earlier resolve crumbled. How she wanted to get to know this man —maybe even to win his love. Her heart danced. At least she'd have a chance since they'd be moving to Maine.

By the time they picked up Brianna's rabbit, Jennifer regained her senses. *I can't get involved again.* She swallowed hard. Moving in with Rob would seal her fate. They couldn't go to Maine. She'd just figure out another way to escape Anton.

Chapter 7

Jennifer grumbled at the rush hour traffic as she waited for the freeway on-ramp light to turn to green. Sirens pierced the hot, stale afternoon air.

Brianna chatted merrily with Nathan from the back seat. "Bunny" sat beside her in a cardboard pet carrier. The animal caretaker had also provided some feed and a container of water for the rabbit's short journey. Nathan sported a new Knott's Berry Farm t-shirt in place of his badly soiled shirt.

An hour later, when Jennifer started to maneuver her station wagon down her street, flashing emergency lights caught her eye. Firefighting equipment and police vehicles jammed her block. Beyond the throng of onlookers and police barricade, firefighters in bright yellow coats coiled their hoses and returned them to two large trucks. Her heart pounded in her ears.

She parked her car in the first available space not too far from Nathan's rental car. "Nathan, would you mind staying with Brianna while I check things out?"

Concern covered his friendly face. "No problem. I hope that isn't...your h-o-u-s-e."

Her mouth felt dry. "I can't tell. Probably not. You know how it is, we always assume ours is the one that's gone." Her laugh sounded hollow to her own ears. "I'll be right back."

Smoke hung in the air. *Father, let everything be all right.* Jennifer noticed a news van across the street. She fought her way through the crowd, searching for a familiar face. A moment later she spotted her surrogate mother talking to a young, female police officer behind the barricade. "Elyssa, what's going on?" She ducked under the police tape and glanced at the officer's name badge.

Officer Hernandez immediately turned and scowled. "You can't come in here." She motioned for Jennifer to get back behind the barricade.

Jennifer spoke with cold dignity. "I live on this block and have a right to know if my property is safe."

The officer's scowl softened. "What's your address?"

When Jennifer told her, she grimly shook her head. "The fire captain will need to talk to both of you. I'll tell him you're here." She spoke a few words into her hand-held radio and waited for a response. "Someone will escort you over."

Jennifer gave Elyssa a helpless look. "What's going on?"

Her friend shook her head. "I just got back from the hospital a few minutes ago." Elyssa's dark eyes mirrored the fear Jennifer felt.

A tall, dark-haired man in plain clothes approached them. From Sergeant Mike Scavone's haggard face, Jennifer surmised the worst. *Oh, Father, it is our place.* Her chest and throat tightened. "Mike, what happened? How bad is it?"

"There was some kind of explosion." He stood before them, his steel-gray eyes etched with pain. He sighed. "I'm afraid there's very little left of your home."

Tears stung Jennifer's eyes. *Why does everything have to happen to us?* She wrapped her arms around Elyssa and hugged her close.

"No. No. I don't understand." Elyssa moaned. "I plugged it in before I left. I was only gone for a couple of hours. How could this happen?

Mike seemed puzzled. "What are you talking about? What did you leave plugged in?"

"The slow cooker." Misery filled Elyssa's eyes. "I wanted to have dinner ready for Jennifer when she got back."

Mike rubbed the back of his neck. "This wasn't caused by a slow cooker; not unless you had nitroglycerin on the menu. Come on. I'll take you back there. Be careful where you step."

The women followed him. Jennifer kept her right arm around Elyssa's shoulder as they stepped past the fire trucks. Water pooled on the pavement beneath the remaining hoses.

Jennifer's left hand flew to her mouth when the house came into view. Jagged portions of the remaining three outer walls leaned precariously against each other, exposing the devastated upper story in the late afternoon sun.

Two firemen stood perched atop of the huge ladder stretched toward the second-story apartment. Twisted metal replaced Jennifer's stove and sink. Sections of the roof dangled from nearby trees and cluttered the once immaculate lawn. Downstairs, wide black streaks marked where the greedy fire had licked the outer walls while consuming the bottom apartment. Nothing remained.

Her trembling fingers tightened on Elyssa's shoulder as the older woman shook with convulsing sobs. Jennifer mentally inventoried her own possessions. The vital documents were in the fire-safe, so they should be all right. Insurance would take care of the furniture, clothing and household items, but what about everything else?

Family members could help replace Brianna's baby pictures. But the baby book, her wedding gown, and mementos of Danny were gone forever. Only the memories remained. Jennifer's tears flowed freely.

Her heart ached for Elyssa as well. She and Roger built that house together. How would she manage now?

Mike's voice broke into her thoughts. "Will you two be all right?"

Elyssa groaned then swayed.

Jennifer grabbed her friend around the waist. "Mike, Elyssa needs to sit down."

"Let's get her to my car." They gently guided their friend to his black sports car and ensured she was safely seated. Mike knelt beside her. "How are you feeling?"

Elyssa's voice quivered. "It's a hard blow, son, but...I'll get through this." She leaned her head against the seat and closed her eyes. "The Lord is my Shepherd. I shall not want..." she softly intoned.

Mike patted Elyssa's hands, then stood up. "She doesn't look good, Jen. Keep an eye on her. I'll have the paramedics check her over."

Five minutes later, while the paramedics attended to Elyssa, Mike introduced Jennifer to the arson investigator, Captain David Morgan.

The stocky man acknowledged her with a slight nod, and then addressed Mike. "Hang around, Sergeant. You can help me take notes." Morgan cleared his throat and turned his attention back to Jennifer. "From all indications, we've got a classic burg and burn."

"A what?" Jennifer interrupted. The man's gruff manner grated her nerves. "Can you speak plain English?"

Morgan ran thick fingers through his thinning sandy-brown hair. "Sorry. Apparently someone broke into the upper apartment and then tried to cover it up with a fire." His voice was expressionless—just stating the facts. "From the evidence, it appears the burglar used the gas to blow the place. With all the windows closed at the time, it was one hellacious blast."

A firefighter motioned Captain Morgan aside. "Excuse me," the investigator told Jennifer. He looked at Mike. "You know the routine, Sergeant."

Jennifer didn't get it. "Why would anyone break into my place? I own nothing worth stealing."

Mike pulled a small black notebook from his back pocket, his eyes unreadable. "Whoever did this probably didn't know, Jen." He flipped through the pad of paper until he found a clean sheet. "I know it's a pain, but I must ask you several routine questions. Where have you been today?"

She answered what she could, and then explained that Brianna and Nathan were waiting for her in the car. When Mike plied for information regarding Nathan, Jennifer told him everything she knew.

Morgan approached them with a furry lump in his hands. "Since the top back bedroom had the least damage, my men were able to dig this out of the rubble. Do you know anything about it?"

Jennifer stared the flat, singed shell of a stuffed animal. "Are you sure this is from my apartment?"

"Yep, and we found several other toy animals slashed open with the stuffing removed."

She stared at the fuzzy carcass for a long moment. This was crazy. *Why....* Fear chilled Jennifer's heart. "Anton! He must have seen me leave this morning."

Morgan scowled. "Pardon?"

Mike's gaze sharpened. "What makes you think Anton caused this?"

Anger coursed through her. "Who else would stoop so low? If it weren't for the stuffed animals, I might think it could be someone else. But the fact that my daughter's things were intentionally destroyed shows that it was an act of pure hatred. This definitely fits Anton's personality, especially after his threats last night."

Mike furrowed his brows. "What threats?"

Jennifer looked at him, bewildered. "Didn't Tina tell you? I called and told her everything this morning."

His gaze hardened. "We didn't have much time to talk, today. She did say to stop by and see you."

Jennifer nodded. Tina hadn't failed her. "I tried to end my friendship with Anton last night. He became furious and threatened to harm me and Brianna if I walked out on him." She watched Mike's eyes narrow as she spoke. "He said he'd be out of town for a week or so on business and that I had better get my act together to suit him by the time he returned. Apparently, he didn't leave town yet."

Morgan grunted. "Could be our perp. Sergeant, get the whole thing from the beginning," he ordered. "I'll see what I can get from the other woman." He headed back to Mike's car.

Fury blazed in Mike's steel-gray eyes. "Why didn't you call me last night, Jen?"

She dropped her gaze and mumbled an apology. Mike had a right to be angry. Since Danny's death, he had become guardian to her and Brianna, protecting them as fiercely as he did his own family.

Yet, a defiant spark of independence remained in her heart. Why should she have to run to any man when trouble came? They were the ones who left her behind—just look at her father and Danny.

Mike's voice cut through her thoughts. "Jen, what is going on here? Have you lost your mind? He could have killed you and Brianna." He motioned toward the rubble of her apartment. "Is this clue enough to what you're dealing with?"

Jennifer's shoulders sagged as she realized Mike was right. She couldn't deal with Anton alone. Because of her obstinance, Elyssa now suffered. She glanced over at Mike's car to see how her friend fared. A paramedic squatted beside the car, checking the woman's blood pressure. Jennifer felt raw and vulnerable. *What have I done to her?* She turned and faced Mike. "What do you need to know?"

Mike's jaw jutted forward, his lips drawn in a tight line. He poised his pencil. "Tell me exactly what happened last night. I want to run him in for questioning."

She reluctantly recounted details of her fight with Anton. Mike scribbled notes as Jennifer talked.

"What happened to the carafe and mug?"

Jennifer shrugged. "I cleaned up the mess and tossed the broken glass into the kitchen garbage."

Mike closed his notebook and shoved it in his back pocket. "Did you take the garbage out or did you leave it in the apartment?"

"I took it out just before we left this morning. I know that the garbage pickup isn't until tomorrow, but I don't keep trash in the house any longer than necessary."

"What kind of bag is it in?"

"A white plastic bag. Why?"

He turned and started to walk. "Prints. Let's retrieve it."

The acrid stench of burnt wood and cloth stung Jennifer's nostrils as she followed Mike behind the building. Wet ashes clung to her shoes and stockings.

When they reached the dumpster, Mike shoved a large piece of roofing out of the way. "Can you see it anywhere in here?"

Jennifer stood on her toes and peered over the side, careful not to touch the edges. "I'm not sure, but it may be the one back there in the left corner."

"All right." He pulled himself onto the dumpster and swung his legs over. "Let's hope this is it."

"Your clothes will get filthy." Jennifer protested.

"Yep, that's the way it goes." He carefully stepped onto the garbage and reached over to grab the bag she had indicated. He untied it and inspected the contents. "Bingo." Mike handed the bag to her and climbed back out of the dumpster.

He took the white garbage bag back from her. "Do you have any pictures of Anton?"

"No. He hated cameras—said it was against his religion to have his photo taken."

"I bet." Mike studied her a moment with an impassive look on his face. "Danny always bragged about your total recall ability. Let's put that to the test. I need a few sketches of Anton from various angles."

She wrinkled her nose. The thought of drawing portraits of someone she detested nauseated her. "I suppose, but I lost all of my supplies in the apartment explosion"

Mike steered her toward his car. "We've got stuff at the station. How long would it take you to do three or four pencil sketches?"

She pushed back a wayward curl. "Maybe an hour, if you don't need portrait quality."

"Excellent. Let's head over there now."

Jennifer's mounting concern for Elyssa eased when her friend and Morgan joined them on the wet sidewalk. Color had returned to Elyssa's face, and she seemed steadier. Jennifer reached out to touch her arm. "Are you all right, Mom?"

"Fine, child. Especially now that those two medics have stopped poking at me." She threw an irritated look at Mike. "I can't imagine who set them loose like that."

Morgan motioned to Mike. "Sergeant, I need you to take these ladies down to the station to go through the mug books right away."

"No problem." Mike looked at Jennifer and Elyssa. "We were heading for the station anyway. I'll walk you ladies to Jennifer's car."

Elyssa assented. "I'd rather ride with her. I won't have a moment's peace unless I can keep an eye on her and Brianna."

They started down the street, each absorbed in private musings. Jennifer worried about her daughter. How could she explain the disaster to her daughter? Her brows met as she grappled with the problem. She gave voice to her dilemma. "Mom, what do I tell Brianna about this? "

"The truth," Elyssa answered. "She'll want to know about her toys and such."

"But what do I say? 'Sorry, our house is gone. We don't have a home anymore?'" Her voice held a note of sarcasm, and she immediately regretted it. Elyssa didn't deserve such disrespect. "I'm sorry for snapping. I've never had to deal with anything like this before and I'm a bit unnerved."

Mike put a protective arm around her shoulder. "It's hard, Jen, I know. God will give you the right words."

With each step closer to her car, Jennifer's feet felt like lead. "Should I let her see the house, or would it be too frightening?"

"She doesn't need to see this," Mike warned. "It would definitely leave emotional scars."

Elyssa squeezed her hand. "I'll help you talk to her. Just know that no matter what we say, she'll want to go home."

How could I be so stupid to let this happen? The bleak thought hammered her. *I should have known Brianna hated Anton for a reason. I just refused to see. This is all my fault.* Her throat constricted. "Will Brianna ever get over this?" *Or will it haunt her like my past does me?*

"She's young, Jen," Elyssa assured her. "With extra affection and comfort, she'll eventually be able to move on."

Jennifer noticed a camera crew following them at a distance. "Mike, do we have to talk to those vultures?" She hated this intrusion in her life. Journalists had plagued her at the hospital immediately following Danny's death. Since then her dislike of reporters bordered on hatred.

Mike looked back, his countenance darkening. "I'll try to keep them away from you. If they're persistent, walk away without engaging."

Jennifer nodded and quickened her pace. When the station wagon came into view, she caught sight of Brianna. The youngster stood on the hood, clutching Bear-Bear and waving wildly at her. *Father, please give me the right words.*

She glanced at Nathan's tall frame and her heart began to hammer inside her chest. *Get a grip, Jen,* she scolded herself. *He's only a man, and men spell nothing but trouble.*

The doctor leaned against the car door. "We were getting a bit worried, Jen," he told her when she joined them. "What's going on?"

Brianna reached for her, dangling her bear by one arm. "Me wants to go home, Mommy."

Jennifer's heart broke. She enveloped her daughter in a tight embrace. "Um, we have to stay somewhere else tonight, pumpkin." Jennifer looked up at Nathan and continued talking to Brianna. "Our house had a bad accident and got hurt."

Nathan's dark blue eyes spoke volumes. "I'm so sorry," he whispered in a husky voice.

She resisted the urge to find solace in his arms.

Brianna tried to struggle free. "Me wants to take Bunny to see my toys," she insisted.

A deep sigh escaped Jennifer. This was so hard. She swallowed the lump in her throat. "We can't, hon, our house went bye-bye. We're going to Uncle Mike's work first. Then Grammy's going shopping with us. Later, we are going to find a nice place to stay for the night."

Brianna stamped her foot on the car hood. "Me go home!"

Jennifer's eyes misted. She looked to Elyssa for help. Her friend stepped forward and diverted Brianna's attention by asking about her new pet rabbit.

While they chatted, Mike reached the car. He motioned toward the camera crew. "They'll back off for now."

Jennifer introduced the two men.

Mike asked Nathan a few pointed questions and seemed satisfied with his answers. He turned back to Jennifer. "We need to get you three a safe place for the next few days."

Nathan spoke up. "Since I'm at the Hyatt, why don't I get them a room there?"

Jennifer smiled sadly. "That's sweet, Nathan, but there is no way that Elyssa and I could afford those rates."

Mike interrupted her. "Jen, given the circumstances, it would be best for you and Elyssa to have someone nearby. Besides, your insurance will cover the hotel costs."

Nathan concurred. "I'll take care of the hotel expenses for now. You can pay me back after you settle with your insurance company."

"But..." Jennifer's protest died on her lips when she caught Mike's no-nonsense expression. "All right. You win, this time." She fumed inside. *Why do I have to be around bossy men all the time?*

A reporter and photographer converged on them from behind. "Mrs. Warner, do you feel this fire has anything to do with your husband's killers?"

Jennifer instinctively grabbed for Brianna. The flash of a camera strobe momentarily blinded her. Her temper flared, but she resisted the urge to slug them.

Elyssa pulled at her arm. "Let's just get out of here."

Mike put himself between the news crew and his friends. "I'll take care of them," he spoke into Jennifer's ear. "Go directly to the station. I'll meet you there." He turned and diverted the newsmen while his friends made their escape.

Chapter 8

Two hours later, Jennifer put the final touches on her fourth sketch. Anton's face burned with anger on the page. Involuntary shivers crept up her spine. She slid the papers across the gray desk to Mike. "Here. This is the best I can do."

Mike took them from her and gave the top one a cursory glance. "Great. Between these and the prints off the handle of the carafe, we've got a good start. Anyhow, I should be able to get the information I need within the hour."

She stood up and stretched. "May I go now? I've got to pick up clothes and stuff and get Brianna to bed." Jennifer looked at her blackened hands. "I might even find a way to get rid of these stains."

"Tina's watching after Brianna at the hotel, so don't worry about her." He tapped the eraser end of his pencil on the table. "Sorry about the ink, but it was necessary to fingerprint you, Nathan, and Elyssa."

She looked at him in disgust. "But our palms, too? I thought fingerprinting meant just that—fingers."

"It's a bit more complicated than that. As for you getting clothes, I've got a gut feeling you're in grave danger, and I'm keeping you under tight wraps. Tina already picked up some necessities to tide you ladies over until we can get a proper list. She's at the hotel right now with Brianna and Nathan."

Jennifer turned away, irritated. She knew never to ignore Mike's hunches again. He had warned her about Anton months ago, and now she'd become a captive of fear. Her lips tightened. She stood at the window and watched cars pull out of the parking structure across the street. *I'll never get hurt like this again, she vowed. No man will ever get close enough to try.*

Mike broke into her thoughts. "I still need some more information from you, Jen."

She turned and gave him a scalding look. *Some friend.* Didn't he care that she was tired and hungry? "I need a break, Mike. My head is splitting and I can't see straight. Do you suppose I could get a burger or something? Or do you only feed prisoners?"

"No need to bite my head off, Jen. I'm trying to help you. My order from Mr. Wong's should be here any minute. I can get you some acetaminophen and water."

"Yes, please." Jennifer sank back into her chair as Mike placed a call for her medicine. She sighed. "What else do you want to know?"

Her friend slid a pad of paper across the desk, and then propped up his feet. "Every little detail you know about Anton. Where he works, where he lives."

Jennifer tried to recall what she knew. It surprised her to realize that Anton had revealed very little about himself. "I'm ashamed to say, I have no clue."

She rested her chin on her fists and watched Mike's right foot wiggle. "He once said he ran some kind of shipping business with his father. When I asked him about it, he said he doesn't discuss business during his leisure time. I dropped the subject." She lifted her gaze to Mike's face. "He does take frequent business trips out of the country."

The detective's dark eyebrows rose. "He told you that?"

""Yeah, he said it was part of his job. I saw one of his recent airline tickets to Italy."

"Anton showed it to you?"

Jennifer shifted uncomfortably in her seat. "No. He was rummaging through his briefcase about a month ago and I got a glimpse of the ticket and itinerary."

Mike's wiggling foot froze in mid-motion. "Do you remember the date and destination?"

She tipped her head. "Milan, August tenth. I didn't ask him anything about it, though. I figured if he wanted me to know, he would have offered the information." Jennifer felt a minor twinge of guilt. "It was awfully snoopy of me to peek at his ticket, huh?"

Mike waved off her discomfort and picked up his notebook. "Dump the guilt. This may be the break we need. What airline? Layovers?"

She wrote down what she knew.

A knock sounded on the door. Mike answered it. He returned with a cup of water and an individual packet of headache medicine.

He waited until she'd taken the pills before continuing his interrogation. "Are you sure you don't know his home or business address? Phone number? Father's name? Acquaintances?"

The flood of questions irritated Jennifer. Each was a vivid reminder of her foolishness. Shame pummeled her with hot fists. She closed her eyes and wished she were miles away. "I'm clueless. Anton always stopped by the store or my apartment, so I never gave it any thought."

Mike blew out a heavy breath. "Besides last night, have you noticed anything strange about Anton's behavior?"

If you had brains, girl, you'd be dangerous, Jennifer scolded herself. If she had talked to Mike weeks ago about all of this, it would have saved everyone a lot of grief.

She focused on the desk as if it held vital answers to her dilemma. Mike would likely blow his stack, but she needed to get this over with. She looked up warily and braced herself. "I'm sure Anton's had me followed for the past month. That's one of the main reasons I ended our relationship."

The detective's feet hit the floor. Fury burned within his steel gray eyes, but his voice remained calm. "Did you confront him about this?"

Jennifer shuddered. "No. I was waiting for the right time. Last night he showed up, angry for my having a life apart from his every whim. It went downhill from there."

Mike ran his fingers over his head, making the short, black hair spikes stand up. Jennifer recognized the pain in his eyes and realized how much she had hurt him by keeping her troubles secret.

Danny had told her about their pact—that if either partner was killed or disabled, the other would care for his family. At the time, Jennifer hadn't comprehended the intensity of each man's commitment to the other.

Now, she understood. Mike had staked his honor on that promise and intended to follow through no matter what. She bowed her head. "I'm sorry, Mike. I should have told you before. I thought I could—"

"Handle it yourself," Mike finished for her. Frustration filled his voice. "When are you going to realize we're on the same side, Jen? I'm not here to control your life or to take away your freedom. I promised Danny that I'd protect you, and help in any way possible."

"I know. It's just hard to depend on someone, Mike. I don't want my world collapsing again like it did when Danny died. It hurts too much."

"Well, your solo act hasn't exactly protected you, either, has it?" he snapped. His gray eyes glared at her.

Jennifer inhaled sharply and her face twisted with pain. "I deserve that," she said quietly.

Mike's demeanor softened. "I'm sorry, Jen. That was inappropriate. You have a right to live as you see fit."

Tears stung her eyes. "No, you're aboslutely right, Mike. My own decisions have led me to where I am. Now, Brianna and Elyssa have to pay for my stupidity."

He shook his head. "You're hardly stupid, Jen—naive as the summer days are long, maybe—but never stupid. I just wish you wouldn't shut out those who really love you."

Jennifer contemplated his words. Despite her quest for independence, she knew she needed her friends. The problem lay in letting them past the walls she had erected around her heart. She smiled weakly. "I'm not sure how to trust anymore, Mike, but I'll try."

He reached across the desk and squeezed her hand. His warm gray eyes spoke comfort. "Just let us help you through this. I want to catch Anton before he does anything else. You must help me out by not keeping secrets."

Jennifer nodded. "All right. Ask away."

Mike released her hand and leaned back in his chair. "Does Anton carry any weapons?"

"I don't think so." She closed her eyes, and went over the details of that day. A vivid picture jumped into her mind. "Wait. He had one the day I saw the airline ticket." She looked up. "There was a handgun in

Anton's briefcase. He said he carried it for protection because of the shipping business. That's why I looked at the ticket."

"What kind of gun?"

Jennifer threw her hands in the air. "I'm no weapons expert, Mike. You know I hate guns. I wouldn't even look at Danny's. I was always afraid that thing would go off in the house." She rubbed the chill from her arms.

Sergeant Scavone motioned to the sketchpad. "Draw me a picture of what you saw."

She scowled, and then picked up her pencil. How long would he keep her here? Jennifer closed her eyes for a moment to see the gun again, then swiftly captured its outline on the paper.

Mike got up and stood behind her. "Have you ever seen a gun like this before?" he asked when she had finished.

Jennifer thought for a moment. "No. I don't think so." She blew out her breath.

The detective returned to his seat and picked up the pictures of Anton. He leaned back in his chair and closely studied the top one. A strange expression crept across his face.

She watched him, frightened by his reaction. "What? Is there something wrong?"

"It...I know I've met him before, somewhere. I just can't place him right now." He seemed dazed as he looked at the other sketches. He bolted upright, his face deathly pale. "Oh, Lord God," he whispered hoarsely. His focus remained glued to one of the pictures.

Apprehension gripped Jennifer. "Mike?" She tensed when he didn't answer. "Mike, what is it?"

His hands shook as he handed over the last sketch she had done of Anton. "He looked exactly that way when he opened fire from the balcony. He was the only one without a face mask."

Her startled gaze met his. "What are you talking about? What balcony? When?"

Mike reached for the gun drawing. His eyes narrowed—his anger visible in the hard line of his jaw. "The ambush."

Chaos roared through Jennifer's brain with hurricane force. She had befriended her husband's murderer? The thought turned her blood to ice. Her stomach churned. No wonder Anton always got out of meeting Mike. *Why didn't I see it?* She licked her dry lips. "Are you sure?" Her voice seemed to come from somewhere far away.

In a low voice, he murmured. "It's him. I'll stake my badge on it." His eyes took on a dangerous glint. "I'll nail him if it's the last thing I do." He nodded toward her. "And you will help."

Confusion clouded Jennifer's mind. "Can't you just pick him up on murder charges?"

"It's not that easy. We need more evidence than just the memory of an amnesia victim."

"What about Sunday's robbery? Can you take that approach? The whole thing seems like a rerun of three years ago."

Mike gave a dry laugh. "The lieutenant won't even let me near robbery detail. He's afraid that with my history of amnesia, the defense would get the whole case thrown out of court. That's why he stuck me on domestic violence."

He leaned toward her, his lips curving wryly. "I'll be a good boy and play by the rules. I'll just work on it from this angle. You'll press charges for assault."

Jennifer stiffened. Didn't he understand what he was asking her to do? "Mike, you know as well as I do that he'd get out on bail and come after me. Then what?"

Mike looked at her, his eyes cool, his tone precise. "You are going to press charges, Jen, and then you and Brianna will disappear. It'll give me time to come up with some hard evidence to link him to the heist and the ambush."

This was crazy! "What kind of evidence?"

"Danny's gun and wallet for starters." Mike pulled his gun out of its holster and laid it on the desk.

Jennifer gasped. It was a duplicate of the one in Anton's briefcase.

Mike motioned to the gun. "We both carried SIG Sauers." He perched on the edge of the desk. "The official news report about Sunday's heist was purposely incomplete. The security guard and courier were both executed with Danny's gun."

Jennifer pressed her hands against her head to silence the screaming inside. *This can't be true.* Her mouth gaped open, but the words froze in her throat.

"How cold can one man get?" Mike's gaze hardened. "You're Anton's latest trophy."

She stared at him, shaken by the intensity of the emotions that gripped her. "Trophy?" Her voice sounded weak and shaky.

"Don't you see?" Mike jumped to his feet and paced the small room. "He took the wallet and gun as trophies of his victory over the cops. Danny always carried pictures. Anton had to know who you were."

Jennifer sagged against the chair. Anton had targeted her? Chilling fear rippled through her. She twirled a lock of hair around her finger. *Father, what have I gotten us into this time?*

Mike sat on the edge of the desk and knit his brows together in deep concentration. "From what we know, Anton's pulled about a hundred robberies, but none in the same city twice." He looked at her. "Except this past Sunday."

He drummed his fingers on the desk. "He's up to something and I'm positive it somehow involves you." He rubbed the back of his neck. "What does Anton know about your relatives?"

Jennifer tried to recall her conversations with Anton. "Nothing, really. He never seemed interested, and I never felt comfortable discussing them with him." She chewed on her lip. "He did meet Michelle briefly when she visited last month, but she didn't offer him any information. Why? Do you think he'd try to hurt them, somehow?"

Mike shook his head. "We need to find you and Brianna a safe hiding place right away. So, Nathan's your brother's best friend?"

"I guess. That's what they've both said."

"Does Rob have room for you and Brianna at his place?"

Jennifer grudgingly gave into the inevitable. "Yeah. Rob wrote me the other day and asked if I would consider moving in with him. He's remodeling a place in northern Maine."

"Does he know about Anton?"

She sighed. "No. Anton was out of the country during Christmas, so I didn't bother to tell him."

Mike gave a curt nod. "Call Rob and tell him you're coming. I want you and Brianna out of here no later than Friday. I'll even make your plane reservations."

"Absolutely not!" Jennifer shook her head. "No planes, ever. I'll drive, but *no flying*."

The phone rang. Mike leaned over and snatched up the receiver. "Scavone here. Yeah, anything turn up?" His expressions began to darken. "FBI? You sure? I see. What about the prints?" He frowned. "That can't be right. Hold on." He put his hand over the receiver. "Jen, was Anton wearing gloves when he used the carafe."

"No. Why?"

"The lab only found your and Elyssa's fingerprints."

Jennifer felt baffled. "His prints have to be on the handle."

Her friend put the phone to his ear. "No gloves. What can you do?" He was quiet for a moment. "Right. All right. We've already got their palm prints. Let me know when Lieutenant Reynolds gets back. Right. Thanks." He hung up.

Jennifer sensed something had gone wrong. "What's going on?"

Mike dragged his hand over his weary face. "This is going to be a long night. For some reason, Anton left no fingerprints on the carafe or mug. We tried to run him down by name, but Cal ID has nothing— not even a driver's license."

"How could he not leave prints?" She leaned forward. "I don't understand. Everyone has fingerprints, don't they?"

"Everyone is born with unique patterns on their fingertips. However, there have been cases where criminals have used various methods to erase those patterns—plastic surgery, caustic chemicals."

"Sounds gruesome." Jennifer shuddered. "If this is the case with Anton, what can we do, now?"

"We *do* have an unknown partial palm print, but it'll take weeks before we can match it up with a file." Mike walked around the desk to stand beside her. "I can't wait on the prints—there's too much at stake. Use your recall skills and give me a description of Anton's car and the license number. I want to know everything you can remember about your involvement with him—times, dates, places."

Jennifer tore off the top sheet of paper from the pad. "I don't know if this is important or not, but Anton has borrowed my car on a number of occasions, including Sunday. Every time he took it, he told me his Porsche was in the shop."

Mike reached for the phone and quickly dialed a number. "Lee, Scavone here. Listen. You know that two-tone station wagon that I parked just outside the door? We need to go over it for prints and other evidence. Right. I'll be down as soon as I can. Thanks." He hung up and went to the window.

Jennifer watched the second hand sweep around the clock, and then she stared at the pencil. Her stomach growled. She gnawed on her lower lip and tried to think. She groaned inwardly as the detective's movements broke her concentration. An impatient sigh escaped her. "Mike, I can't think with you pacing around."

Someone knocked at the door. Mike answered, and then set a white bag and a can of root beer on the desk. "Here's your supper. I've gotta talk to the lieutenant. I'll be back." He gathered up her notes and sketches, and then left the room.

The fragrant odor of spiced chicken tickled Jennifer's nose. She opened the bag and peered into the cardboard containers. Her mouth watered as her search revealed Kung Pao chicken, stir-fried vegetables, and spring rolls. Pleased with the menu, she helped herself.

Once she satisfied her appetite, Jennifer dragged her eyes back to the blank page. She searched her memory and began to write. Within fifteen minutes, she had filled both sides. After going over the list again, she scooped up the paper and opened the office door. Sergeant

Scavone met her in the hallway with a couple of large books tucked under his left arm.

Jennifer shoved the paper into his free hand. "Here. If I remember anything else, I'll let you know."

He motioned her back into the room. "We're not finished yet. I need you to go through these mug books."

She crossed her eyes at him in frustration, and returned to her seat. "Who am I looking for?"

Mike dropped the books on the desk. "See if you recognize anyone in there. You may have seen them at the store, at a restaurant, near your home, wherever. Perhaps we can identify whoever Anton had following you."

She nodded and opened the first book. Mike took a seat and started reading the list in his hand. After a few minutes, he broke the silence. "When you went to Bernard's, did Anton pay with cash or credit card?"

Jennifer looked up. "Credit card, why?"

"If we're lucky, we might be able to trace him through it. Where were you seated?"

She told him then dropped her gaze back to the book.

An hour later, Mike ushered Jennifer into the lobby where Elyssa sat waiting. "I've never seen so many faces in one place before," the older woman complained, massaging her forehead. "My head hurts from looking at all of them."

Jennifer blinked her eyes. "I know the feeling." Even now, the faces whirled before her. What a waste, she hadn't recognized anyone. She manipulated her neck to release the tension that had built up. How she wanted a chance to collapse and cry. "Can we go now, Mike?"

He nodded and led them out to his car.

Chapter 9

"You ladies are to stay in the room until I tell you otherwise." Mike escorted Jennifer and Elyssa into the empty hotel elevator. "I thank God that Nathan was able to make arrangements to give you his room." The elevator doors shut.

Jennifer's mind snapped to attention. "His room? Why did he give up his room?"

"With all of the conventions this week, every room in the area is booked solid," Mike explained. "One of Nathan's buddies agreed to let him bunk in on a cot."

Elyssa smiled at Jennifer. "I'm quite impressed with that young man. He's a rare breed. What do you think, Jen?"

Jennifer clenched her teeth, not trusting herself to speak right away. She knew she should feel grateful for Nathan's chivalry, yet anger surged inside of her. "He's merely doing what Rob would do in his place," she stated flatly. "I do appreciate the fact he's given up his room." *Elyssa had better not get any ideas on matchmaking. I'm certainly not interested in any more heartache.*

Mike interrupted. "Speaking of Rob, Jen. You'd better call him right away and get the arrangements set. It would be best if you let him know what was going on, as well."

Jennifer rolled her eyes. "Great, this just gives Rob more reason to play the mother hen."

"How about someone filling me in?" Elyssa asked. "My home gets destroyed, the police ask me about a delivery man and no one bothers telling me what is going on."

"Delivery man?" Jennifer echoed. "You mean the one that delivered the bear yesterday?"

The elevator doors slid open.

Mike silenced them. "Let's wait until we get inside your room before discussing this further." He walked up to a door and knocked. A tall, willowy brunette unlocked the door and let them step inside.

Tina smiled a greeting, and her large brown eyes twinkled. "I'll be with you in a minute." She returned to sit on the bed with Brianna, where the youngster was gleefully beating her at a game of Fish. "Brianna, how do you know what cards I have all the time?" She handed over her last three cards.

Brianna squealed. "Me win!"

Tina unfolded her long shapely legs from the double bed. "You have the makings of a real card sharp here, Jen."

"I'm getting worried. I have no idea where she's picked up this talent." Jennifer eyed Elyssa with suspicion. Mike snorted.

Elyssa raised her hands in surrender. "Grammy confesses. I've taught her everything I know about 'Fish'." She bowed her head in mock humility and wrung her hands. "This doesn't mean you're severing visitation rights, does it?"

"I don't know," Jennifer said with a straight face. She tapped her foot for a moment. "All right. You can stay, on one condition—no gambling or pick pocketing."

Elyssa waved a hand at her. "Aw, you sure know how to take the fun out of everything."

Mike and Tina laughed. Jennifer smiled, but wanted to cry. How would she and Brianna manage without Elyssa? Sadness lapped against her heart and tugged at the corners of her mouth. Elyssa meant so much to them. Since they had moved into her vacant apartment nearly three years ago, she had become mother and grandmother. *Life won't be the same without her. I don't want to say goodbye.*

Elyssa looked around the room. "Where's Nathan?"

Tina stretched and yawned. "He had a meeting. He'll stop by in the morning to have breakfast with you. Here's his number if you need him." She gave a slip of paper to Elyssa.

Mike picked up Brianna and gave her a big hug. "Love you, pumpkin." He looked over at Jennifer and Elyssa. "We need to go pretty quick, but we want to pray with you before we leave."

They all bowed their heads. "Lord," Mike began, "thank you for keeping our loved ones safe today. Please let Your angels stand guard over each of us here. Extend that protection to Nathan, Rob, and the rest of Jennifer's family. Give the police department and the FBI wisdom and discernment in pursuing this case. God, do whatever it takes to bring the suspects to justice. Please prevent them from harming any more people. Most of all, Lord, remind each of us here how much you love us. In Jesus' name, Amen."

Tears moistened Jennifer's eyes when Mike finished praying. She took Brianna from his arms and tried to concentrate on his instructions.

"Remember to stay put," Mike told them. "Room service will deliver your meals. If you'll put a clothing list together, Tina can take care of it for you first thing in the morning."

He wrote something down on a piece of paper and handed it to Jennifer. "Here's my pager. I'll be scrounging tonight, so don't hesitate to call if you need me." He pointed to a three-digit number. "Use this code if there are any problems. If there's an emergency, dial 9-1-1 first, then call me and punch this code into my pager. Otherwise, I'll be stopping by to see you tomorrow. Lock the door behind us, and don't let anyone in but Tina, Nathan, or myself."

After the Scavones left, Brianna began to fuss for her own bed. Jennifer and Elyssa tried to comfort her and finally got the tearful youngster to sleep. The women then sat at the small round table, drank tea and quietly discussed that evening's Bible study.

Jennifer nervously fingered the new Bible Tina had bought her. She didn't want to resurrect the events of the day, but she had some loose ends that needed tying together. "Mom, earlier you mentioned the police were asking you about a delivery man. What was that all about?"

Elyssa set down her cup of jasmine tea. "A man stopped by this morning after you left for Knott's Berry Farm, wanting to know when you'd be back. He said he had a package he needed to deliver to you personally. I didn't like his looks, and since he wasn't wearing a uniform, I told him I couldn't say exactly when you'd be back."

Jennifer stiffened. "What did he look like?"

The older woman shook her head. "I've never been good at remembering faces unless I've seen them a few times. I just have a vague recollection of dark hair graying at the temples and shifty brown eyes. I couldn't close the door fast enough. Does Mike think he's got anything to do with the explosion?"

Jennifer shamefacedly caught Elyssa up on what she and Mike had pieced together.

The older woman's voice snapped angrily. "That lout. For two cents I'd shoot Anton myself and save the police the effort."

"I'm so sorry for dragging you into this." Jennifer told her. "If it weren't for me, you'd still have a home."

Elyssa waved her off. "Nonsense. Anton's a professional criminal. He's responsible for his own actions and he'll certainly pay for them. Mark my words."

Jennifer sighed. "Mike will drive himself into the ground until he's tracked Anton down. Anyway, now you know what we're up against. As much as I hate the idea, Brianna and I have to go into hiding."

Elyssa's dark eyes reflected her despair. "Where will you go? Will I be able to contact you?"

"I don't know, Mom. I'm afraid Anton might come after you for information, so the less you know, the better off you'll be."

Tears streamed down Elyssa's face. "But you're my family. How will I know if you're all right? I don't want to lose you."

Jennifer allowed her own tears to fall. "There's got to be a way, Elyssa. I don't want this to be the end of our relationship, either. We love you too much."

She hugged her friend. "If only..." Jennifer's words died as the glimmer of an idea began to take shape. She grabbed Elyssa by the shoulders. "I know. Why don't you come with us? Brianna needs her Grammy, and I need my mom." She crossed her arms. "In fact, we refuse to leave without you."

Elyssa remained silent for a few moments. "Where would we go?" she asked, finally.

Jennifer told her about Rob's offer. "I know he'd be more than happy to let you come, too. You won his heart a long time ago by the way you loved Brianna and me."

Her friend balked. "I don't know, child. He's a nice boy, but he doesn't want to be saddled with an old woman."

"Nonsense. For one thing, you're not old—that's something you'll never be. You're too feisty. Besides, Rob told me he really likes you."

"I just don't want to be an imposition."

"You won't be, really. Just let me ask him, all right?"

Elyssa sighed. She shook a finger at Jennifer. "All right, but don't you try talking him into anything. Ask him outright. If he needs convincing, I won't go."

"Fair enough. Now let's get some sleep."

The next morning, Jennifer placed an early call to her brother and explained the events of the previous days. She had considered leaving out some information, but knew that Mike would probably call Rob himself, so she came clean.

"Anyhow, if it's all right with you, Elyssa will come with us too," she said after assuring Rob no one had been injured.

"Of course she's welcome, Jen. You didn't need to ask," Rob told her. "Tell Grammy I've got the perfect room for her. It has a view of the hills and trees. I'll get it ready right away. How soon can you get here?"

Jennifer smiled and nodded at Elyssa, who sat nervously on the edge of her bed, cuddling Brianna. "Mike wants me to head out no later than Friday. I'll talk to Elyssa and see if she'll come out with us then." She discussed a few more details with Rob, and then hung up.

She watched her friend's face brighten when she relayed Rob's message. "Would you like to leave with us on Friday to drive there?"

"I wish I could." Elyssa sighed. "I've already talked to my insurance company about the fire. They need me to settle a few things in person. I could fly up there in about two weeks, though." She reached for her purse and took out a brochure. "Before I forget again, I think it would be best if we turned powers of attorney over to Mike. He can handle any of our additional personal business, but we can't be traced."

Jennifer agreed. "I kept wondering how to handle everything. That would solve my problems on that end."

Later that morning, Sergeant Scavone stopped by with a copy of the local newspaper, a small blue suitcase, and Jennifer's somewhat warped security box. "I wish those newshounds would back off when they're told," he growled, tossing the paper on the table. "Anton will have gone deep underground, now."

Jennifer picked up the newspaper. The front-page headline blared, "Murdered Cop's Family Victims of Arson Blaze." Centered above the story was a large picture of herself with Brianna in her arms, holding Bear-Bear. The camera had captured the agony in Jennifer's eyes. She felt disgusted. *Why couldn't they just leave us be? Now, we'll never catch Anton.* She handed the paper to Elyssa.

Mike set the rest of his load on the table. "I located your security box. It's a bit damaged, but should have done its job. If you have the key, it would be a good idea to take a look inside and be sure."

Jennifer located the keys in her purse and opened the box. The papers didn't even smell of smoke. "Praise God, they're fine. She shuffled through the documents. "At least I won't have to go through all the trouble of replacing them."

Elyssa peered over Jennifer's shoulder. "I should get one of those. I've always kept my important papers in the bank security deposit box."

Mike motioned Jennifer aside. "We went over your car with a fine-toothed comb, hoping for some new clues. We didn't get much. At least we know for sure he didn't stash any of the jewels in it. That's about all I can tell you."

He insisted they alter their original travel plans. "I'd feel a lot better about your trip if we made some changes. I'll trade your car in for another one and register it in my name so you can't be traced. Go ahead and sign over the title to me this morning so I can get everything worked out."

They sat at the table and filled out the necessary paperwork. When they finished, Mike pocketed the documents. "Once things settle down, Jen, I'll transfer the new title to you. Now, your new identity is Lynne Tyler. I'll have some new I.D. made up for you by Friday. Also, you and Brianna need disguises," he continued.

He opened the suitcase he had brought. "Everything you need is here. I want you to cut and dye Brianna's hair and dress her like a boy. As for you, we'll be changing your style of dress and you'll be wearing a wig and glasses."

Jennifer found the changes distasteful. She'd preferred classy shirts to the drab pants and shirts Mike had provided. She gave in since this could mean the difference between life and death for herself and her young daughter.

When she put on the dark wig, the wire-framed glasses, and darkened her eyebrows, Jennifer peered at a complete stranger in the mirror. *Thankfully, this is only temporary. I'll be glad when things can get back to normal.*

It broke her heart, however, to cut off Brianna's long, curly blonde hair. At least Mike had agreed to a compromise. He'd drop the boy disguise for Brianna if Jennifer made the other drastic changes. She complied and used a toothbrush to apply the temporary black dye to her daughter's short ringlets.

Brianna turned the entire event into a game, even enduring the dyeing process with a grin. When Nathan stopped by that evening, the little girl showed off her new look.

Nathan stood in the doorway, with a plastic bag in his hand, looking somewhat shocked. The doctor quickly put on a smile. "You look very pretty, princess." He set the bag on the floor, and reached back into the hallway. "Look who's come for a visit."

Brianna squealed her delight when she spotted the large square wire cage. Bunny had arrived.

"I figured Brianna might get a bit stir-crazy," he explained, "so I thought the rabbit might help her pass the time," he told Jennifer. "She has her own potty box and knows how to use it."

Jennifer thanked him for his thoughtfulness and quickly found a spot in a corner for the black lop-eared rabbit. She spread newspapers on the floor to protect the carpet.

Nathan set the cage in its designated spot. He explained to Brianna that Bunny could only stay with her in the hotel room until it was time to leave for Maine. Then, when Nathan was ready to go home, the rabbit would then go with him on an airplane. "Bunny will be waiting for you at your Uncle Rob's."

For the next two days, Jennifer, Elyssa and Brianna remained confined to the hotel room. Entertaining the toddler proved a difficult feat. The youngster had so little room in which to run around. Television shows helped a bit, but Brianna rarely sat still for long.

Elyssa came up with the idea to let Brianna and the rabbit play together on the large bathroom floor. "It isn't right for Bunny to stay cooped up like that. This way, the two of them can have some fun and we won't have to worry about Bunny soiling the carpet or beds."

Jennifer agreed to the plan on trial and was soon pleased with the results.

Mike came by with a special camera and took Jennifer's picture. "I'll have your new driver's license by tonight. Put your current license away somewhere and don't use it until I tell you otherwise."

Jennifer nodded and concealed her driver's license in a hidden flap in her purse. Since she had no credit cards, she didn't have to worry about replacing any. She'd pay for their lodgings with cash.

When she got her new license, she checked it over carefully and slipped it into her wallet. For the entire trip, she would have to remember use her new name and only refer to Brianna as Brie.

Nathan joined the fugitives for breakfast and supper, but his attitude toward Jennifer seemed to have chilled. He was still polite and caring, but the camaraderie she felt with him at Knott's Berry Farm had all but vanished.

Jennifer couldn't shake her humiliation. *He probably thinks I'm a real dingbat. After all, what kind of woman makes a friend of her husband's murderer?* Maybe he even couldn't stand the sight of her.

By the time she and Brianna headed out of Long Beach Friday morning, Jennifer had severely questioned the wisdom of moving so close to Nathan. *Good, grief, Jen,* she scolded herself as she settled Brianna in her car seat. *It's not like you'll be living with him.* She'd probably never see him. Still, she felt uneasy.

Chapter 10

When she reached Albany, New York, several days later, Jennifer decided she'd dump the disguises. They'd reach Misha's soon, and no one had shown any interest in them during their trip.

Brianna's temporary hair dye had already lightened during their cross-country trip. Jennifer assured her daughter that her hair would grow longer fast enough. In the meantime, she looked adorable with the circlet of pale brunette curls framing her face.

Jennifer spied a discount clothing store right across from their motel. She and Brianna scurried over to buy new clothes for both of them. She found several skirts and sweater tops for herself. Brianna fell in love with some colorful pantsuits with matching hair bands.

In a burst of rebellion, Jennifer tossed the old clothing into their bathroom trash can, relieved to get rid of them. However, she packed away the wig and glasses, intending to mail them back to Mike.

The next day, Jennifer and Brianna finished eating breakfast just outside Brattleboro, Vermont. Wisps of fog danced in the cold mid-morning breeze as a light rain began to fall. Jennifer shivered in her thick white cardigan sweater; thankful she had thought to buy warmer clothing. She buckled Brianna into her car seat then shut her door.

Jennifer spent a few minutes picking leaves from the windshield of the light blue Ford Taurus. She wiped her wet hands on her black denim skirt and got in the car.

Thankfully, now, she wouldn't have to answer any questions about the disguises. While Misha and Rob knew the whole situation, Jennifer had sworn them to silence. "I won't have Uncle Peter and Aunt Sarah worrying about any of this," she had insisted.

The windshield wipers slapped an awkward beat as Jennifer steered the car onto the rain-slick highway and headed toward New Hampshire and Portland, Maine.

"Michelle will expect us tonight," she calculated aloud. "Then, in three more days, we'll finally be home with Uncle Robby." Jennifer tuned the radio to a public broadcasting station. Strains of Stravinsky's "Firebird Suite" filled the air. They crossed into New Hampshire.

"Bear-Bear cold," Brianna announced as she busily dressed the bear in a pair of her new footsie pajamas.

"Well, we don't want that. Let me turn up the heater."

Half an hour passed in partial silence. Jennifer glanced back to see what Brianna was doing. The child's short curls lay against the stuffed bear. Her breath fell softly. The early morning starts were tough on the youngster. She'd often fall asleep within half an hour of starting down the highway, and then wake up some time later wanting to play.

The cross-country journey had seemed arduous, with all the stops necessary to accommodate Brianna. It could have been worse, Jennifer thought. At least she didn't sleep all day and stay up all night.

While the youngster had gone back to wearing pull-up diapers since they lost their home, her sleep patterns had not changed. She still slept like a log. Nothing short of a major disaster or Anton's voice would wake her up.

Just outside of Keene, New Hampshire, Jennifer looked into her rear-view mirror in time to see a dark sedan converge on her bumper.

He must be in an awful hurry, she thought, glancing in the mirror at the other driver. His short black hair grayed at the temple, and his face seemed a hardened mask of rage. *Who is he angry at?* If the man wasn't careful, he'd likely cause a nasty accident.

She looked for a place to move out of his way. Without warning, the sedan pulled onto the right shoulder and slammed into her car. "What is he doing?" Jennifer shrieked amidst the sickening sound of metal scraping metal. *Father, help me! He's trying to kill us!* Her knuckles went white as she struggled to maintain control of her car. Brianna woke up and added her screams to the chaos.

The stranger rammed his car into hers again, forcing the Taurus onto the opposite shoulder. Then, as suddenly as the attack began, it ended. The stranger gunned his engine and shot down the two-lane country highway.

Flashing lights in Jennifer's rear-view mirror revealed the cause of her assailant's flight. A two-tone police vehicle whizzed by in pursuit of the dark sedan.

Jennifer steered her car to safety and shut off the engine. She reached back and released Brianna from her seat. Her frightened daughter climbed into her lap. "It's all right, now, baby," Jennifer cooed, despite her own pounding heart. "We're safe. The police will make sure of that."

Inside, Jennifer's thoughts raced. This was no accident. Had Anton sent someone after them? Was he the one who had destroyed their home? There was something vaguely familiar about the driver, but she couldn't quite put her finger on it. *Oh, why can't I remember?*

A knock at the driver's window made Jennifer jump. She moved to the middle of the seat and clung to Brianna. How had the man escaped the police so fast? Her mind searched frantically for ways to protect them from this lunatic.

"Ma'am, are you all right?" a voice called.

Jennifer glanced out the driver's window and saw a weather-beaten New Hampshire State Trooper peering into her car. His dark blue uniform brought relief to her anxious heart She reached over and opened the door.

"Are you two all right?" the middle-aged officer asked again.

"No injuries that I'm aware of. Just shaken up." Jennifer pushed open the door and stepped out of the car with Brianna in her arms.

The trooper helped her stand. "Are you sure?"

"Yes. I'm...I'm just wondering how my car has fared." Brianna grasped her neck as Jennifer walked around the vehicle to view the damage. A cold breeze whipped at Jennifer's black denim skirt. The passenger's door looked like a crumpled piece of aluminum foil.

"It doesn't look too good," the trooper told her. "Do you want me to call for a tow truck?"

"Do you think the damage will interfere with driving?" Jennifer bit her lower lip, bracing herself for the worst. She couldn't afford the cost of major repairs. Besides, they would have to delay their trip by a few days. "We've got to get to Portland tonight. We'll be safe there.

The trooper evaluated the extent of the damage. "I'm no expert, but from what I can see, the wheel well and axle look fine. I mean, this door is useless, but it shouldn't affect the mechanics of the car."

"Good." Relief washed over Jennifer. "We really need to reach our destination tonight."

He took out his notebook. "I'm afraid I must delay you a bit longer. I need to get some information from you. May I see your driver's license, registration, and insurance, please?"

Jennifer set Brianna on the ground near the driver's door. "Stay here." She retrieved her purse and paperwork from inside the car. Realizing her new I.D. wouldn't match her current looks, she fished out the real license then handed it to him.

"Is this your current address?" the officer asked.

"No, I'm in the process of moving, but I won't be getting to my new home for a few more days. You can reach me through a friend of mine in California who owns this car." She handed him the registration and Mike's business card. "He'll know where to contact me."

The officer looked over the information. "I'll be right back."

Jennifer scooped Brianna into her arms again while the trooper ran her details.

The toddler whined to chase a nearby cat.

"No, honey. He could be sick." Jennifer hoped they could get back on the road soon. She engaged her daughter's attention by pointing to some deer on a nearby hill.

The trooper returned and gave the paperwork back to Jennifer. He questioned her further about the accident. Several minutes later he closed his notebook. "That's all I need ma'am. We'll be getting in contact with you later if we need you to testify. In the meanwhile, please drive carefully."

Jennifer's hands shook as she pulled back onto the highway, but she kept her composure. *Brianna's still upset*, she noted. Although the child was quiet, she was literally squeezing the stuffing out of her teddy bear.

Cotton batting peeked through a small hole in the bear's right arm as Brianna crushed the animal in a tight embrace.

I sure did it, this time, Jennifer scolded herself as she put the miles behind them. Mike had his reasons for the disguises and she should have stuck with them until the end of the trip.

As the hours slipped by, mother and daughter began to relax. The rain had stopped when they drove into Concord, New Hampshire. Ssunshine broke through the hazy sky. Jennifer stopped at a restaurant for lunch. She considered calling Mike, but decided to wait until she got to Rob's. *We'll work out the repairs and such then.* The state police would call him if they needed him sooner.

By the time Jennifer's car pulled into her cousin's driveway on the outskirts of Portland, the sunset had erupted into a blaze of color. Michelle ran out of the house to greet them.

"It's about time you got here," she scolded as she hugged Jennifer. "Rob's called four times already. Even Pop was worried, and you know how steady he is."

Jennifer blew out her frustration. "Good grief, I said I'd be here by sundown. You guys are just a bunch of worry warts." She smiled at her dark-haired, dark-eyed cousin and rumpled her hair. "Pop" was a rugged sea captain, just as her own father had been.

Michelle was like them in her boundless energy, yet appeared so frail and delicate. Layered brown hair framed a pixie face and fell just beneath young shoulders. Jeans, a lavender oxford shirt, a white sweater vest, and penny loafers made here look much younger than her twenty-two years.

"Here, I'll get Brianna." She scurried to the other side of the car to release the child from her car seat. Michelle stopped short when she saw the mangled doors. "What happened to your car?" she demanded. "This looks fairly recent."

"Someone rammed us this morning." Jennifer opened the passenger door on her side, reached across the seat and unbuckled Brianna. "The police chased him, but we don't know whether they caught him yet. I just thank God that we weren't hurt." *No thanks to me.*

"Why would someone do something like that?" Michelle picked up Brianna. "Boy, you're getting big, pumpkin."

Brianna giggled and hugged her in return.

Michelle settled Brianna on her hip and turned back toward her cousin. "Does this have anything to do with your apartment?"

Jennifer shrugged. "I don't know. I got a look at the driver. It's weird, but I have this feeling...there's something...I don't know...familiar about him." She pulled the two suitcases from the trunk. "Anyhow, the police said they'd contact me if they need me to testify."

"I'll get Pop to look at the car. Maybe he can pull some strings and get the door replaced right away."

Jennifer shook her head. "I'd rather you didn't. There's no need to upset him with the accident. The important thing is that we're all right, and that we got here safely. Thanks anyway."

They headed up the stone walkway with Michelle in the lead. "So, besides the accident, how was the trip?"

"Pretty good. Brianna enjoys riding in the car. Potty training is completely out the window for now, though. I can't blame her with all she's gone through lately. She's still upset."

Her cousin studied Jennifer's face. "And you?"

"This whole thing has been unnerving. It's still hard to believe we lost everything. It's almost like I expect I could go back and everything would be like it was when we left for Knott's Berry Farm that morning. At least we weren't there when it happened." Jennifer followed Michelle inside. "Where are the folks?"

Michelle set Brianna on the floor and held her by the hand. "Mom is still in Naples. She was hoping to come back today, but Grandma Bolton fell and broke her leg last night, so she'll be delayed a few weeks. She said to tell you she's sorry she missed you. Pop had to go down to the docks. He'll be home in half an hour."

She led them upstairs to Rob's old bedroom that Misha had converted into a makeshift nursery.

Jennifer placed the baggage on the floor and stretched. "This sure has been a long week. I never knew driving could be so tiring."

Her cousin smiled. "Well, why don't you two get settled in, and then join me downstairs."

Brianna yawned loudly. Bedtime had come early for her.

Jennifer picked up her daughter. "If you don't mind, I'd like to fix her a light supper first, then get her bathed and ready for bed."

"No problem," Michelle replied. "The bathroom's still around the corner. I'll get the water ready while you raid the fridge."

"You are such a love. Thanks." Jennifer deeply appreciated her cousin's thoughtfulness.

After she had settled Brianna down for the night, Jennifer joined Michelle and Uncle Peter in the dining room downstairs.

"You're just in time for supper, Jen." Michelle set down a large bowl of steaming clam chowder beside the crackers, chef salad and coffee.

"Thanks, Misha." Jennifer slid onto a chair across from her uncle. "I'm famished!"

Uncle Peter asked the blessing, and then remained silent until he had finished eating. Jennifer watched him take a long draw of his pipe and lean back in his chair. His ebony eyes studied her from beneath bushy black brows. *I hope Misha didn't tell him anything.*

"I got a letter from your father today," he said finally. He puffed on his pipe. "He's coming home and wants to see both you and Rob."

The news hit like a bomb. Jennifer's resentment emerged. "It's too late for that, don't you think?"

After her mother had filed for divorce, Jennifer's father had left without a word. That was nineteen years ago. From her bedroom window, seven-year-old Jennifer had watched her father walk away. For days, the child had watched the mailbox for the letters her daddy usually sent her when he went out to sea, but none came.

"You can't hang onto your bitterness toward your folks," Uncle Peter gently told her.

Jennifer felt the color rush to her face. How could her uncle take their side?

He leaned forward. "There are a lot of things about your parents that you don't understand."

"I don't care. Nothing can excuse their heartless behavior," Jennifer argued. "No child should be abandoned in a boarding school ."

Uncle Peter made eye contact with her. "I know you had a rough time of it, Jen, but your father had nothing to do with putting you and Rob into those boarding schools."

Jennifer crossed her arms. "Well, he certainly did nothing to stop it. We never even got as much as a postcard from him. If it hadn't been for you and Aunt Sarah, I couldn't have survived those years. You remembered Rob and me on our birthdays and holidays. When you finally talked Corrine into letting us spend vacations with you, I didn't feel so isolated anymore. And you gave us a home when she abandoned us completely."

She slumped back in her chair. "I wish our parents had loved us just half as much as you did. Why did they even bother to have kids?"

Uncle Peter looked as if he was about to say something, but he stopped himself and closed his eyes. "What's past is past, Jennifer. You can't change the events that lay behind you. Be warned, your anger and unforgiveness will harm your own life more than theirs."

Jennifer stared past the clock on the mantle. Vivid memories of those miserable days at the girls' school marched before her. "I can't make the pain of those years go away. I waited day after day for him to come and claim us. For three years I cried myself to sleep. I loved him, Uncle Peter. He was my daddy, and I thought he loved me. After those three years, I had no tears left to cry."

She tried to relax her clenched fists. Old wounds had reopened. Over the years a seed of bitterness had replaced the sorrow in her tender heart and firmly taken root. "The only reason Corrine finally gave you custody of us was because she ran out of money," she murmured. "That's a hard thing for a fifteen-year-old to handle. I'm sorry, Uncle Peter, I don't mean to be rude. I just can't act as if nothing happened. What they did was wrong, and I won't pretend otherwise."

Her uncle reached across the table and touched her arm. "I don't expect you to, Jen. All I'm asking is that you let go of hatred and give your father a chance to make amends."

She shook her head and pulled away. "You're asking the impossible! How can I risk all that pain again? It's just not worth it."

Uncle Peter's voice remained gentle. "Won't you even try?"

Jennifer studied the wooden floor beneath her feet. "I can't...not now. The wounds are too deep. As far as I'm concerned, both of my parents are dead."

Disappointment marked Uncle Peter's face. He stood up. "I'll ask him not to come for a couple of weeks, then. I pray that, perhaps, someday you'll change your mind."

As Jennifer watched him go into his study, she could sense his sadness. He didn't understand. Life didn't always have happy endings. *If only it did.*

"Don't forget to call Rob," Michelle reminded her, coming in from the kitchen. She had cleared the table and washed the dishes while Jennifer and Uncle Peter had talked.

Jennifer had a lengthy conversation with her brother, but did not mention the accident. There was no sense in worrying him, she told herself after hanging up. He couldn't do anything about it, anyhow.

She tucked the slip of paper containing the directions to Rob's house into her wallet, checked on Brianna then showered and got ready for bed.

Tears fell unbidden as she sat on the edge of the bed in her old bedroom and towel-dried her hair. What a mess she'd made. Images of the past two weeks flashed in her mind. Would she ever really get to start over again?

Michelle sat beside her cousin and laid a comforting arm around Jennifer's trembling shoulders. "Jen, are you all right?"

Jennifer expressed her frustrations to her cousin. "I'll be okay, Misha," she sighed when she finished her tale. "I'm just tired and discouraged, I guess."

"About Anton?"

Jennifer wiped her eyes with the damp towel. "I sure picked a winner, didn't I? What kind of woman hangs out with her husband's murderer? How could I have been so stupid?"

"What were you supposed to do, Jen, read minds? You had no way of knowing. Good grief, the cops didn't even suspect him. You had no idea things would turn out this way. So, don't blame yourself."

"Who else is to blame? I had enough clues to know he wasn't the loving man he first portrayed. Brianna hated him from the day they met. She saw right through him. I didn't. Even after I suspected he was having me followed, I stuck in there. What did I need, a baseball bat upside the head?"

Michelle patted her shoulder. "Love can blind us sometimes."

Jennifer looked her cousin squarely in the eyes. "That's just it, Misha. I never loved Anton. I made sure he knew that all along. I used him to make the loneliness go away."

She dropped her gaze and plucked at the towel. "You know, I don't think I'm even capable of loving a man anymore. All of those feelings died with Danny."

Michelle handed Jennifer a box of tissues. "Jen, Anton is the only man you've been involved with since Danny. You can't judge the future on this one mistake. There's someone out there for you. You'll find him when the time is right."

"I'm not willing to take that risk. When men get too close, they have the power to hurt you. Besides, I'd never find anyone like Danny again."

Michelle crossed her legs Indian-style. "Maybe you're not supposed to. Perhaps God has someone completely different planned for you. Not all men are cads, Jen—look at Pop and Rob."

"God doesn't make men like that anymore."

Michelle tossed her head in disgust. "How do you know? You haven't exactly given yourself a real chance to look. Listen, I'm not saying that you didn't have a terrific marriage with Danny, but that's in the past. He's gone. Those two years are a small part of the rest of your life. You're not being fair to yourself or Brianna by quitting." Her voice fell to a whisper. "Every little girl needs a father. You should know that better than anyone."

Jennifer withered inside at her cousin's words. Was she robbing Brianna of that, too? She rejected the notion. "Men are nothing but heartache. Look what Brianna's going through because I got involved with Anton, Misha. That wasn't fair to her. I do appreciate your concern, but I guess I can't see outside my own little box right now."

"I understand, Jen. I won't push you. It'll come in time, you'll see." Michelle hugged her then went to take her shower.

Jennifer picked up her Bible and read her nightly devotions. A while later, she gave into exhaustion, turned out her light and fell asleep.

Multi-colored mist swirled around Jennifer's feet. She stood at a crossroad, but was unable to decide which way she was to go.

"But where are the signs?" she asked herself aloud.

"There aren't any," a familiar voice sneered. "You have to figure it out all by yourself."

Jennifer turned and saw Anton. He held a can of black paint and a brush. Beyond him, Jennifer saw four signposts, but the messages had been blotted out.

She pushed past Anton and tried to wipe off the paint with her handkerchief, but found herself stuck to the first sign like glue.

"Help me!" she cried in desperation.

"Jennifer," her husband called.

She turned toward him. "Danny, you have to help me."

"I can't," he told her. "The dead can't help the living. You have to go on." Danny's figure faded away.

Her father appeared before her, but turned away despite her calls for help.

"Don't leave me here!" she pleaded.

Anton's laugh turned cruel. "No one will help you. You and Brianna are at my mercy."

Suddenly, Brianna appeared in his arms and began to cry. "Don't let him take me, Mommy."

"Help me," Jennifer shrieked. "Help me, Rob!"

Anton's face changed to that of the assailant in the dark sedan. "You can't escape. You told Mike you didn't know me, remember?" His laughter echoed as he and Brianna disappeared.

"No! God, help me, please! Help me!" Jennifer's screams shattered the night stillness.

Michelle shook her. "Jen, stop it! You're okay, wake up!"

Beads of perspiration slid down Jennifer's forehead. "It's him," she cried. "I've got to call Mike right away."

Her cousin stared at her. "What are you talking about?"

"The man who tried to kill us. I remember now." She pulled away from Michelle.

Michelle stepped in front of her. "Calm down, Jen. It's two in the morning; Mike will be asleep."

"It doesn't matter, he's got to know. I've got to call him now."

"What's going on?" Uncle Peter demanded from the doorway. "Jen, are you all right?"

"Just a bad dream, Pop," Michelle explained as her cousin headed down the stairs.

Jennifer dialed the phone with shaky hands. *God, let him be there.* She nervously listened to the phone ring several times.

Finally, her friend picked up. "Scavone here."

"Mike, this is Jennifer. I have to talk to you."

He cleared his throat. "It's about time you called. I just got off the phone with the New Hampshire State Police. Why didn't you tell me about getting run off the road today?"

"I didn't figure it was important." Jennifer pushed her hair out of her face with her free hand. "He just seemed like a disgruntled driver. But I just remembered his face. He was one of the men in the mug shots you showed me."

Mike blew out a ragged breath. "I know. Lou Strombolli. A positive I.D. was made of the body a few minutes ago."

Her mind raced. "Body?"

"Strombolli's car went over a bridge. The troopers chased him up near Barnet, Vermont before he lost control of the car and went careening into the Passumpsic River. Needless to say, he *didn't* survive." Mike's frustration crackled over the phone. "You should have called me, right away, Jen."

She ignored his terseness. "Why was he after *me*, though? I never had any contact with him."

"All we know at this time is that he fits the physical description of one of the gunmen from the two jewelry heists in Long Beach. The FBI has taken over the case."

She twisted a lock of hair around her finger. "How did he find me?"

"Strombolli had your address book."

What? "Impossible. I had left that on my coffee table the day of the..." Her voice faltered. "He's the one who blew up my apartment?"

"It's a possibility, Jen. According to the files, Strombolli specialized in arson blazes." His voice became insistent. "Now, will you answer my question? Why didn't you bother to let me know about the assault earlier, and why did you take off your disguises?"

She hesitated a moment. How had he known about that? *Oh, the driver's license.* "Uh, I thought we wouldn't need the disguises anymore since no one had bothered us that whole way. As for calling, I was going to as soon as I got to Rob's. I figured that the police would call you if they needed to talk to either you or me."

Mike's voice rang with frustration. "Jen, you're enough to give a guy ulcers! If you keep this up, you'll get yourself and Brianna killed. Listen to me. You're up against professional killers." He paused a moment. "Since you blew the disguises, we'll have to abandon that strategy."

"It's just as well," Jennifer confessed. "I...I threw away the clothes and I'm out of dye for Brianna's hair. I really didn't think we'd need them any longer."

Mike growled. "You *certainly didn't* think! Jen, how can I protect you when you keep doing your own thing? From now on you will do as I say and you will call me any time anything suspicious happens, got it?"

Jennifer shrank against his words. She hadn't meant to offend him. "I understand. I will call you from now on."

"You had better! Now, I know you planned to stay with your uncle for a couple of days, but you'd better head on up to your brother's as soon as it's light." He paused a moment. "Do you think your uncle can loan you a car?"

She bristled. "I don't know. Why?"

"Since we don't know who else might be involved with this quarrel, you must stop using the Taurus. If Strombolli found you, someone else might be onto it as well."

Jennifer balked. "But if I leave the car here, wouldn't my uncle and his family be in danger?"

"I've already contacted the sheriff's department up there and alerted them to what's going on. What I *need* you to do is tell your uncle to remove the plates and keep the car in the garage until further notice."

Panic washed over Jennifer. "How am I going to explain all this to him? He'll think I've gone off my rocker."

Mike wouldn't relent. "Then wake him up so I can explain it to him."

Jennifer glanced toward the stairway and cringed. By the look on Uncle Peter's face she knew Michelle had already filled him on her secrets. "You can speak to him right now." She offered the receiver to her uncle. "A friend of mine needs to talk to you on the phone. It's important." She sat at the kitchen table waiting for the inevitable.

Deep pain marred Peter Tyler's weatherworn face when he finished his call with Mike Scavone. "Jen, why didn't you tell me before? Don't you realize how much I love you and that I want to help?"

"I really didn't know what was going on until Mike told me just now. It just didn't seem important enough to bother you with before."

Her uncle winced. "Someone has tried to kill you and Brianna twice and you didn't think it was important enough to tell me? What has happened with you? Have you lost trust in your entire family?"

Jennifer stared at her feet. "No. I just didn't want to over-react, since I didn't really know what was happening."

Uncle Peter drew his breath. "I'd better get the van ready for you. It would be best if you left no later than sunup. No one would expect you to be on the road so early."

The sun sat just above the western horizon as Jennifer spotted the gas station and side road that Rob had described. Between a flat tire, an overheated engine, and Brianna's need for activity, the five hour journey had stretched into ten. She turned her uncle's blue van off the highway. Less than a mile later she saw a weathered two-story house on her right. A familiar gold car sat in the wide driveway

"I guess this is it," Jennifer announced. "There's your Uncle Robby's Chevy Impala."

Brianna rubbed sleepy eyes. Jennifer pulled into the dirt driveway and parked. She grabbed the diaper bag and unbuckled her daughter. "Come on, baby." She gently lifted the drowsy child from her car seat. Let's get you inside."

With both hands full, Jennifer made her way up the outdoor steps and lightly kicked the door with her right foot Breathlessly she listened to the footsteps bounding down some stairs. Relief flooded through her. They were home at last. The door opened. Her mouth dropped open in surprise as she looked up into a familiar face—but not that of her brother.

Chapter 11

"You...!" Jennifer gasped.

Nathan leaned against the doorway. "It was me the last time I looked in the mirror." He opened the screen door. "Have I changed that much in one week?"

"What are you doing here?"

"It's good to see you, too. I live here. Are you going to come inside or not?"

"I...I...must have the wr...wrong house," she stammered and began to turn away.

"Nope, this is it. Rob should be home in about two hours. He had to drive up to Edmundston on business." He led her through a room and up the stairs.

"Why didn't you tell me?" Jennifer demanded.

"Rob was already gone when your uncle called this morning to tell us you were on your way up. Since you had already left, there was no way to let you know that he wouldn't be home until tonight."

"No. I mean, why didn't you tell me that you lived here?"

"Didn't I just say that?"

"When we were in California!" Jennifer felt frustrated. Didn't this man give anyone a straight answer?

"This way. Watch out for Bunny. She's running around here somewhere." Nathan guided her through a hallway. "I was sure that I'd frighten you away if you knew then. Besides, Rob made me promise to keep my mouth shut."

He flipped on a light switch and ushered Jennifer into a room on the right. "This is Brianna's room. Rob had it done up just for her. Now, if you'll hand me your keys, I'll unload your car. The bathroom is down the hall, second door on the right."

Jennifer handed them over, grateful for the help.

Nathan pocketed her keys and started for the door. He turned. "Oh, you'll find clean clothes for Brianna in the dresser."

Jennifer laughed. "Nice thought, but my brother forgets that children grow very fast."

"They do, indeed." Mischief twinkled in Nathan's eyes. "That's why I made sure we got her current size and the next one up." He headed back down the stairs.

Brianna's room had a pleasant feel. Candy-striped wallpaper brightened the walls. A balloon print coverlet and matching pillows sat on a low captain's bed, nestled against the far wall. The windowsills, tiny desk, and polished wooden floor teemed with stuffed animals. Frilly pink curtains framed the windows.

She let the diaper bag drop on the floor, carefully lay Brianna on the bed, and removed her shoes. The child yawned and stretched, but did not awaken. Jennifer rummaged through the oak dresser for some pajamas. She draped them over her right shoulder and took a pull-up diaper from the bag.

"Let's get you ready for bed, baby," she coaxed her daughter. "Mommy's going to wash your face and hands. We'll give you a full bath in the morning. Uncle Robby bought you some pretty pink-and-purple jammies to wear, but let's get you into the bathroom first."

Brianna sat up and leaned sleepily against her mother. Jennifer removed her soiled clothes and diaper then took her into the bathroom. She washed the child with a warm washcloth, brushed her teeth and helped her into a clean pull-up diaper and pajamas.

The little girl was fast asleep when Jennifer laid her beneath the blankets with her brown teddy bear. She tucked her in, kissed her forehead, and silently left the room.

Jennifer had just closed the door when Nathan returned with two large suitcases and an overnight bag. "What happened to your disguises? And where's the Taurus? It took me awhile to realize the van was yours. I thought you might have parked out on the street or something."

Uncle Peter didn't tell him about the hit man. The words formed on her tongue, but she held them back. *He already thinks I'm an airhead. I don't want to give him any more reason to despise me.* "We don't need the disguises now. As for the car, we had a slight accident in Vermont. No big deal. Anyhow, Uncle Peter told us to take the van."

"Closed subject?"

She resisted the urge to tell him the truth, to ask for his protection. "Closed subject!"

An unreadable expression crossed Nathan's face then vanished. "I'll show you to your room." He led her down the hall and set her bags inside a doorway, then turned on the light. "You have a built-in bathroom right through there," he said, pointing. "Do you want something to eat?"

Jennifer noticed the rest of her luggage neatly lined up on the bedroom floor. "We ate at McDonald's in Houlton, but I guess I could use a snack." She followed him back down the hall.

A howl sounded outside. Nathan cocked his head. "I need to tend to something downstairs. I'll meet you in the kitchen. It's the room on the right, over there."

"Is it all right if I call my uncle and let him know we arrived safely?"

"Sure. You'll find the phone on the wall next to the breakfast bar." Nathan headed down the steps.

Jennifer called Uncle Peter, then took a seat at the breakfast bar. She idly spun the spice caddy. *I did want to see Nathan again*, she told herself, *but I didn't ask to live with him.* Would this arrangement with Rob even work out? Her brother had some serious explaining to do.

Nathan strode into the kitchen, placed a shiny brass kettle on a burner, and turned up the flame. "Would you like some decaf Cafe Francais? I make a good cup or two, if I do say so myself."

"If it's not too much trouble." Jennifer watched him so she could learn the recipe. She giggled when Nathan opened a can of imported instant coffee and spooned some of its contents into two mugs.

"See, nothing to it." He grinned as he poured the steaming water. "Would you like something to snack on?"

"What do you have?"

"Oh, bits of this and slivers of that. How about hot tomato soup, raw baby carrots, cheese, and toast?"

"Sounds great. Can I help?"

"You have not faith in ze great chef?" Nathan scolded in mock French, waving his hands as he spoke. "I am, how you say, offended."

Jennifer laughed. "Sorry, chef. I'll leave the kitchen if you will show me the way to the living room."

Nathan pointed the way. "Make yourself at home."

Jennifer picked up her mug and walked through the darkened dining room. She wandered into the living room. where a cozy fire glowed in the stone fireplace. She wryly noted a dozen or more photographs of herself and Brianna on the polished wood walls. Many of them had been taken the previous Christmas when Rob had visited for three weeks. In the space above the mantel hung the portrait Jennifer had painted of Brianna and herself.

An antique radio stood in the corner beside the window. Jennifer switched it on, and to her delight, recognized the opening strains to one of her favorite symphonies. She settled herself on the cream-colored sofa and tucked her calf-length plum skirt around her legs.

A few minutes later, Nathan carried in a large serving tray and set it on the coffee table. He took a white linen napkin off the tray and laid it over his left arm. He made a sweeping bow. "Dinner is served, milady."

"Do you usually eat in here?" Jennifer accepted a deep bowl of soup.

"When my favorite radio programs come on. They're the highlight of my evenings." Nathan sat beside her and asked the blessing. He picked up his own bowl, raised it to his lips, and sipped the hot liquid.

Jennifer followed his example. "I take it you don't believe in silverware," she teased.

He smirked. "I confess, I minimize my dishwashing efforts."

Jennifer picked up a thick piece of toast from the tray and took a generous bite. "This is homemade bread. Don't tell me you made it."

"No, I confess. Queen Maggie down the street kindly does most of our baking."

"Queen Maggie?"

"A dear, sweet woman who has taken pity on a couple of helpless bachelors. But now we'll have to rely on your cooking skills. She's going to be too busy for us because of harvest."

Jennifer reached for a slab of cheese. "I don't know that I can match her culinary skills."

"According to Rob, you could put her out of the kitchen."

"Rob's a dreamer."

"So am I."

Jennifer's gaze met his. Was there some hidden meaning in his words? Her cheeks flushed with embarrassment, and she pulled her attention back to her food. Why did she have to be attracted to him? *I'm not going to get involved. I won't! He'd only let me down.*

Bunny hopped up to Nathan and nudged his leg. The doctor took a carrot from the tray and held it out for her. The black lop-earred rabbit closed her eyes in obvious ecstasy and nibbled away at the treat. "She really likes carrots and apples," Nathan explained. "I have the rabbit care manual for you to look at. Would you believe rabbits aren't supposed to have lettuce or cabbage?"

Jennifer raised her eyebrows. "You're kidding. That's the first thing I'd think to give her. I'll take a look at that manual first thing tomorrow." She watched the furry little creature. "She seems to have really made herself at home. Where do you keep her food and stuff?"

"Her water and food bowls are against the wall in the kitchen. Her litter box is in the cloakroom near the stairs. She basically sleeps where she wants to, but usually she's behind the couch. I guess it seems like a huge rabbit hole to her."

Jennifer watched Bunny for a few miinutes. "Was it overly hard to rabbit-proof the house?"

"We had to rearrange some furniture and bundle the wires out of her reach." Nathan handed Bunny another carrot. "Oh, I found that magician's hat I was looking for. She kinda likes it, so I'm thinking about maybe training her for the rabbit-in-the-hat trick."

Jennifer pondered his news. "You really think you can train her?" She held a carrot out to Bunny.

"Why not? She's really smart, and I've already taught her to come when I stomp the floor once with my foot."

Jennifer watched the black rabbit's nose twitch as she nibbled at the carrot. At the sound of a closing door downstairs, Bunny hopped away.

"Do I smell food?" a voice called from the kitchen, moments later. "Nathan, I sure hope you made some for me."

Rob Tyler ambled into the living room. Curly black hair tumbled carelessly around his ears and forehead. Keen green eyes rested on Jennifer. "Jen! I saw Uncle Peter's van and couldn't figure out why it was here. When did you get here? If I'd known you were coming today, I would have postponed my trip." He knelt beside her and hugged her close. "I hope this clod hasn't bored you all evening, Sis."

Jennifer smiled at Nathan. "Not in the least."

"See, someone appreciates me, Rob," Nathan gloated.

Rob smirked. "I'd appreciate you if you ever left me any food."

"Roomie, the fixings are on the shelf. Surely, an architect can use his hands for something as simple as warming up some soup."

"What, and have to slave over a hot stove? Isn't that your job, Doc?"

Nathan scowled. "Use the microwave, Rob. That's why we bought it."

"Oh, yeah, I forgot. Can I steal you away for a few minutes, sister, dear?" Rob coaxed. "We have a lot of catching up to do."

"Sure." Jennifer set down her mug. Rob helped her stand then hugged her again.

"It sure is good to have you here, Jen." He turned toward Nathan. "We'll be back in a few minutes. Do you want anything from the kitchen?"

"Another cup of decaf coffee, if you're inclined to make any."

"Coffee, it is." Rob picked up the mugs. "You're wanting the fancy stuff, right?"

"Yeah, I left the tin on the shelf."

"We'll be right back." Rob led the way into the kitchen and began throwing various items into the microwave. "You won't mind taking care of a couple of lonely bachelors, will you, Jen?" He sliced some bread. "I'm so tired of eating from a can. We only eat healthy once a week at the queen's house."

His sister laughed. "I can hear the violins in the background." Her voice turned serious. "Why didn't you tell me about your roommate?"

Rob looked up from his task. "I was afraid you might not come if I told you. I figured that once you got up here and saw the place, you wouldn't mind. He lives downstairs. I hope you're not too angry."

"It did come as quite a shock." Jennifer turned the flame up under the kettle. "Where'd you meet him?"

"Right out there on the front lawn. I was house hunting. We both saw the 'for sale' sign at the same time, and stopped to look the house over. After talking for a while, we decided to divide the house, top and bottom floors, and share the kitchen. Once we moved in, we became the best of friends."

Given her brother's introverted personality, that spoke volumes.

Rob searched his sister's face for a reaction. "I'm sorry I didn't tell you about Nathan before. He's good people, Jen. Really. Please stay. I mean, he lives downstairs and all."

Though Jennifer felt rather uneasy with the arrangement, she realized she really didn't have anywhere else to go. Besides, Elyssa would join them soon.

I'll have to trust You on this one, God, she prayed silently. Aloud she said. "I'm grateful that you asked us to come, Rob. You've always been a pretty good judge of people, and Nathan does seem to be nice. We'll give it a go."

"Great! You won't regret it, I promise."

Jennifer spooned the instant coffee into the mugs and stirred in the hot water. "Are there any other surprises I should know about?"

"Nope. That was it." He loaded up a tray with his supper and the coffee mugs. "Come on, I'm starved. By the way, why do you have Uncle Peter's van? What happened to your car?"

There's no sense in worrying him with it tonight. I'll tell him later, if he needs to know. "I... we had an accident in Vermont. We weren't hurt or anything, but one of the doors needs to be replaced. Uncle Peter loaned us the van."

Jennifer hoped he wouldn't ask for details as they left the kitchen and was glad when he didn't press further.

"We're saved," Rob shouted to Nathan from the dining room. "She's going to stay."

"Shhh! Brianna's asleep. I'm afraid if she hears your voice, she'll wake up and then be too excited to go back to sleep."

Rob cringed slightly. "Sorry. You made pretty good time getting here from California, Jen. How'd Brianna take the trip?"

Jennifer sat on the sofa. "She's done pretty well. Moving has confused her quite a bit. She doesn't understand why we can't stay at the apartment anymore. I think she'll adapt pretty well, though. It will just take her a few months. However, potty training's completely out the window. We'll have to try again in a few months."

"I'm sorry I wasn't here to greet you," Rob set the tray on the table and sank into the beanbag chair Nathan had brought in for him.

"I understand, Rob," Jennifer responded. "It was a good thing that I met Nathan in Long Beach. At least he was a familiar face, if an unexpected one, when I got here."

Doctor Pellitier laughed. "This man is the biggest worry wart. He's been a nervous wreck since he got the news you were coming. I had to call him right after you left California, so he could figure when you'd be at Michelle's."

"Rob, I didn't realize you cared that much," Jennifer teased. "No wonder you're my favorite brother." She quickly ducked when Rob tossed a wadded paper napkin at her. "He always reacts that way when I say that. I just can't figure out why."

"You're not being very nice, Rob," Nathan scolded lightly. "It would have been worse if she had said that you were her least favorite brother."

"You're probably right, Doc. Although sometimes I think she has placed me in the latter category. Like the day I stole her teddy bear a—"

"You're heading on that ground right now," Jennifer warned. "No childhood stories!"

"You were seventeen, then. Does that count?"

She threatened him with a couch pillow. "Rob!"

Nathan tactfully changed the subject. "Did you get those supplies delivered all right, Rob?"

"Oh, yeah. Thanks for the loan of the truck. There's no way I could have gotten that stuff in my car." Rob dunked a piece of bread into his bowl of soup and stuffed it in his mouth.

Nathan waited for Rob to finish chewing. "Did you get the contract?"

Rob nodded enthusiastically. "I've been selected to design the new Edmundston mall."

"Hey, that's great news." Jennifer beamed. "When do you start?"

"As soon as I finalize the blueprint changes for Bangor."

Rob and Nathan began to discuss the architect's projects at length.

Jennifer's eyes began to droop as she listened to the two men. Weariness weighed on every muscle.

"Hey, sleepy." Nathan nudged her. "Maybe you'd better get to bed."

Rob pulled her to her feet. "I'll even escort you to your room."

"Thanks. See you in the morning, Nathan, and thanks for the wonderful snack."

Nathan smiled warmly at her. "Goodnight, Jen. Sleep well."

Rob hugged Jennifer outside her door. "It's so good to have you here, Jen. I hope you'll see it as home."

"Thanks for making a place for us." A yawn seized her.

"Get some sleep. We'll talk later."

Jennifer prepared for bed, read her Bible, and then spent time in prayer. When she lay down, sleep came quickly for her. Tonight, no dreams disturbed her.

Laughter outside Jennifer's window awakened her the next morning. Sunlight streamed through the curtains and danced playfully around her head. She pulled on her robe and glanced out the window to the scene below.

Brianna, dressed in blue pants, pink sweater, and sneakers, ran around the yard, chasing bubbles. Her short golden curls bounced with every step. Nathan, clad in jeans, a plaid shirt, and loggers' boots, sat crossed-legged on the ground, blowing the soapy marvels through a small wand. A few landed on his dark hair.

"Mo', mo'," Brianna demanded.

"Why don't you blow some for me to catch?" Nathan showed Brianna how to dip the wand in the liquid and then blow through the hoop to create the bubbles. The child laughed gleefully.

Jennifer smiled and turned from the window to start her shower. After toweling dry, she pulled on her forest green corduroy skirt and a soft, gray sweater. She dried her hair with a blower, and then combed her auburn locks until the air cracked with electricity.

When she entered the kitchen, the troubled look on her brother's face disturbed her. His fingers clenched his dark curls in apparent frustration. Rob looked up.

"Mike Scavone called while you were sleeping and told me what happened. Why didn't say something last night?"

Jennifer poured herself a cup of coffee and sat across from Rob at the breakfast bar. "I didn't want to bother you with it."

"Bother me?" He stood and paced the room. "Some idiot tries to kill you and my niece, and you're worried about bothering me with it?" He raised his voice in anger. "I'm your *brother*. I expect to know when anything like this happens."

"What good would it have done last night, Rob? The man's dead. Besides, I...I thought it would be best if I handled it myself."

"That's what Mike figured. You don't have to, Jen. That's what family is for." Rob sat on his stool and leaned over the bar. "I know we didn't have much 'family doings' when we were growing up, but we had each other. We still do. You can trust me. I want to know when things are going wrong so I can be beside you and help in any way I can. Please don't ever shut me out again."

Jennifer covered his hand with her own. "I never meant to shut you out, Rob. I just...Corrine always said I had to learn to take care of myself. That no one else would."

"What would she know? That woman never gave us the time of day." Bitterness tainted Rob's voice. "Some mother—all wrapped up in herself. We couldn't call her anything other than Corrine because it might ruin her social standing. Well, I'm breaking the cycle. I'm here for you. Even when I'm out of town, if you call, I'll drop everything and come right home. I mean it. Nathan is here to protect you, too. He's good people, or I wouldn't allow him anywhere near you or Brianna."

"I know." Tears glistened in Jennifer's eyes. "I couldn't ask for a better brother than you."

The back door slammed and heavy footsteps raced up the stairs.

Bunny scurried from her hiding place and hopped into the kitchen.

"Mommy, Mommy, wook at me!" Brianna's happy face appeared above the banister. Blueberry juice stained youngster's mouth., She held tightly to Nathan's head as she rode on his shoulders.

Jennifer relieved him of his lively burden and set her on the floor. "Nathan, I think you've made a friend."

"We gonna make boobewwy pancakes, Mommy!" She stooped to pet Bunny's black fur.

"With what berries we have left, munchkin." Nathan placed the wicker basket on the floor. "She must have eaten more than half of what we picked."

Jennifer wiped her daughter's mouth and hands with a wet paper towel. "She never could resist fresh berries." She shooed Brianna off to her bedroom to play for a while. Bunny hopped after the child.

"Nathan, have a seat," Rob instructed his friend. "We've a bit of a problem to discuss. You too, Jen."

Jennifer chewed her lower lip while Rob relayed the information Mike had given him that morning.

"Did I leave anything out?" His keen green eyes echoed his question.

"That about covers it," she murmured, ashamed that Nathan had to hear about the latest incident. She avoided meeting his eyes. As one of her hosts, he had a right to know what was going on. Still, she wanted to hide her troubles—afraid others would judge her by her mistakes.

Nathan broke into her thoughts. "Did you tell anyone else where you were going?"

She shook her head. "No. You, Elyssa, Rob, Misha, Mike, and Tina were the only ones who knew I was leaving Long Beach. Mike instructed me to only give the information he had written on his card if needed."

Silence reigned for a moment before Nathan spoke again. "Did you leave a forwarding address with the post office?"

"Just Mike's. He said he'd forward any mail."

Rob glowered. "How did that guy find you?"

"Mike said he had my address book." Jennifer weighed that significance and shuddered. "I'm so glad I put your letter in my purse before we left for Knott's." She sighed. "He also may have been following me before I came up here. Anyhow, he's dead."

Her brother grunted. "Well, little sister, I'm not taking any chances." He glanced at his roommate. "Nathan, would you be their bodyguard until I get back from Bangor tonight?"

Dr. Pellitier smiled. "No problem. I was hoping to show them around the neighborhood."

Out of the corner of her eye, Jennifer glimpsed her daughter crawling beneath Nathan's stool toward the blueberries. Before she could say anything, Nathan had snatched the basket away from Brianna's pilfering fingers and set it on the breakfast bar.

"Good timing, Nathan." Rob laughed at the proceedings.

Jennifer scooped up her daughter. "Save the berries for the pancakes, sweetie."

Rob glanced at his watch. "Listen, folks, it's seven-thirty. I've got a plane to catch." He scribbled a number on a piece of paper and handed it to Dr. Pellitier. "Here's where I will be. If you need me at all, don't hesitate to call. Take care of my ladies, Nathan."

"You bet, roomie. Now, I have a pancake-making date with my favorite little munchkin."

Rob kissed his sister and his niece. "I'll see you tonight at the bonfire." He hurried down the steps.

Jennifer released Brianna to help Nathan. She stepped to the dining room window and watched Rob's car pulled out of the driveway. *The last thing I need is Nathan Pellitier as a bodyguard.* Anxious thoughts flooded her mind. Several minutes later, she returned to the kitchen.

Chapter 12

Brianna stood on a wooden high chair and stirred pancake batter with a large plastic spoon. A trail of flour marched down the front of her sweater, over a makeshift towel apron, and ended in a small pile on the floor beneath the chair. Nathan cracked another egg and dropped it in the bowl. Brianna stabbed it with the spoon and mixed it into the batter, splattering the countertop in the attempt.

Jennifer sat on a stool and marveled at how a man could take such delight in spending time with a small child.

"What are you sitting down for, Jen?" Nathan admonished her. "Heat up the grill so we can cook these masterpieces."

Jennifer obeyed. *Brianna sure has taken to him,* she mused. *He can seem quite irresistible.* She had to ensure she didn't allow herself to get involved with him. *It'll only lead to disaster.*

"We are expected at the queen's court today," Nathan announced as he poured batter on the grill.

"Fantasy time," Jennifer murmured.

"No, I'm serious. I spend my days off at the queen's. Rob and I assist her and Franz with projects," he explained.

"What kinds of projects?"

"Today it's harvesting the majority of the vegetables from their garden." Nathan sprinkled fresh blueberries on the bubbling batter then began flipping each pancake over. "We're expecting frost in a few days. Between that and upcoming potato harvest, we've got to take advantage of this weekend."

"That sounds interesting. Can we help?"

Nathan tossed a pancake in the air. Brianna cheered when it landed back on the grill. "That, milady, is precisely why we are going over. I would, however, recommend that you put on a flannel shirt and jeans."

Was he kidding? "But I don't have any, show-off."

He scanned Jennifer's figure. "Well, the shirt, I can remedy. The pants are another matter, but we'll worry about that after we eat."

Jennifer set the table while Nathan piled the golden cakes onto a platter that Brianna held. When the three had gathered around the table, Nathan asked the blessing and began to serve breakfast.

"Not bad, for a man," Jennifer teased, popping another forkful of pancake in her mouth.

"I surprise myself sometimes," Nathan replied. "Besides, I had the capable assistance of this young lady."

Brianna grinned.

When they had finished breakfast, Nathan cleared the table, set the dirty dishes in the sink, and then headed down the stairs. "I'll be back in about ten minutes," he hollered.

Jennifer loaded the dishwasher as Brianna looked on.

Nathan returned shortly with a pair of faded jeans and a red flannel shirt. "Here, use these. Go ahead and change. I'll meet you the kitchen."

"Thanks. Should I change Brianna's clothes?"

Merriment danced in his blue eyes. "Why dirty another set?"

"You're right." Jennifer laughed. "Nathan, you'd make an excellent parent some day."

"I'm working on it." The phone rang. Nathan answered it while Jennifer took the clothes to her room.

"What did he mean he's working on it?" Jennifer mumbled as she changed. The plaid shirt felt soft and comfortably broken in. She ran her hands along the sleeves. Nathan was unmistakably well-built. The phone rang again. *Where did he get the jeans?* Did he have a girlfriend? The thought weighed heavy on her heart. She didn't want to even imagine another woman in his arms, someone who would be the center of his attention.

"This is nonsense!" She blindly rushed into the hall and collided with Nathan.

He recovered from the sudden impact. "What's nonsense?"

"Um...umm...nothing," she stammered. "Let's go." She picked up Brianna and started toward the stairs.

He stopped her. "We have to make a detour to the hospital first. Minor crisis. It'll give me a chance to show off the medical center."

Jennifer blinked. Her daughter wasn't dressed to go into town. "Oh, no! Brianna's sweater!"

"I'll grab a clean top. Wait for me downstairs." He joined them a moment later on the landing. "Turn her around and I'll swap these" In an instant, Brianna sported a blue teddy bear sweatshirt.

Curiosity got the best of Jennifer. "Why do you have to go to the hospital? Is there an emergency?"

"One of my patients is threatening revolt, and I have to rescue the nurses. Nothing a little intervention won't cure." Nathan grabbed the car seat and installed it in the back seat of his blue pickup truck. "Here you go, sweetpea." He buckled in Brianna.

Jennifer climbed into the front seat, anticipating the ride into Caribou. Rolling hillsides blushed with brilliant autumn colors. Farmhouses dotted the countryside. The crisp, fresh air was a welcome relief from Southern California's foul smog.

Nathan maneuvered his blue pickup into the parking lot of the medical center, located on the outskirts of the town.

"I'll get Brianna." Jennifer got out, opened Brianna's door. and unstrapped the child from her car seat. "You'll have to mind us while we're in there. Do you understand?"

Brianna nodded and reached out for Nathan. "Me wants piggy-back

The doctor carried her to the Cary Medical Center entrance and placed her on the ground

The toddler seemed fascinated with the electric doors and tried them out several times.

"Come on, baby," Jennifer scooped the child into her arms. "Let's go see where Nathan works."

A nurse walked by, assisting a patient in a wheelchair. Brianna clapped her hands in delight. "Me, too, Mommy! Me, too!"

"I don't think so, Brianna."

"Maybe you can have a ride on the way back," Nathan told the youngster and led the way down the corridor to the surgical ward.

A stout gray-haired nurse stood behind the nurses' station, scrubbing a large brown stain on her uniform with a wet cloth. "Dr. Pellitier, I can't tell you just how glad I am to see you," she said when she saw Nathan. "Big Jake is simply horrible this morning. Look at this!" She pointed to the stain. "Beef broth! I have a notion to send him the cleaning bill!"

"A good morning to you, too, Edna," Nathan teased the woman. "I thought you said he was just a little upset. What happened?"

Jennifer moved herself and Brianna out of the way.

A sudden crash resounded from down the hallway, and a slender young man bolted from the third room on the left, clutching a brown overnight bag.

"Here it is, Edna," He tossed the leather case on the counter. "Mr. Rahn is now in with Mr. Campbell. We moved him just in time. Jake's trying to tear the bathroom door off its hinges." The male nurse pushed a curly chestnut lock from his forehead.

Nathan raised his eyebrows. "Getting a little bit of exercise this morning, Terry?"

"You look a little busy yourself, Doc." Terry assessed Jennifer and Brianna with his dark brown eyes. "Care to introduce me to these lovely ladies?"

Nathan waved him off. "Maybe later. Fill me in, first. What's going on? I have the vague impression that he's slightly upset about something."

"That's an understatement," Terry scoffed. "He's raging angry about the liquid diet you placed him on. He wants a 'real breakfast.'"

Edna handed Nathan a metal clipboard. "Here's his chart. I tried to explain that his stomach wouldn't be able to handle the load yet, but he wouldn't listen. Instead, he started throwing things, aiming at staff members." Edna sniffed her disapproval.

Terry scowled. "He dumped apple juice over the head of an orderly then threw his broth at Edna when she entered the room. We managed to smuggle out his roommate after I locked Jake in the bathroom. I reinforced the door with a chair until we can get him subdued."

Nathan reviewed the patient's chart. "Sounds like he's reacting to his medicine. What about his stitches? Did he tear them?"

Terry balked. "Doc, nobody in their right mind is going to get close enough to find out. Unless you're already packing a tranquilizer gun."

"Remind me to order one." Nathan stepped behind the nurse's station. "Meanwhile, we've got to get in there and check him out. Edna, see who all you can scare up to lend a hand."

Edna broadcast the request for assistance over the intercom.

Loud bangs reverberated from down the hallway. Terry raked his fingers through his unkempt brown hair. "Do we get hazardous duty pay for this? I'd kind of like to live at least long enough to see Christmas—a hundred years from now."

"Is he that dangerous?" Jennifer shifted Brianna to her other hip. The conversation now worried her.

Terry turned to face her. Anxiety filled his brown eyes. "He's a slightly abbreviated version of Goliath."

"Actually, he's more like a bull in a china shop, so he won't be too bad," Nathan countered. He scribbled a few sentences into the patient's chart. "Terry, get a few large metal trays. We'll use them as shields. Edna, get me a hypo of sodium amytal. Hopefully that'll keep him quiet for a while. Who said a doctor's life was easy?" Nathan excused himself and went into his office. When he returned moments later, he wore his white lab coat.

Several nurses and orderlies converged on the ward and waited for instructions. Terry came back with the aluminum trays. Edna joined the group a few moments later.

Jennifer watched the proceedings with growing anxiety.

Nathan took the syringe and instructed Edna to stay at the nurses' station. He led the other medical personnel down the hallway.

"I hope he doesn't get hurt," Jennifer told Edna. "Does this type of thing happen often?"

"No, this patient is unusual, but don't worry. Dr. Pellitier can hold his own." Edna picked up the patient's chart again and began to write.

Sounds of a major skirmish erupted from the room in question, followed by explosive swearing. Edna dropped the chart and ran to help. Brianna clung tightly to her mother as Jennifer stared down the hall and whispered a prayer. Minutes later, silence fell.

Dr. Pellitier emerged from Jake's room, carrying a tray and the spent syringe. Blood oozed from above his right eye.

"Nathan?" Jennifer hurried to his side. "You're bleeding."

Brianna patted his shoulder. "You got a boo-boo."

"It's just a small cut," he assured them. "I'll let you doctor it up if you like. I've just got to make a phone call first." He dialed a number and spoke several orders into the receiver.

After he hung up, Nathan submitted to Jennifer's care. He winced as she cleaned the wound with the iodine pads that he had handed her.

Brianna stood beside him, holding his left hand. "Mommy make you all better," she clucked soothingly.

The rest of the medical staff headed back to their own duties as. Edna and Terry guided a laden gurney toward the nurses' station. Jennifer gasped as she viewed the gigantic figure lying before her.

"Lumberjack," Nathan explained. "I have to repair some stitch work on our friend here. Why don't you and Brianna wait for me in the front lobby?"

Jennifer pressed a bandage in place. "Is it safe to work on him?"

"He'll be as gentle as a baby just as long as that sedative works." Nathan dropped a kiss on her cheek. "Thanks for worrying, though. I'll be done in an hour if the damage isn't too extensive."

Jennifer touched her cheek with trembling fingers as the medical team pushed the gurney toward the operating room. Nathan's kiss had been light, but it left Jennifer's senses reeling. She felt weak. *Stop behaving like a schoolgirl,* she scolded herself. *You've been kissed before.* She led Brianna to the waiting room at the front of the hospital.

While her daughter busied herself with some picture books, Jennifer tried to read a magazine. Her thoughts wandered back to Nathan's kiss. Why had it affected her so strongly? Danny had given her a sense of security during their marriage. Nathan caused a rising turmoil in her that frightened, yet excited her at the same time. She wondered wistfully what it would be like to be held in Nathan's strong arms—to have the love of such a man.

I won't get involved with him, she reminded herself silently, attempting to push Nathan from her thoughts. *The man seems too perfect. He's got to be hiding some flaw; something that will bring me heartache. My life is complicated enough as it is. I don't need to add on any more problems. No, I will not fall for Nathan Pellitier!*

A light tap on her shoulder made Jennifer jump. "Welcome back to earth, Jen," Nathan teased. "What planet were you visiting?"

Why, oh, why do his eyes have to be so blue? Jennifer sighed, her heart fluttering wildly.

"Are you all right, Jen?"

She regained her composure. "I'm fine. Is it time to go?"

"Not quite," he announced. "It's wheelchair time!"

Brianna cheered.

Jennifer rolled her eyes. "I'm beginning to wonder who's the kid in this group."

Nathan laughed and unfolded a wheelchair. "You might as well enjoy the ride, too, Jen. Your chariot awaits."

"I'll pass this time."

Doctor Pellitier sat in the chair. "In that case, we'll ride and you can steer." He placed Brianna on his lap. "Onward," he commanded.

"But I don't know which way to go," Jennifer protested. She wished he'd abandon this idea and take them back home.

"Go that way."

Jennifer pushed the wheelchair in the direction Nathan indicated.

"Go down this corridor," he instructed.

When Jennifer noticed that the walls were adorned with neat rows of paintings, she slowed to view them. "Who painted these?"

"Mostly local artists," Nathan explained. "I even know a few of them."

Jennifer's heart faltered when she recognized a familiar ocean scene with her own signature at the bottom. Her face felt hot. "How did this get here?"

"Ah, my favorite." Nathan beamed. "Your brother kindly loaned it to me, so I could enjoy it while I'm here at the hospital."

How could Rob do this to me? "He told me nothing about it!"

Nathan chuckled. "Would you have allowed me to hang it here?"

"Of course not!" Her tone came out harsher than she expected.

"Exactly why he didn't tell you. Besides, it was his birthday gift. I had asked him to loan me the portrait of you and Brianna, but he refused. You do good work, by the way."

Jennifer blew out her frustration. "Brothers!"

"I think his version was 'Sisters'." He tapped the arm of the wheelchair. "Shall we get on with the tour?"

Nathan guided them through the hospital, and then back toward the front lobby. "Would you two lovely ladies care to stop at the gift shop?"

Brianna clapped her hands and squealed with delight.

"Nathan, it's not a good idea," Jennifer warned.

"I'm sure she'll be fine." He stood.

Jennifer raised her hands in surrender. "All right, then. I refuse to take any responsibility for what happens."

"It's a deal." Nathan set Brianna on the floor, took her by the hand, and entered the shop. Jennifer leaned on the doorframe and chuckled as Brianna thrust every toy she could reach into Nathan's arms.

Dr. Pellitier motioned frantically at Jennifer and silently begged for help. After a moment, Jennifer stepped forward. "Brianna, stop."

Her daughter dropped a cloth doll and looked at her mother.

Jennifer exhaled. She wouldn't completely rescue Nathan, but she intended to retain the progress she'd made with the toddler. "You can choose only one toy. Do you understand?" She left off the price limit to teach him a lesson.

Brianna nodded and started looking at the various toys.

"How about two—" The words died on Nathan's lips when Jennifer scowled at him. He returned his armful of toys to their shelves.

Finally, the child chose a large stuffed horse as large as herself.

"I know, I know," Nathan muttered as he lugged the toy toward the truck. "Rule number one: Mother always knows best."

"You're catching on." Jennifer scooped up Brianna before they stepped into the parking lot. "How much did she take you for?"

Nathan seemed hesitant to speak. "Uh, one fifty."

"A hundred and fifty dollars!" Jennifer scoffed. "At least I rescued you. Rob paid over three hundred. That's what made Brianna lose control in shops. My brother insisted she chose everything she wanted, and wouldn't take no for an answer."

"I'll get him," Nathan vowed. "He's created a monster."

"Der's a monsta?" Worry clouded Brianna's face. She clung tighter to her mother.

"No, honey, Jennnifer explained. "Mr. Nathan just made a mistake that he won't repeat."

Dr. Pellitier balanced the toy horse across his shoulders. "Teach me, oh master. What are your specific rules?"

"Tell her she can have only one toy, and the amount she can spend."

Nathan quirked his eyebrows. "You didn't set a price limit today."

"Because you didn't give me one." Jennifer rolled her eyes. "Give me the receipt. I'll send it to the insurance company for reimbursement. The toys lost in the fire were covered."

Nathan. stooped to pluck a large daisy from a nearby flowerbed and held it out. "Peace offering?"

"One flower?" Jennifer playfully accused. "You blow over a hundred dollars on a stuffed horse for my daughter then try to bribe me with one flower that you *stole*?"

Nathan grabbed her left hand and knelt on the pavement. "Please forgive me, Jen," he feigned grief. "I'll never make it through the day if you're angry at me."

An elderly couple walked by and smiled as Jennifer frantically tried to pull her hand out of Nathan's grasp. Her cheeks burned.

"Fine. Just stop embarrassing me." She snatched the flower from his other hand and walked swiftly to the truck.

"I can't take you anywhere in public," she complained when Nathan caught up with them.

He unlocked the doors and placed the horse next to Brianna's safety seat in the center of the back seat. "I'll try to do better, Jen. I just lose control when you're around." He took Brianna from Jennifer's arms, and then danced wildly around the truck with the youngster.

"Good grief," Jennifer lamented. "Are you going to act like this at the queen's house?"

Nathan got Brianna buckled in. "Heavens, no! I have a reputation to consider. To her I'm an outstanding, responsible, kind—"

"Spare me," Jennifer interrupted with laughter. She climbed into the front passenger seat. "All I ask, Nathan, is that you be on your absolute best behavior."

"All right," he groaned as he slid behind the steering wheel.

"You gonna cwy, Nafan?" Brianna asked.

"I just might," he told her, pouting. "Nobody loves me, or even cares when I have a bad cut. Everyone just picks on me."

"Po Nafan," Brianna crooned. "Me woves you."

Jennifer groaned. "Give me a break, Nathan."

He wiggled his eyebrows at her, his bandage moving wildly. "I'm pretty good at melodrama, don't you think?"

She fastened her safety belt. "It's a good thing you went into medicine; otherwise you'd be starving in some bare apartment in the middle of New York City."

"I'd prefer California."

She looked at him and cocked her head slightly. "Then, what are you doing here?"

He grinned. "I didn't want to put all of those actors out of work, so I did them a favor and became a surgeon."

Jennifer smirked. "Hollywood will be forever grateful."

"Ouch!"

"Owie hut?" Brianna asked.

Nathan shook his head. "Just my ego, sweetpea."

Brianna moved her arms like wings. "You got a eagow?"

"Uh, no." Nathan tried to explain to the wide-eyed child. "My e-g-o."

"It's what makes men think they're big shots," Jennifer added.

Nathan gave Jennifer a warning look. "You're not being very nice, princess. I always pay back with interest."

Jennifer laughed at him. "Oooo, threats, now?" From everything she'd seen, he posed no real danger.

"Promises, princess. Promises." Nathan rubbed his hands together and chortled. Mischief filled his eyes.

Yeah, right. "I'm shaking in my boots." Are you going to start the engine or not?"

He slapped the steering wheel. "Whoops, I forgot something. I'll be right back." Nathan hopped out of the truck and ran into the hospital.

Jennifer and Brianna sang the child's favorite songs until Nathan returned ten minutes later.

"Miss me?" he asked them as he slid back into the driver's seat.

"Oh, yes!" Brianna declared. Jennifer merely smiled.

"It's off to the queen's house, then."

Chapter 13

Just before ten o'clock, Nathan parked in front of a sprawling white farmhouse just down the street from his own home. He ushered Jennifer and Brianna past the roomy wrap-around porch and held back the low branches of a weeping willow. As they walked around the side of the house, an oak tree showered them with a handful of colorful leaves and some acorns.

Jennifer shifted Brianna's diaper bag and drank in the kaleidoscope of sights. Her fingers itched to sketch. A split wood fence crisscrossed the property and stretched into the distance. Autumn-kissed maple, oak and birch trees dotted the landscape. She felt invigorated by the fresh autumn air. On a day like today, Jennifer felt she could easily forget her troubles.

A noisy squabble drew her gaze to two plump turkeys fighting in a pen in front of the large red barn twenty feet away. "I've never seen turkeys that big before."

"They're also mean," Nathan warned. "One's for Thanksgiving, and the other's for Christmas."

"How do you decide which is which?"

He shrugged. "We draw straws." His eyes took on a wicked glint. "Sometimes, though, the one that makes us mad goes first."

A crash of metal cans came from the nearby old weathered shed.

"Queenie, are you back here?" Nathan called.

"In here, Nathan," a muffled voice answered from inside the shed. "I'll be right with you. The milking machine broke and Franz needs a couple of parts to get it going again."

A smirk covered Nathan's face. "Isn't it a little late for the milking? Those cows must be in a lot of pain."

The voice sounded exasperated. "Don't sass me, young man. I milked them all by hand, first thing, and I don't want a repeat performance tonight." The clattering resumed.

"How many cows do they have?" Jennifer asked.

Nathan did a quick calculation. "At last count, there were twelve." He raised his voice several notches. "I brought reinforcements for the harvest, milady. Rob had to fly to Bangor again."

A plump, silver-haired woman in a pair of old blue jeans, a green flannel shirt and scuffed tennis shoes emerged from the doorway. Rolled-up sleeves bared her tanned arms strengthened by years of hard work. She jiggled a handful of metal and plastic washers in her right hand. "It's about time you showed up. We expected you earlier."

"Sorry." Dr. Pellitier shrugged. "Duty called. I had some emergency stitching to tackle first."

The woman's keen blue eyes surveyed the newcomers with interest. "Seems to me these lovely young ladies would be a much better distraction, son."

Nathan bowed with a flourish. "Queenie, this is Rob's sister Jennifer Warner and her daughter Brianna. Ladies, this is Maggie Michaud, affectionately known as the queen."

Maggie rolled her eyes. "You boys have quite an imagination. Humph! Queen, indeed."

"Boys!" Nathan complained. "We could be eighty-nine and she'd still call us boys."

Jennifer looked at him, surprised. "I thought you said—"

"I admit to nothing," he interrupted.

Maggie shot Jennifer a knowing look. "You wouldn't think he was a grown man if you could see him hover over my cookie jar."

"Or play with soap bubbles or ride in wheelchairs," Jennifer added.

Nathan nudged her arm. "Hush! My reputation is being ruined before my very eyes."

Maggie shook a finger at him. "Nathan, you'll know what a ruined reputation is if you don't make yourself useful." She thrust the washers into his hand. "Take these to your uncle and meet us at the west shed."

Uncle? Jennifer watched Nathan sprint to the barn, and then turned toward Maggie. "You're Nathan's aunt?"

Maggie nodded. "Yep, his mother is my youngest sister." She guided them past a tall, round, white-washed stone building, and through an open wooden gate.

Jennifer noted that the building was at least seven feet tall. "Is that some kind of silo?"

"Smokehouse." Maggie led them toward a larger shed at the west end of her property.

"Pwetty," Brianna stopped to gather red and gold leaves.

Maggie looked down at the youngster and chuckled. "She's quite a little doll. Would you mind if I taught her how to preserve those?"

"Not at all. I'd be glad to learn as well." She hesitated. "It's been a long time since I've done anything like that. I didn't realize just how much I've missed Maine."

"You either got it in your blood, or you don't, that's for sure. Linda, Nathan's mom, she doesn't have it in her blood—prefers Pennsylvania. Her boy shows sense, though. He came back here to live."

Nathan joined them just as they reached the gray wood shed. "You'll want to avoid walking too close to that." He motioned to a smoking mound of dirt nearby."

"What is it?" Jennifer peered at the curiosity.

Nathan chuckled. "It's a secret. You'll find out later today." He and Maggie unbolted the shed doors and pulled them wide open, revealing several wheelbarrows, some large baskets and an array of gardening tools. Jennifer set Brianna's diaper bag on the ground.

"Me have wide?" Brianna asked when Nathan brought out a medium-sized wheelbarrow.

"That's a great idea," he agreed heartily. "I think you'd better ride this time, Jen. We'd be too heavy for you to push."

Jennifer placed several tools in a basket and looked to Maggie for rescue from the doctor's wild proposal.

"I agree, Jennifer." The older woman's eyes twinkled. "He is heavy."

Nathan tried again. "I'll just give you a ride up to the field, then I'll come back for the other wheelbarrow," he prodded.

"Wouldn't it be easier if I just pushed the other wheelbarrow over? It would only take one trip, then." Jennifer suggested.

"That wouldn't be near enough fun," Nathan argued. "Come on, live it up." He unceremoniously picked up Jennifer, deposited her into the wheelbarrow, and sat Brianna on her lap. "Wanna ride, too, Queenie?"

"No, Nathan. My old bones can't handle those games anymore." Maggie picked up two medium-sized baskets. "I'll just take these to the other side of the field and start picking the last of the peas.."

"We'll have all the fun, then." Nathan turned the wheelbarrow toward the field, and then started running.

Jennifer screamed and shut her eyes. She clung to Brianna with her left arm, and to the edge of the wheelbarrow with her right hand. *The guy is nuts!* Wind whipped her hair across her face as the ride jostled her and Brianna from side to side.

Brianna shrieked in glee and begged Nathan to run faster. Jennifer finally opened her eyes and began to enjoy herself. Scenery whizzed by in a colorful blur. Nathan circled the edge of a small pond a few times, weaving wildly. A sudden jolt tipped the wheelbarrow, spilling Jennifer and Brianna onto the soft grass.

"Do it again, Nafan," Brianna begged, laughing. She tried to crawl back into the wheelbarrow.

Nathan rushed to Jennifer's side. "Are you all right?"

"I'm fine," she assured him as he helped her to her feet. Jennifer's skin tingled under his touch. She quickly pulled away and brushed off her clothes, avoiding his gaze. "Aren't we supposed to be working?"

"Soon enough." Nathan righted the wheelbarrow. "We're determined to get everything in today."

Jennifer scanned the large field, ringed by bright marigolds. Tall stalks of sweet corn divided the growing area in half. Rows of ripening pumpkins and other types of squash dotted one side. Herbs, tomatoes, broccolli, cucumbers, bush beans, and other vegetables stretched across the other side.

She felt overwhelmed by the enormous task. "I don't see how we can even put a dent in it." A brisk breeze swept by, giving her a deep appreciation for her warm work clothes.

Nathan followed her gaze. "We won't be working alone. Tons of help will arrive this afternoon. We'll get it done. Meanwhile, let's start with the acorn squash and zucchini. I'll go back for another wheelbarrow and the rest of the equipment."

As Brianna chased a dusky butterfly, Jennifer drank in the autumn goodness around her.

Nathan returned with Brianna's diaper bag and other supplies. He handed her a bushel basket and a pair of gloves. "I'll cut the stalks. You and Brianna can load the veggies into the containers," he explained. "The zucchini will go in the wheelbarrow, the acorn squash will fit in the baskets.

Brianna proudly marched the first acorn squash to a basket beside the wheelbarrows and placed it carefully on the bottom. Before long, she became bored and decided to chase the cats playing nearby.

Jennifer felt uneasy with Brianna wandering around. "Uh-oh. I'd better keep an eye on her. I don't want her falling in the pond."

"I've got the perfect solution." Nathan took a small metal whistle from his pocket and blew into it. A few minutes later, a huge gray animal trotted out of the adjoining woods.

Jennifer gasped as the wolf headed straight for them.

"Relax, Jen, it's only Spirit," Nathan assured her. "He's half husky, half wolf, and a real gentleman." He bent over and stroked the dog's head. "Spirit watches out for the family. He'll keep Brianna safe while we're working. He's the best babysitter around. Come on, get acquainted with him."

Jennifer squatted down and began to pet Spirit's thick coat. He definitely had the markings of a wolf, yet had bi-colored eyes, and a mouth that seemed to curve into a grin. "Why does he have one brown and one blue eye?"

"It's a genetic thing with huskies," Nathan told her. "I think it gives him real character." He knelt beside Spirit and pointed at Brianna. "Protect," he commanded. Spirit bolted to the girl's side.

Brianna made fast friends with Spirit. The animal didn't seem to mind the child's play and even allowed her to ride on his back. Wherever she went, her appointed guardian followed, tail wagging.

Intrigued, Jennifer watched them from the squash patch. "Over here, sweetie," she said waving, when her daughter turned and began calling for her.

Spirit tagged along as Brianna ran to her side. "Mommy, see my new fwiend? Can I keep him, pwease?"

"I'm afraid not, honey. He belongs to Nathan."

The child's smile faltered a bit, and then brightened again. "Can I bawwo him?"

"We'll see."

Nathan grinned. "You can borrow him as much as you want, sweetpea. Just be nice to him."

Brianna squealed with delight and ran off with Spirit at her heels.

"She couldn't shake him now if she wanted to." Nathan chuckled.

Jennifer's gaze followed her daughter. Spirit definitely acted like the youngster's shadow. "He's quite an animal. Where did you get him?"

Nathan knelt down and chopped at another stalk. "Well, first you have to understand that Spirit sees himself as superior to us. Second, he thinks he's my owner."

"You're kidding, right?"

He raised his right hand. "On my honor. Spirit chose me just before his previous pet, Tom Westley, died."

Jennifer lifted a large zucchini into the large wheelbarrow. "He really thinks he owns you? How did he pick you out?"

Nathan continued cutting stalks. "Tom was one of my patients and became a dear friend. He stayed at home for as long as he could, but the tumor took its toll. Toward the end he agreed to enter the hospital if I'd watch after his house and Spirit."

He stared off into the distance. "The two of them had been partners in the Air Force K-9 unit at the old Air Force base, just north of here. When Tom retired, Spirit retired as well. The night Tom died, Spirit showed up on my doorstep in Caribou. He's been with me since—about a year, now."

"You mean Spirit's a trained police dog? What if he attacks Brianna?" She scanned the area for her daughter.

Nathan noticed her alarm. "Don't worry, Jen. He's too well trained to attack a child. Spirit's one of those animals with an instinctive sense of a person's character. Tom always said he could trust Spirit's judgment. If he didn't like someone, Tom kept an eye out. Eventually, he'd find out what Spirit already knew."

Jennifer relaxed a little. The dog did seem quite gentle with Brianna. The duo came into view with Spirit in the lead. Brianna's light brown curls blew about her merry face. "It looks like we're in for another shoe hunt." She pointed to the child's muddy bare feet. "I just hope they're somewhere out in the open."

"We'll find them," Nathan assured her. "Spirit's great at tracking."

"Did you move out here because of him?"

"Actually, because of the neighbors. Spirit can be a bit intimidating and he's not one to stay put. He'd patrol the neighborhood, but people didn't care too much for that. So, out of respect for their fears, and for Spirit's independence, I started house hunting."

Jennifer glanced over at their weathered gray house. "Well, God gave you and Rob quite a find. It's a really nice house."

Nathan wiped his brow with the back of his hand. "That's for sure, and it's not too far from the Westley place, either, so Spirit can visit his old haunts." He pointed to a farmhouse on a hill just barely visible beyond the forest. "It makes it convenient for me, too, because I'm taking care of Tom's place until his son comes back from overseas."

As the morning wore on, Jennifer rolled up her shirtsleeves. By one o'clock, every container overflowed. She placed the last ripened acorn squash beside a basket. "Now what?"

"We'll unload them on the back porch. Tomorrow, the women will start freezing and canning the produce. Though I dare say some of those zucchini will definitely become bread." Nathan stood up and stretched. "I don't know about you, but I'm starved. Maggie's got dinner waiting for us inside."

Jennifer's stomach rumbled. "That sounds really good. I'll have to wrangle Brianna, first."

She located the youngster, Spirit, and the child's mud-drenched shoes beside a large puddle on the other side of the barn. "You need a bath before we do anything," Jennifer told her, picking up the shoes. Brianna rubbed her muddy hands on her pants and grinned back. They walked back to the patch.

Nathan chuckled when he saw Brianna. "I'll help you tackle the mud monster when we go in," he told Jennifer. "We can put her clothes and shoes in Maggie's washer so they'll be ready by the time we head out again." He handed a small acorn squash to Brianna, and then tilted the large wheelbarrow onto its wheel. "Jen, if you take the small wheelbarrow, I'll get this one."

"Sure thing." Jennifer had little difficulty pushing her load while Brianna walked beside her. After parking the wheelbarrows next to the porch, they made three trips to gather the baskets, diaper bag and stray squash.

"Come on in the house for dinner, and take a load off your weary bones." Maggie called through the kitchen window.

The trio trudged up the back steps into the house.

"This way." Nathan led Jennifer and Brianna to a large sink just opposite the door. Various coats hung from pegs along one side of the room. Rubber boots lined the baseboard beneath them. A washer and dryer hugged the outer wall.

Brianna squirmed and complained as her mother scrubbed the child's face, hands, arms, and feet.

"I can never figure out how kids manage to get so filthy in such a short time." Nathan tossed Brianna's clothes and shoes into the washer, poured in some soap, and turned on the machine.

Jennifer laughed. "It definitely takes talent, but I'd say she had a head start with that big mud hole beside the barn." She quickly changed Brianna's pull-up diaper. "We're just lucky she didn't shed the rest of her clothes as well. I'll have to keep a better watch on her."

"Sorry about that. Spirit will keep her from getting hurt, but unfortunately, like most kids, he loves mud holes."

Jennifer chuckled. "Don't feel too badly, she has a penchant for mud. I learned a long time ago to only give her baths at night and do minor swipes during the day. Otherwise, I'd go absolutely nuts."

"Thanks for the warning." Nathan opened a side door.

"Something sure smells good," Jennifer carried Brianna into the country kitchen that doubled as the dining room. The tantalizing odors of freshly brewed coffee and home fries browning on the large wood-burning stove tickled her nose. Her mouth watered from hunger.

Maggie placed a platter of ham and cheese sandwiches on the cherry-wood table. "The weather's beginning to turn. I just hope the rain holds off until we finish harvesting." She motioned for them to sit.

Jennifer accepted the chair Nathan had pulled out for her. He grabbed a highchair, set it beside her, and then picked Brianna up. "A royal dinner throne for a little princess."

Brianna clapped and slid into the seat.

"Where's Franz?" Jennifer surveyed the room. "We haven't met yet."

Maggie set a dish of fresh sliced tomatoes on the table next to the sandwiches. "He already ate and went back to the barn. He'll be out there for the rest of the afternoon, he said. I guess the milking machine still doesn't work right."

Nathan took a seat to Jennifer's left and stifled a laugh. She questioned him with her eyes. He leaned over and whispered in her ear. "Uncle Franz already fixed the machine. He's staying in the barn because he doesn't want to help with the harvesting." He winked and put a finger over his lips.

Jennifer nodded. *Franz sure sounds like a character.*

Maggie added a plate of home fries to the fare, then sat down and asked the blessing.

The woman's prayer warmed Jennifer. *She speaks as if God is right here at the table with us.* Elyssa had a lot in common with Maggie. Perhaps they'd become good friends.

Nathan began to pass the plates of food while Maggie pinned a cloth around Brianna's neck to serve as a bib. Jennifer cut up a sandwich for the youngster and poured her a glass of milk. Brianna quickly stuffed her mouth with food.

"She's not much of a talker, is she?" Maggie observed a bit later.

Jennifer laughed. "She rarely speaks during meals. Eating's much too important to waste time doing anything but chewing. Brianna's like a hummingbird. She eats to have strength to eat. Nothing goes to fat."

Brianna grinned and continued eating.

Chapter 14

Lunch, talk revolved around the afternoon plans. "The gang will arrive in about an hour to bring the rest of the garden in," Nathan told his aunt. "School let out yesterday, but potato harvest starts Monday."

He turned toward Jennifer. "This is a family harvest," he explained in between bites. "The Michaud-Pellitier clans are extensive and each household has a share in the produce. Most of the families live in town, but everyone lends a hand planting and harvesting. You'll get to meet a bunch of my cousins this afternoon."

"Sounds like an ideal way to farm." Jennifer cut up another sandwich for Brianna. "You said school's out? Is there some kind of special holiday?"

Nathan shook his head. "Schools close here for about three weeks during this time of the year. Most kids have to help their folks with the potato harvest. The districts allow them off, since the classrooms would be nearly empty, anyhow."

Maggie speared some tomato slices with her fork. "Even though most of the workers get paid during harvest, the kids will gladly return to school. Potato picking is backbreaking work."

"Sometimes dangerous, too." Nathan piled more food on his plate. "I don't know how many times some fool-hardy kid gets careless and ends up with a foot or hand caught in a harvester. This is definitely not my favorite time of the year." He handed a strawberry tart to Brianna.

Maggie shook her head in sympathy. "I guess that means you'll be on call for emergency surgery this season."

"I'll be fine if someone keeps the coffee on for me." Nathan looked at Jennifer.

Jennifer met his gaze. "If you mean me, I'll be happy to, as long as the word 'please' falls somewhere in the asking." She refilled Brianna's cup of milk.

Maggie laughed. "You'll educate him yet, Jennifer. Then our whole family will be happy."

Not another matchmaker. She sidestepped the woman's comments and placed another sandwich on her plate. "Maggie, I don't remember when I've been this hungry. I'm afraid I'll make it a habit."

"Farm work always builds one's appetite like that. But don't worry." She cut her sandwich in half. "It also helps you work it off."

Dr. Pellitier opened his mouth to speak.

"Don't even remark on that, Nathan," Jennifer warned.

"Not a word." He looked at his watch then stacked his dishes in the sink. "You're out of baskets, Queenie. We've got a few stacks in the shed next door. Be back soon. I'll get Brianna's things into the dryer."

He headed for the laundry room, and then he stepped onto the porch and let the screen door shut behind him.

As Nathan's truck started up the road, Jennifer carried her own dishes to the sink. She refilled her coffee.

"I see that the jeans fit you," Maggie put down her cup. "Nathan does fairly well at guessing sizes."

"Oh, you loaned these to him?"

Maggie nodded. "Katie won't mind me putting them to good use. Most of my local grandchildren are in the habit of leaving some of their work clothes here for their weekly visits; it saves them from hauling extra stuff around."

"Sounds logical." Jennifer glanced over at Brianna. The child's head rested on her tray and her breath came in soft even rhythm. "She'll be out for awhile."

"She's adaptable to just about anything, isn't she?" Nathan's aunt watched the sleeping youngster and smiled.

Jennifer reseated herself and reached for a tart. "She does pretty well. How many children and grandchildren do you have?"

"Well, let's see, seven children, and...five, eight," her fingers touched the air as she counted, "eleven, sixteen, eighteen, twenty, twenty-one grandchildren."

Jennifer couldn't fathom the challenges of such a large family. "I bet you have stories to tell, as Elyssa would say."

"Indeed. We've had a roller coaster ride of joys and sorrows." Maggie took another sip of tea. "As newlyweds, Franz and I believed if we were faithful Christians, we'd have nothing to worry about." She chuckled. "Babes that we were, we had overlooked Jesus' words in John 16:33. 'In this world you will have trouble. But take heart! I have overcome the world.' We had plenty to learn, but God showed his faithfulness through financial hardship, illnesses, a devastating barn fire, and the loss of our oldest son."

She lost a child? Jennifer's heart reached out through her own pain. "I'm so sorry. What happened to him, if you don't mind me asking?"

Maggie's eyes took on a faraway look. "Neal was our wild child. He and some of his friends went snowmobiling up the road near Thomas Park. On a dare Neal blindly jumped a snowbank and landed in the path of a snowplow. He was fourteen."

"That must have been devastating." Jennifer understood that kind of pain. "How did you cope?"

"One day at a time. While the pain lessens over the years, it never completely disappears. There are times I wonder what he might have become." The older woman sighed. "Franz had given Neal permission to take the snowmobile. We had no idea our son would pull something so risky. Since then, Franz has refused to let anyone under the age of twenty-one ride any of our equipment without an adult present. He's very adamant about it."

"That makes a lot of sense. My brother was rather reckless in his teens. I'm surprised he survived."

Maggie sipped her tea. "Yes, Rob has told me about some of his shenanigans. I'm glad that you'll be looking after him and Nathan. They're a couple of lost souls without a woman to care for them."

Jennifer snorted. "They're mature enough to get by on their own."

"They may get by, but in my experience, I've learned that men need women around to make their house a home. You're making progress already from what I can see."

Matchmakers should be outlawed. Jennifer stirred her coffee. "Rob didn't tell me about his housemate when he invited me here."

Her hostess shrugged. "Perhaps he wasn't sure that you'd be interested in the information, or that maybe you would have refused to come if you knew."

"That's what he said, but..."

Maggie patted her arm. "Rob loves you very much. He's been acting like a little boy at Christmas since he found out you were on your way."

Jennifer sipped her coffee. "He'll never know just how timely his offer was for me. God's hand definitely guided the planning."

"You'll be a real blessing to both those boys." She looked Jennifer in the face. "You mentioned God. Are you a born-again Christian?"

"Yes I am, though I must confess I didn't get truly serious about my faith until recently."

"If you don't mind my asking, what changed your mind?"

Jennifer set down her cup. "When Misha, my cousin, came to visit a few months ago, I noticed there was something about her—something that I wanted for myself. I discovered her secret was a personal relationship with God. Misha's faith is an intricate part of her life, not a once-a-week ritual. She just drew me in, and now I wonder why I waited so long." Jennifer thought about Mike, Tina, and Elyssa. Why hadn't she responded to their witness? Perhaps they reminded her too much of Danny.

"Your cousin's proof that living your faith is the best witness. It catches people unawares." Maggie patted her hand. "I'm so glad you're one of His. That makes you part of a very large family, you know. Rob and Nathan are both committed Christians, too."

Rob gave his heart to Christ? When had that happened? "That's great to know," she said out loud. "It's good to have other Believers around. I need all the encouragement I can get." *But not in the romance department.*

"If you're interested, I host a cottage fellowship here at the farm each week. We have Bible study and prayer as well as a chance to get to know other Christians. The boys are a regular part of the group, when they're not out working."

Jennifer stifled a laugh. Maggie's use of the word "boys" tickled her. "I'd really like to come. And I'm sure Elyssa would too. She's a dear friend who's moving in with us next week."

"Then, it's settled." Maggie pushed her chair back from the table. "Now help me tidy up, then we'll get a quilt for our little doll and head back to the field."

After she helped clear the table and wash the dishes, Jennifer re-dressed her sleeping daughter. She picked up Brianna and followed Maggie outside. The older woman spread a colorful patchwork quilt in the shade near the large tomato garden. Jennifer gently laid the child upon it. Spirit immediately lay beside Brianna and rested his head on his paws.

Jennifer and Maggie equipped themselves with some remaining baskets and began picking ripe tomatoes.

"We've had an excellent crop of these this year," Maggie told her. "If there's not a heavy frost, we'll be picking tomatoes for another month"

Numerous green tomatoes hung on each of the many bushy plants. "It would be a shame for them to go to waste."

Maggie smiled. "Don't worry. If we get a heavy frost warning, I'll pull the plants up by the roots, then hang them upside down from the porch roof. The tomatoes will finish ripening on the vine."

The thought had never occurred to Jennifer. "That's amazing. I had no idea they could ripen that way." She looked forward to learning much more from this woman.

Half an hour later, Nathan's truck pulled into the driveway, followed by two small repurposed school buses hauling full loads of jean-clad young people.

"That's the Michaud clan, or at least some of them," Maggie explained. "Many are my grandchildren; the rest are their cousins." As she spoke, a large van came into view. "Those are the Pellitiers. We'll have plenty of help today."

The groups tumbled out. "Hey, Queenie," Nathan hollered. "Look what I found." He tossed a basket to each person as they filed past him.

Jennifer counted thirty people coming toward them. Terry, the young man from the hospital, made a beeline for Maggie.

The older woman embraced him. "Terrance, where have you been? I've missed you something awful."

He kissed her on the cheek. "I've been working double shifts at the hospital, Grams."

Maggie laughed. "At least it keeps you out of trouble, my boy. Jennifer, this is my oldest grandson, Terrance."

"We sort of met at the hospital." Jennifer extended her hand.

Terry lifted her hand to his lips. "I'm glad such a lovely lady is a friend of my dear Grams."

Jennifer blushed. This one was quite a charmer.

Nathan stepped between them. "I want you to meet everyone else, Jen." He drew her away and began introductions. Jennifer felt overwhelmed by the names and new faces.

"Maybe we should wear name tags," said Katie, a lovely young lady with hazel eyes, and glossy black hair caught up in a long French braid.

Jennifer laughed. "That might help, but since I'll be here for a while, I may get the names right with practice."

Nathan clapped his hands. "All right, gang, let's get to work," he ordered good-humoredly. "We've an entire field of crops to bring in today. Then we'll have a bonfire."

The young people descended on the field and began to fill their baskets. After a quick word with Maggie, Nathan escorted Jennifer toward the rows of corn.

"Queenie said she'd watch over Brianna this afternoon," he told her. "Since all the kids are here, my aunt isn't needed for the field work."

Jennifer felt uncomfortable. "Are you sure that won't be a bother? I mean, Brianna can be quite a handful sometimes."

"Don't worry about it. Maggie loves children. Anyway, she said she wanted to show Brianna how to preserve leaves."

"Oh, that's right. She mentioned that earlier." Jennifer sighed with relief. She watched Maggie settle into a chair near Brianna's sleeping form. "I'll be interested to see how the craft project turns out."

The afternoon flew by. Nathan offered Jennifer a drink from his canteen. "Ready to take a break? It's already two-thirty."

"It doesn't seem that long." She took a few sips of the cool water. "I think I'll keep on going."

"You'll feel it tomorrow, for sure," he warned. "It always catches up to you the next day."

Two hours before dusk, the group lugged full baskets in from the fields, hauled most down the ramp to the farmhouse's root cellar, and returned the tools to the shed.

Nathan went back to the truck and brought out some light jackets for Jennifer and Brianna. "You'll be needing these before long."

The teenage boys chopped down the cornstalks and piled them toward the edge of the field. Several girls wrapped potatoes and ears of corn with aluminum foil and carried a large basketful to the fire pit halfway between the house and the barn.

Jennifer and Brianna helped lay bricks in a large circle. The girls placed the potatoes and corn in the center. then covered them with more bricks. They mounded dry leaves, sticks, and firewood on top of those until they had three-foot pile. Soon a cheery fire winked in the late afternoon sun.

Once the fire had reduced to glowing red coals, Nathan hammered two iron poles into the ground on either side of the fire site and lay a long metal spit, laden with several whole-baking chickens, across them. Franz Michaud, a gray-haired, bewhiskered man, settled himself in a comfortable chair nearby to monitor the meat.

Terry and a couple of the young men hauled a large, hand-hewn table out near the firepit, while the young women followed with bowls of potato and macaroni salad, plates of sliced tomatoes and cucumbers, carrot sticks, celery, cakes, tarts, and Maggie's vat of hot apple cider. Several straw bales served as seats.

Apples floated merrily in a metal washtub of water while many of the workers tried their skill at capturing them with their teeth.

"I always knew your mouth was good for something, Terry," one of the teen boys teased as the male nurse won the competition, getting six apples in succession.

Rob arrived just in time for the festivities, carrying a guitar case and a much smaller case that Jennifer couldn't identify.

"Unca Wobbie's home," Brianna squealed, She ran to greet her uncle with open arms.

"Hey, kitten." Rob set down the cases and caught his niece in his arms. "This is the welcome a man needs after a hard day at work."

"Missed you." Brianna hugged him.

"I missed you, too, sweetie." He hugged Jennifer with his free arm. "So, how'd everything go today, gang?"

Nathan playfully nudged Rob's shoulder. "It's amazing how you always manage to dodge manual labor."

His housemate shrugged and grinned. "Talent, I guess. I'll do my part this week, Doc, I promise."

"You can start now. I can use a hand." He handed him a shovel and led him to a spot near the shed.

A few minutes later, Nathan and Rob pulled a huge covered pot of baked beans from a smoking pit and set it next to the large table.

After brushing off his hands, Rob rejoined his sister. "What all did you get finished this afternoon?"

"Everything's in except the pumpkins, onions, carrots, turnips, and apples," Jennifer said. "We'll tackle those on another day."

"Next week's project will be preparing pumpkin," Nathan told Rob. "That means you, too, buddy. If you're anywhere around."

Rob shrugged. "I can't promise anything. I've got to meet with a few of my clients regarding their blueprints, including the one in Bangor."

"You poor soul." Nathan patted him on the back. "No pumpkin peeling, no pumpkin pie for you."

Jennifer took pity on her brother. "Brianna and I can help, Nathan."

"I think Maggie's counting on it." Nathan wagged a finger at her. "No smuggling pie to this bum, though."

When the food was ready, Franz asked the blessing and thanked God for the willing harvest workers. The group soon piled their plates with food. Excited chatter filled the air.

Jennifer thought the roasted corn tasted better than any she had eaten in the past. In fact, she enjoyed the whole meal immensely. *Pleasant company really does make all the difference.*

Nathan, Rob, Terry, and Katie discussed the morning activities at the hospital. Jennifer learned the young woman had her eye on becoming a pediatrician.

Brianna ate her fill, and then busied herself with charming the group with her antics.

"Jen, when Brianna's older, can I marry her?" Tim Michaud called out from a nearby straw bale.

"You'll have to clear that through me, first," Rob growled at the sandy-haired teen.

"Don't forget me, buddy," Nathan reminded him.

Jennifer looked at the two men impatiently. "I'm her mother. Don't I have a say in this?"

"No!" both men answered in unison. Laughter resounded through the group. Jennifer bit her lip and kept quiet. She'd set them straight once they got home.

"Me marry Nafan," Brianna announced.

"Sorry, kitten, he's already got someone else in mind," Rob told the youngster. "You've got plenty of time to worry about that stuff later."

A pang of angry sorrow stole across Jennifer's heart. So, Nathan belonged to someone already. *That two-timing...I should have known!* Why should she care, anyhow? But for some reason, she did. Jennifer was glad when the three-legged race started. She could get her mind off of Nathan by concentrating on the activities at hand.

The last of the sunlight soon faded from the sky. Nathan lit the bonfire at the edge the field as the group gathered around it. Rob pulled up a wooden crate and began strumming a soft notes on his well-worn guitar. Uncle Peter had given it to him for his tenth birthday.

"Give us something lively, Rob," Tim shouted.

Rob began to play a fast-paced tune. Nathan pulled a fiddle from the small case that Rob had brought and added strong clear notes to his friend's music, while Franz accompanied with his harmonica. Jennifer joined the group in clapping along. Soon, she was caught up in a square dance. One of the younger girls held Brianna as the group whirled to the music.

When the musicians played a lively Scottish melody Maggie kicked up her heels, her skirt twirling about her legs. Franz danced with her, still playing his harmonica.

When the dancing subsided, everyone sat around the fire and sang while Rob accompanied them on his guitar. Jennifer put on her jacket and helped Brianna into the other one. She held the child on her lap and rocked her gently as they sang along.

Nathan placed his fiddle back in its case and sat beside Jennifer. "Happy?" he asked, leaning close.

She nodded, smiling. "I never knew anything could be so much fun." She shivered against the cool night breeze and held Brianna closer.

"I should have brought heavier jackets for both of you," Nathan said. "I may be able to remedy the problem, though." He put his arm around her shoulder and pulled her to his chest.

Jennifer stiffened. She felt uncomfortable with his arm around her, but couldn't think how to pull away without being awkward about it. She hoped he wouldn't notice the loud pounding of her heart. *You'll never learn, will you, Jen? Give it up; he's spoken for.*

"Relax, princess," Nathan whispered. "I'm not going to hurt you."

Jennifer hardened her resolve *You'd better believe it, mister. No one will ever hurt me again.*

As the group continued to sing, Jennifer listened to Nathan's rich tenor. Brianna snuggled deeper into her mother's arms and soon slept soundly. Jennifer, too, felt tired.

"I'd better put Brianna to bed," she told Nathan, pulling away from him. "Please tell Rob where I've gone and let Maggie know that I've had a lovely time." Jennifer balanced the child in her arms as Nathan gently assisted her to her feet.

Just as she reached the road, Jennifer heard someone running behind her. She tensed, thinking it was Nathan.

"Wait up Jen," Rob called, catching up with her. "Here, let me carry Brianna. You must be exhausted."

As they neared their house, Nathan's truck pulled up beside them. Terry occupied the passenger seat. "Bad accident near Limestone," he shouted out the window. "I don't know what time I'll be home. Better pray. Those kids need it." He waved and drove off.

"Let's go ahead and pray now, Jen," Rob suggested.

Her brother's request surprised her, but Jennifer bowed her head and joined him in asking God's mercy on the accident victims and those rushing to help them.

Chapter 15

Jennifer gently closed Brianna's bedroom door and headed for the living room. An old collage of photographs in the hallway caught her attention. Each scene brought back hazy, warm memories from her childhood, and she basked in the glory of them. As she viewed the pictures, Jennifer realized that her parents appeared in none of them. *I guess Rob's written them off, too.*

Her mind fingered Uncle Peter's announcement regarding her father. As angry as she felt, she couldn't help but wonder what brought him back after all these years. What did he want from them? What would Rob say when he found out?

Jennifer joined her brother in the living room. He sat on the couch, reading, while a pleasant fire crackled on the hearth. She sank into the easy chair across from him. A sweet fragrance tickled her nose. "Am I losing my mind, or do I smell flowers?"

"It's probably just the rose bushes outside," Rob replied. "The window's cracked open a bit, so the scent is most likely coming in on the breeze." He placed a page marker in the book and set it on the stand beside him. "So, how was your day at the farm? I didn't get much of a chance to ask you earlier."

"I loved it. Maggie's a real peach. There's something so inviting about her. It's almost as if she has an inner light that draws people in."

Her brother agreed. "She and Franz are about the best you can find. They and Nathan led me to the Lord a few months ago."

Jennifer smiled. "Maggie mentioned you were a Christian, and your eagerness to pray earlier surprised me. I hoped it meant you had truly accepted Christ. You see I got serious about my own relationship with Him few months ago, myself."

Rob leaned toward her. "That's great! Nathan and I have been praying for you since the night I got saved."

It warmed her heart to know her brother cared that much. She smiled. "God really does answer prayer, doesn't He?"

Her brother could not contain his excitement. "You're certainly a living example. Just wait until Nathan hears this."

Jennifer gestured with her hands. "I can hardly believe that God has really brought me here. It's almost like having a fresh start at life."

Concern crossed Rob's face. "Sis, are you sure you don't mind the arrangement with Nathan living downstairs?"

She shrugged. "It'll take some getting used to, but I guess it will be all right. Especially since Elyssa will be here within a few days."

"He's good people, Jen. Really."

She wasn't convinced about that after hearing Nathan already had a sweetheart. Still... "Brianna adores him, and that says a lot."

"And you?"

Jennifer shrugged. "He's nice."

"Just nice?"

She gave Rob a warning look. "Beware of matchmaking, brother, mine. I'm not interested. Besides, Nathan belongs to someone already."

Rob seemed puzzled. "Do you know something I don't?"

Jennifer's frustration mounted. "Rob, at the bonfire you said he was already planning to marry someone."

Her brother laughed.

"What's so funny?"

Rob sobered a little. "I hate keeping secrets, but I promised not to tell. You'll find out soon enough."

She felt uncomfortable with the conversation and decided to change the topic. "Rob, is there an empty room around here where I can set up some easels? I want to start sketching and painting again."

"Sure. There are a couple of rooms downstairs that are just being used for storage, right now. It wouldn't take much to convert them into a studio. We can just move the boxes into the loft. If you want, we can get started this coming week."

"Oh, I can do most of the work myself, Rob," Jennifer offered. "Just show me where you want the boxes and such, and I'll take care of it from there."

He slapped the couch arm. "Nonsense. This will be a family project. We'll all lend a hand. In fact, let me get a sketch pad so we can make our plans."

During the next hour, Jennifer and Rob sat together on the couch and designed the studio. "Why don't we make this adjoining room a playroom for Brianna," Rob suggested. "That way you'll be able to keep an eye on her while you are working."

Jennifer went over the plans again. "That sounds like a great idea. I don't want Elyssa to feel she has to always watch Brianna." She stifled a yawn. "Could we talk some more about the plans tomorrow?"

"No problem." Rob set down the sketchpad and switched on the radio. Jennifer settled back and listened to *The Abbott and Costello*

Show. It seemed amazing that the 1940s show was still on the air after all of these years Though she enjoyed the comedy, her mind wandered back to her father's reappearance. She needed to talk to Rob about it, but how would he respond?

When the show ended, Jennifer gathered up her courage. "Rob, have you talked to Uncle Peter over the past couple of days?"

He eyed her, curiosity written on his face. "No. Just Misha. Why? Is something wrong?"

She ran her hands along her pant legs. "I'm not sure how to say this, so I guess I'll take the blunt approach." She took a deep breath. "Uncle Peter said he heard from Dad—that he's coming back to Maine."

Rob stared at her. "You're kidding, right?" When Jennifer shook her head, he stood and walked over to the window. He remained silent for a few minutes then turned to face her. His eyes revealed the battle raging within. "Did he say when?"

"In two weeks."

His voice faltered. "Is...is Dad all right?"

Jennifer shrugged. "I don't know. I didn't want to press Uncle Peter for information. It came...as quite a...shock to me."

She studied her shoes; afraid of what her brother might think of her answer. "It's strange, Rob. As a girl I dreamed of this day—thought of what I might say; how I might act. I would have accepted him gladly without reservation, then." She crushed a small sofa pillow to her chest as memories stabbed her with renewed pain. Her voice fell softly. "Now —now I don't care to see him again. I've discovered that old wounds hurt worse the second time around."

Silent agony blanketed the room. Rob turned back toward the window. "I want to see him, Jen," he said, finally, his voice heavy with emotion. "I have to find out what kind of man abandons his children. I need to know why he left us."

Jennifer gazed at the flickering flames. Raw grief tore through her. She could still remember the plaintive wail of the wind as she pressed her nose against the windowpane and watched her father go. He hadn't even said goodbye.

"Oh, Daddy, I love you," the child had cried through her tears. He stopped briefly and looked up at her. Then, with the wind whipping at his overcoat, he had turned and walked out of her life. Nineteen years later, his actions still tortured his two children.

Jennifer rested her head in her hands. Would this pain ever go away? She felt her brother's warm touch on her shoulder.

"We'll get through this, Jen," he told her. "We've got each other, and most of all, God."

A few minutes later, Jennifer bid her brother good night. As she turned on her bedroom light, she stared in disbelief. Bouquets of flowers—everything from daisies to roses—covered every shelf and her dresser top. On her bed sat a large cream-colored bear with a dozen pink roses between its paws. A pink satin ribbon around the bear's neck held a gold-colored card. Jennifer opened the card and read: "Peace offering? Nathan."

Easy girl, Jennifer warned herself. *Beware of men bearing gifts. The pain isn't worth it.* She tossed the card on the bed, and then began to unpack the rest of her suitcases.

"Jen," Rob called softly from outside her door.

She placed her night clothes into the dresser. "Come in, Rob, I'm just getting settled."

"I forgot to ask," he began, entering her room, but then burst into laughter. "This looks serious, Jen. Anyone I know?"

"No big deal, Rob," She placed her clothes into her dresser. "It was a...well...a slight misunderstanding."

Her brother's eyes mocked her. "A slight misunderstanding? Life is definitely going to get interesting around here."

Jennifer glared at him.

"All right, Jen." Rob raised both hands in surrender. "I'll butt out."

"Good boy." She hung some dresses in her closet. "What were you going to ask me?"

"Huh?" Rob thought for a moment. "Oh, yeah. I'm heading into Presque Isle tomorrow to get some drafting supplies and to see about another job. If you'd like, you and Brianna could come along. It'll give you a chance to stock up on your paints and stuff."

"That sounds tempting, but I really have to finish unpacking. Besides, I promised Maggie I'd be over tomorrow afternoon. Could we make the trip on another day and include shopping for some winter clothes? By then, I should know what all we'll need."

"Sure, no problem. I must get my supplies tomorrow, but we'll make a shopping day later this week." Rob told her goodnight and left.

Jennifer put her suitcases away, took a long, relaxing, hot bath and prepared for bed. After reading her Bible, she spent some time in prayer, and then crawled under her covers.

The next morning, Jennifer, Brianna and Rob ate together in the dining room while Bunny wandered about. Since Jennifer planned to help out on the farm, she decided to wear the jeans again, this time with one of Rob's green sweatshirts. As Nathan had predicted, Jennifer's muscles did indeed protest from the previous day's exercise.

She accepted the pain good-naturedly and just moved a little slower than usual while making breakfast.

Rob looked slightly uncomfortable in the conservative blue suit, white dress shirt, and black tie he reserved for job interviews. "I hate to leave you alone, Jen," He said between mouthfuls of scrambled eggs. "I don't know when Nathan will be back."

"We'll be fine," Jennifer assured him. "After we finish here, we'll be at Maggie's, so there's no chance of boredom. We'll just see you when you get home."

Rob put his plate in the sink then grabbed his coat and briefcase. "Are you sure?"

Jennifer nodded.

"All right, then, kiddos, I'll see you this afternoon." He kissed Brianna on the forehead. "Maybe we can do something on Sunday after church or on Monday."

"We'll have plenty of time together." Jennifer kissed Rob's cheek. "Now, get out of here. It's already seven-thirty."

Rob ran down the stairs then raced back up. "Keep the door locked and don't let anyone in, all right?"

Jennifer rolled her eyes. "We'll be good, worry wart. Drive carefully."

When he had gone, Jennifer wiped the peanut butter off Brianna's face and hands, and then set her on the floor. "Let's get you dressed, then we'd better get our beds made before I load the dishwasher."

Brianna picked out a pair of pink and purple overalls and insisted on wearing a dark blue and green checked turtleneck shirt with it. Jennifer grimaced at the choice of color, but bit her tongue. *Choose your battles. This one's not worth it.*

Once the chores were finished, the toddler scurried away to explore her new toy box and to play with Bunny.

Jennifer felt grateful that Brianna could entertain herself for longer periods of time. She quickly looked in on her daughter, and then took advantage of the quiet to go through the rabbit care manual.

Once she felt quite familiar with the rabbit's needs, she decided to get better acquainted with her new Bible. Thumbing her way through the pages, she came across a section of memory verses. "'I have hidden your word in my heart that I might not sin against you.' Psalm 119:11," she read aloud. That was a good idea, but where would she begin?

She slid her finger down the list of verses until one in particular caught her eye. "Jude twenty to twenty-one? Is this for two whole chapters?" Jennifer used the index to locate the book. "Oh, it's verses twenty and twenty-one. What a short book. I'll memorize these first."

Jennifer read the verses aloud and repeated them a few times. She copied them on a sticky note and put the paper on the cupboard just above the sink where she would see the verses often. She repeated them again. "'But you, dear friends, by building yourselves up in your most holy faith and praying in the Holy Spirit, keep yourselves in God's love as you wait for the mercy of our Lord Jesus Christ to bring you to eternal life.'"

She put on some water for coffee. The phone rang. Jennifer answered on the second ring and giggled when she recognized her brother's voice. "What'd you forget, Rob?"

"Hold on, I've got my note right here." He was quiet for a moment. "Oh, I went ahead and bought you a basic art kit to tide you over for now. It's in a large black case somewhere in my attic office. I really hope you like it."

"Thanks, Rob. How much do I owe you?"

"Nothing. Consider it a welcome home gift."

"That's so sweet of you. I really appreciate it." After she hung up Jennifer checked on Brianna, and then headed for Rob's office. She easily located the black case on his drafting table and took it down to the kitchen. *Rob's always been so thoughtful.*

"Basic kit, my eye," she exclaimed when she examined the contents of the case. Oil pastels, water colors, paintbrushes, charcoals, drawing pencils, rubber erasers and various sketch pads lay in orderly rows and stacks. "He spent a fortune on this one." Jennifer knew better than to confront Rob on it. He'd feel thoroughly insulted. "I'll figure out some way to pay him back."

She turned off the stove under the whistling kettle and made a cup of coffee for herself. A vehicle pulled into the driveway. Jennifer peered out the dining room window. Her heart gave a little dance. *Nathan's come home.* She felt disconcerted to realize how much she was attracted to him, especially since he was spoken for. *Besides you've sworn off of relationships, remember?*

Nathan dragged himself up the stairs and into the kitchen. His face bore the weight of his exhaustion and his shoulders slumped in discouragement. "Hi. Would it be possible to get a good breakfast here? I'm starved and half beat."

He looks like something the cat dragged in. It's amazing he could even drive himself home. She kept her thoughts to herself, however and smiled. "Sure, what would you like?"

"Anything but coffee. I think I drank three potsful and my stomach can't bear the thought of anymore." He grimaced and leaned against the kitchen doorway.

"You look like you've had better days," Jennifer admitted lightly, bringing him a tall glass of grape juice. "You were up all night, right?"

He yawned. "Mostly. I grabbed a short nap on a gurney—worst sleep I've had in ages."

Jennifer motioned toward the breakfast bar. "Have a seat. I'll have your food ready in a few minutes."

Nathan winced as he eased himself onto a stool.

"The accident was really bad, then?" Jennifer asked, taking some eggs and cheese from the refrigerator.

Nathan dropped his head into his hands. "Yeah. Some fool teenagers decided to drag race near the old Air Force base and managed to flip the car several times. We lost a sixteen-year-old girl around midnight. Her parents are taking it real hard. Her brother was driving. His surgery was tough enough on his folks. They thought they were going to lose him, too. He made it, though. I just wonder how he's going to take the news of his sister's death."

Jennifer grieved with him. "It will be hard on the family. I'm so sorry this had to happen, Nathan."

"That's just it, Jen. It didn't have to happen." He pounded his fist on the breakfast bar. "One foolish act has ruined so many lives."

"How many kids were in the car?"

"Six, and only one had sense enough to use a seat belt. One kid's legs may be permanently paralyzed from a back injury. When will people learn?"

Jennifer heated the skillet and poured in the egg mixture. "Nathan, you've done all you can. All we can do now is pray for the families and for those who survived the accident. God can still work in their lives."

Nathan forced a smile. "You're right, Jen. I get a bit carried away sometimes. Forgive me for my outburst."

"No forgiveness needed." She popped a couple of pieces of bread into the toaster. "You have to let your feelings out. Bottling them up doesn't do any good. I know. I've been an expert at it."

"Does that mean I'm forgiven for yesterday morning? I'm really sorry for embarrassing you in front of those people."

She turned the omelet. "I've been meaning to talk to you about that. You really shouldn't have spent your money on those flowers. It's...it's not right."

"I can't think of anyone else I'd rather spend it on."

The spatula slipped from her hand and clattered to the floor. Her heart pounded. Jennifer realized now what Rob had meant. She was the one Nathan had set his heart on.

She chewed her lower lip. *Now what am I going to do?* Jennifer didn't want to hurt his feelings, but also didn't want him to get the wrong idea. She quickly washed off the spatula and filled a plate with the hot food.

Jennifer gathered her courage. "That's really sweet, Nathan, but I'd rather you didn't." Her hands shook as she set his breakfast before him. "Let me know if you want any more eggs." She busied herself at the sink. "I hope you plan to get some sleep this morning. You look like you really need it."

"What I need is a new back." He finished his grape juice. "I think a nice hot shower will help, though."

Jennifer fixed some more coffee and drank it as Nathan devoured his food. She could tell his back really hurt by the expression on his face. "I think all of that hard work yesterday probably added to the strain in your back. You need a good massage, and Rob says I do pretty well at it."

"You don't have to twist my arm. I know a good thing when I hear it." He finished his breakfast. "Just let me grab a quick shower, first." Nathan headed down the stairs.

Jennifer cleared the dishes. *I won't fall for him,* she reminded herself. *He'd leave me just like Daddy and Danny did.* Her heart ached. She knew her husband didn't choose death. Still, he had broken his promise that day, and then left her behind. She washed off the breakfast bar and the counter then started the dishwasher.

Brianna ran into the kitchen. "Me wants cookies and waisins and milk and bunny food," she announced.

Jennifer poured milk into a sipper cup. "Are you having a tea party for your toys?"

The child shook her head solemnly. "Me feeding Bunny."

"Cookies and raisins aren't on her menu. You can share your cookies with Bear-Bear and I'll give you some carrots and an apple for Bunny." Jennifer fixed a plate of goodies, helped Brianna take her snack into her bedroom. She returned to the kitchen and continued her cleaning chores.

When Nathan returned upstairs, he handed Jennifer a tube of liniment then pulled off his blue sweatshirt. "You can't know how much I appreciate this. It gets a bit wearing on the body to stand over a patient for hours on end."

Jennifer squeezed liniment onto her hands. "And I don't think sleeping on the gurney helped you any."

He brought a chair in from the dining room. "No, but I needed to stick by the hospital in case there were any more complications." He sat on a stool and leaned forward against the table, exposing his back.

Electricity surged through Jennifer's veins as she smoothed the liniment over Nathan's rippling muscles and warm skin. She worked the knots out of his shoulders and mid-back. Despite her resolve, she longed to nuzzle her cheek against his neck and to be held in his strong arms.

As if he had read her mind, Nathan stood up and faced her. He cupped Jennifer's face in his right hand, gently stroking her cheek with his thumb. She gazed into his eyes, lost in their blue depths. Nathan's lips touched her ever so lightly. Jennifer trembled as he drew her into his arms. He claimed her mouth with his, and she responded willingly, wrapping her arms around his neck. Her heart beat wildly as she was crushed against his bare chest.

Suddenly, Jennifer pulled away. "I'm sorry, I can't," she whispered breathlessly.

"Who are you frightened of, me...or you?" Nathan kept his arms around her waist.

She mentally fought the effect his velvety voice had on her pulse. "Please. Nathan, you don't understand."

He looked at her with smoky blue eyes. "I understand that you feel something for me or you wouldn't have kissed me like that."

Jennifer pulled free. "Mere physical attraction is not enough for me. There has to be much more."

Disappointment dripped from his voice. "I never pegged you for someone who played games, Jen."

She could sense that his voice masked contempt. "I...I'm not...I... don't." Jennifer wrapped her arms around herself as if to protect her from his disapproval.

"Then what?" His eyes searched her face. "You're still in love with that Anton guy?"

Jennifer felt sick. She adamantly shook her head. "No. I've never loved him."

Nathan studied her. "I don't get it, Jen. You don't play games, but you dated Anton even though you didn't love him."

"I didn't date him. We...the whole thing was...a...a mistake. One I won't repeat—ever." She struggled to keep her composure. Why couldn't he understand? How she wished he'd break through the barrier of her fear. "I cannot get involved with you, Nathan—not with anyone." She cringed as a hint of anger washed across his face.

"As you wish." His voice turned lifeless. Nathan picked up his sweatshirt and turned to leave. "I think I'll have that nap now. Thanks for breakfast and for the massage. I'll be up in a few hours to help with the queen's project." He headed down the stairs to his room.

Jennifer watched him go. Tears slipped down her cheeks. An endless gulf stood between them now. Her heart ached in confusion—torn between her desire for his love and fear of abandonment. "I'm going to be strong about this," she whispered. "I have to be."

Chapter 16

Maggie and Katie had started shelling peas when Jennifer and Brianna joined them on the back porch of the farmhouse. Spirit tagged along and now lay content beside the porch steps.

"Mornin'," Maggie wiped her hands on her jeans. The sleeves of her blue flannel shirt were rolled up just below the elbows. "Katie and I decided to get an early start on the tedious work. My daughters will be coming over in the next few days to process the rest of the harvest. Then we'll tackle the pumpkins and root vegetables once potato harvest is completed."

Jennifer noticed that Katie also wore blue jeans, and a long-sleeved blue and turquoise flannel shirt. *I guess that's the norm up here.* It would make more sense for her to get some jeans of her own rather than wearing skirts in situations like this.

While Jennifer released Brianna's hand, she kept an eye on her daughter. "I hope you don't mind us coming over so early. Nathan just got in a little while ago from the hospital, so I thought it would be best if we came over here and let him sleep in peace."

"How bad was it?" Katie's warm hazel eyes held a note of concern.

Jennifer relayed Nathan's update. "It's going to be rough on all of the families involved."

"Sounds like this is a prime opportunity to pray." Maggie bowed her head and asked for God's intervention.

When the prayer had ended, Jennifer wiped tears from her eyes. "What can Brianna and I do to help out here?"

"You have your choice of shelling peas or shucking corn," Maggie said. "The peas will be quickest to process since we can easily blanch them and immediately set them on the screens for freezing. The corn will take extra work, since after blanching, we must slice off the kernels before freezing them."

After weighing the pros and cons, Jennifer chose to work on the peas. She and Brianna settled in chairs next to the huge basket of pods. Jennifer patiently showed Brianna how to extract the tiny round balls from their oblong casings.

Her mind wandered back to her fiasco with Nathan. *I can't believe he thinks I'm a user. I've got to make him understand.* She decided to try to talk to him again later—if her courage didn't fail.

A much-subdued Terry joined them mid-morning. His grandmother immediately put him to work shucking corn.

The time passed quickly. Maggie's tales of her life in northern Maine served to keep Jennifer's mind occupied. She was grateful for the distraction. Jennifer finished one bushel of peas, then reached for the next basket. "Have you met any unusual people up here, Maggie?" she asked, hoping for another story.

"About twenty years ago I met a woman whose great-grandparents imigrated here from Sweden in 1870. She said back then that the only access one had to this area in the winter was by dogsled or by cross-country skis."

"Do you mean it still isn't," Terry teased his grandmother. Maggie gave him a warning glance.

Jennifer raised her eyebrows. "Are the winters here really that bad? I'm only used to the southern part of Maine."

"Not too bad," Terry told her, inching away from Maggie. "The snowdrifts only get to about twenty feet or so."

Katie kicked her cousin's foot. "Knock it off, or else."

"Don't you listen to him," Maggie told Jennifer. "My grandson can work yarns better than any weaver I know. There's nothing to worry about as long as you use common sense." She finished shucking an ear of corn and set it in a basket filled with others. "We'd better stop for lunch before Terrance starts any more storytelling."

Later that afternoon, while Brianna napped in her room, Jennifer wandered through the living room, lost in thought. Perhaps it would be best if she and Brianna found another place to live. At best, her relationship with Nathan would be an awkward one. If only he understood what she was going through, then perhaps they could become good friends.

A movement in the doorway startled her. Her eyes widened in panic.

"It's just me, Jen," Nathan stepped into the room. He looked concerned. "I'm sorry. I had no intention of frightening you."

Jennifer drew a breath of relief. "I'm all right... just still a bit jumpy, that's all." She noticed he still wore the blue sweatshirt and jeans from earlier. *It should be a crime for a man to look so good.*

Nathan sat on the couch, his long legs stretched out in front of him. "I owe you a major apology, Jen. I had no right to make the accusations I did this morning."

She knit her brows together, not quite believing her ears. "It was my fault as much as yours. I guess I did a poor job of explaining myself."

Nathan shook his head. "You shouldn't have to explain. After what you've been through I can understand you not wanting to jump into a romantic relationship. I judged you from my own limited experience, and for that I apologize."

Jennifer stared at him. "I'm not sure what to say."

"How about, 'Let's call a truce and start over as friends?'"

Friends? Anton had twisted that very word and used it to hurt her. *Nathan's nothing like Anton,* she told herself. Brianna wouldn't care so much for him if he were. She smiled shakily. "All right. Friends."

A black ball of fur suddenly scurried past Jennifer's feet with Brianna, crawling on all fours on the rabbit's heels. "Whoa, little one," Jennifer grabbed the youngster and swung her up into her arms. "Why are you chasing Bunny like that?"

"We pway tag, Mommy." Brianna explained with exaggerated patience. "Me chase Bunny and Bunny chase me."

On cue, the rabbit peered from behind the armchair and stamped her hind feet.

"She wants me chase Bunny," Brianna implored. "We want to pway.

Jennifer looked at Nathan.

He merely shrugged. "Sounds reasonable to me."

"I'll take your word for it, Brianna." Jennifer set her daughter down.

The rabbit stamped her feet again and took off through the dining room. Brianna laughed and chased after her as before, dodging the chairs as she made her way under the table.

A few minutes later, Bunny chased Brianna through the living room. Jennifer surveyed the odd sight in amazement. "Doctor, I'm beginning to question my sanity."

"Aren't we all?" He answered with a laugh. "Aren't we all?"

Jennifer realized she needed to start supper, so she excused herself and headed for the kitchen. She took a quick mental inventory of the cupboard contents, and then rummaged through the freezer. "Good grief, Nathan, when's the last time you went grocery shopping?"

"I think it was the week before I went to the conference," he answered from the living room. "Why?"

"Ice cream, believe it or not, will not make a good main dish. Don't you have any meat?"

"Sure. It's in the freezer."

"Where?" Jennifer stared at the stacks of ice cream cartons before her. Not a sign of meat could be found.

Nathan ambled into the kitchen. "Oh, I'm sorry. All of the healthy food is in the big freezer downstairs. We only keep the important stuff close by. What kind of meat do you want?"

"Maybe fish would be better. Do you have any?"

"Sure, what kind? We've got haddock, cod, flounder, sole, and trout."

She decided to keep it simple. "Anything that's already cleaned and boned. Are the frozen vegetables down there, too?"

"Yep. Anything in particular?"

"Broccoli, cauliflower, and carrots, if you have them." Jennifer knew her daughter would love the combination.

"Okay I might have a few packages." He headed down the stairs, then returned a few minutes later. "Two fillets of sole and your veggies, ma'am. Let's see, that comes to two hugs—"

"Do you want to eat?"

Nathan backed away. "No charge. Do you need some help?"

"I could use a glass casserole dish."

He produced one from the cupboard and placed it on the counter. "Do you know how to use this microwave?"

Jennifer preheated the oven. "Not this model. I'll be ready for my first lesson in about five minutes, though."

The phone rang. Nathan grabbed it before the second ring. "Dr. Pellitier. Who's speaking please? Just a minute." He handed the receiver to Jennifer. "It's Michelle."

"Hi, Misha!" Jennifer greeted her cousin. "What's up?"

Michelle's voiced sounded strained. "I hate to tell you this, but Anton called earlier today, looking for you."

A chill crept up Jennifer's spine. *How did he get Misha's number?* She took the phone into the hallway for privacy. "What did he say?"

"Just that he was worried about you. He wanted to know if I had any idea where to find you."

"What did you tell him?"

"I said to check your apartment in Long Beach. When he said you weren't there, I told him that of course you were—I had talked to you just a few weeks ago and was planning to go see you at Thanksgiving."

Jennifer smiled at her cousin's quick thinking. "How did he take that bit of news?"

"He swore and hung up." Michelle cleared her throat. "Someone really ought to clean his mouth out with some of Grandma's soap. Anyhow, I thought you'd want to know."

"Did you call Mike?"

"Pops called him from the docks, just in case Anton tried to call back. We didn't want to make him suspicious. Anyhow, the FBI is monitoring the phones, now."

Jennifer twisted a lock of hair around her finger. Michelle had bought her some time, but how much? "I just wish they'd catch him."

"Don't worry, they will. You're safe where you are. Besides God's watching out for you. After all, He has brought you this far safely."

"I know, but I can't help thinking about everything that's happened so far. Elyssa lost her home because of me. How do I know that Anton won't try to hurt you or the rest of the family?"

Michelle's voice remained steady. "Jen, stop taking the weight of the world on your shoulders. God is perfectly capable of taking care of us all. Remember, our Father never gives us more than we can handle with *His help*."

Jennifer sighed. "I know the words, Misha. It's just hard to apply in person, sometimes."

"Maybe that's why God has allowed you to go through so much," her cousin prompted. "Perhaps this is His way of helping you grow."

A groan escaped Jennifer. "I must be incredibly hard-headed, then. I can't imagine willingly putting Brianna through this much suffering."

"Don't think God isn't moved by your tears, Jen," her cousin continued. "He hurts with you. You know, like when Brianna split her chin open and you had to hold her down while the doctor stitched her up. You cried about as much as she did."

A glimmer of understanding poked through Jennifer's confusion. "It's something for me to explore, I guess."

"Oh, before I forget, Mike said Elyssa will be in Presque Isle tomorrow afternoon. Can you pick her up?"

"Definitely! Oh, thank God. Did he say where she'd be flying out of?"

"No, but I do have the flight number and time. She does have an escort to as far as Portland, from what Mike said." Michelle quickly relayed the flight information. "By the way, what do you think of Dr. Pellitier? Is he as gorgeous as he sounds?"

"Yes, but don't quote me, I'll deny everything."

"Details, I want details."

Jennifer rolled her eyes. "There are none."

"Come on, Jen. You've got to have some impression."

"No comment."

Her cousin laughed. "Well, if you decide you don't want him, let me know when I come for a visit."

"When are you coming?"

"Not before Christmas. I don't want to invoke the wrath of my university professors by ditching classes. It's highly detrimental to earning good grades."

Jennifer snorted. "You and your big words. I'll be waiting to hear from you. I can't wait to show you the area. It's fabulous."

"Write me and fill me in on what you're up to. I can't wait to find out what the doctor is like. Send a picture, if you can."

Jennifer bit her lower lip. "I don't know about writing, Misha. If Anton has your number, he'll have your address by now, too. I can't risk him finding out where we are."

"Oh, I hadn't thought of that. I figured with the FBI hanging around, he wouldn't dream of trying anything."

"Think again. Remember, he murdered Danny in cold blood, and then planted himself into my life. That kind of man is not only crazy, but also a maniac. Watch your step, Misha. I don't want anything happening to you or your parents."

"Don't worry Jen. The FBI agent assigned to us said he'd make sure we were protected. I'll talk to him and find out the best way for us to keep in touch with each other, all right?"

"Thanks, Misha. I'll wait to hear from you." Jennifer hung up and returned to her casserole. Her hands shook slightly and her stomach roiled with anxiety.

"Everything all right?" Nathan tore up lettuce for a salad.

She braced herself against the counter. "Anton called my uncle's house this morning looking for me. Misha told him I was in California." She closed her eyes and fought back the terror clawing at her mind. Would Elyssa get away safely?

Nathan put his hands on her shoulders. "That was good thinking on your cousin's part. Did she contact Mike?"

"Uncle Peter called him from the docks, just in case Anton tried to call back. The FBI are monitoring their phones, now."

"Hang in there, Jen. This will all work out fine. But until they catch him, you're not to answer the phone. We'll use an answering machine to screen the calls. I'll talk to Rob about it when he gets home, okay?"

Jennifer smiled weakly. She hated answering machines. However, in this instance, maybe she could tolerate one—for now. "I guess that would be all right." It felt nice to have someone to lean on. She told him about Elyssa's expected arrival and made arrangements for him to go with her to the airport.

"I'll make her feel just like a queen," he assured her.

She laughed and poured a mixture of cream of mushroom soup and milk over the sole fillets.

Nathan looked over her shoulder. "What are you making?"

"Fish Divan. Do we have any french-fried onions?"

"Second shelf on the left."

Jennifer generously sprinkled the onions on the top of the casserole. She slid the glass baking pan into the oven, and poured the vegetables into a covered glass bowl, "I'm ready for my lesson."

Nathan opened the microwave door, and then showed her how to work the unit. "If you have any questions when I'm not here, the owner's guide is in this drawer. Rob only knows the basics."

Footsteps bounded up the stairs. "The basics of what?" Rob demanded. "Something smells good."

"Using the microwave, roomie."

"Oh, okay." He peered through the glass of the microwave. "Are we eating healthy tonight, Jen? Nothing beats real food."

Jennifer playfully scolded her brother. "Didn't anyone ever tell you that it's best to reserve judgment until you've tasted the meal?"

"I have great faith in you, sister dear," Rob countered. "Oh, could we have homemade biscuits, too? I liked the way that you made them when I visited you last Christmas."

"I'll make them if you keep an eye on your niece."

"Fair enough. Where is she?"

"In the living room. She's also been quiet for some time, now, so you'd better find out what she's been up to."

"I'll set the table," Nathan offered.

"Hire that man, Rob," Jennifer teased. "And make sure you give him a raise."

"What's twenty percent of zero?" Rob asked Nathan as he headed toward the living room in search of Brianna.

"Zero."

"Take a raise, roomie."

They ate supper by candlelight. Nathan had arranged a centerpiece of fresh cut roses in an Oriental vase for the table.

"It seems you have more talents than just medicine, Dr. Pellitier," Jennifer fingered some of the flowers.

"That? You can give credit to Maggie. Her projects rub off on me, I guess." Nathan buttered another biscuit. "Speaking of talent, I had an interesting discussion with a gallery owner last night. He noticed your seascape at the hospital and wanted to know if he could see some more of your work. He's quite impressed and is considering showing some of your paintings at his gallery in Caribou."

"Glenn Loring wants to show Jen's work?" Excitement lit Rob's face. "Jen, he's a very famous artist in these parts. In fact, his work has been shown in many of the best galleries across the country and in Europe."

"I'm sure he was just being kind," Jennifer poured some milk for Brianna. "I'm not that good."

Nathan spoke up. "Glenn thinks so, and believe me he doesn't hand out compliments lightly. At least let him take a look at some of your other work. That is, if you are interested."

She looked at him in disbelief. Could he be telling the truth?

"Sis, this could be your big chance," Rob urged. "Don't let it pass without grabbing it."

Apprehension gnawed at Jennifer's heart. Dare she put her hope in this? "I...I have nothing recent. Everything was lost in the fire."

Rob was undaunted. "I've got plenty of your paintings here, and then you have a bunch at Uncle Peter's."

Jennifer's hand gestures mirrored her frustration. "You don't understand. My style has changed a lot this past year. What if he doesn't like the way I paint, now?" She chewed on her lower lip.

"I'll pray about it," she said, finally. "If this artist is really interested in my work, he'll wait. I'll let you know what I decide soon."

After clearing the table, Jennifer bathed Brianna and got her ready for bed. Before tucking the child in, she read her a story from her children's Bible, and then prayed with her.

Jennifer turned off the light, hopeful that her daughter was getting into a good bedtime routine. She returned to the kitchen to finish cleaning up. Nathan and Rob were nowhere to be seen. As she rinsed off the dishes, she heard banging below.

"What in the world?" She wiped her hands. The banging stopped, and then started again. "What are those two up to?"

Jennifer hurried downstairs, following the loud noises until she found the men. "Isn't it a bit late at night to be doing construction...or destruction." Glaring light from a shadeless brass floor lamp cast stark shadows across the cluttered room. Several boxes lay on the floor. A dozen or more painting canvases leaned against a bare wall.

Rob handed a mounted canvas to Nathan. "We're getting a head start on your studio."

Jennifer stepped over a large mound of debris and inspected the room further. Nathan carefully hung a portrait she had done of Rob and Brianna. Even in the harsh light, one could tell the painting was a good one.

As she viewed the other canvases, she recognized them as among those she had shipped to her uncle's house just after Anton entered her life. "Uncle Peter said he'd put most of my paintings in storage."

Rob cocked his head to one side. "He did, but I couldn't bear the thought of all of those masterpieces hiding in a dark attic. So, I liberated several to keep here." He combed his fingers through his dark curls. "You're not upset, are you?"

Jennifer laughed. Rob's boyish charm always managed to catch her off guard. "No, just surprised as usual."

"Well, what do you think?" Nathan motioned across the room with his arm. "Of course, it's far from finished, but it's a beginning."

Those two are something else. "It'll be great. You're both so sweet to go to all this trouble, and I hate to sound ungrateful, but could we possibly work on it another day? Elyssa's coming tomorrow and I want to make sure everything is ready for her."

"Sure, Jen," Nathan agreed. "Well, roomie?"

Rob shrugged. "Sounds good." He turned out the light and the three trooped upstairs.

Jennifer turned in just before midnight. After a warm bubble bath and preparing for bed, she repeated her memory verse, read her Bible, and spent some time in prayer. Michelle's news crowded into her mind. "God, I realize you have been protecting me, but I just don't understand why these horrible things keep happening," she prayed. "When will it all end?"

Chapter 17

Elyssa's flight arrived on time the next afternoon. Jennifer nervously peered out the window at the tiny airport, anxious for the sight of her friend. Nathan and Brianna walked back and forth, counting the number of blue and yellow chairs in the small waiting room. When Elyssa finally disembarked and walked through the arrival gate, Jennifer and Brianna enveloped her in hugs.

"Thank God you're here," Jennifer told Elyssa. "It seems ages since we saw you last. I thought something might have happened to you. How was your flight?"

The older woman clutched Jennifer's arms and shuddered. A mix of anxiety and relief filled her brown eyes. Wisps of graying brown hair escaped her trademark bun. "I honestly feel like kissing the ground. I don't mind flying in those big planes, because you can't really tell you're flying unless you look out the window. But those puddle jumpers —you can't help but know you're in the air—they drop suddenly, climb again, only to drop a few minutes later. I'm grateful I didn't have to sit in one of those cross-country."

Nathan took her overnight case. "They take a bit of getting used to."

Elyssa reached into her purse and brought out her luggage claim tickets. "Well, I don't plan on getting used to them." She handed the tickets to Nathan. "They're not real airplanes, they're remote control toys. I'm staying on the ground after this."

She picked up Brianna and smothered her with kisses. "How's Grammy's girl?"

"Me missed you."

"Well, I missed you, too, pumpkin. You'll have to tell me all about your trip and show me around the house."

Jennifer steered Elyssa toward the luggage area. "You must be really tired, Mom. What time did you leave California this morning?"

"Actually, I left yesterday and spent the night in Washington, D.C." Elyssa beamed. "You wouldn't believe it, but I had the most wonderful time this morning with my escort. I have so much to tell you, but it will have to wait until we get home."

On their way home, Jennifer asked Nathan to take a detour to the post office so she could get some money orders to send Mike. "I'll be just a few minutes."

Jennifer got out of the van and hurried into the post office. She made her purchases, and then went over to a nearby table. She addressed an envelope, stuffed in the money orders and wrote a quick note of explanation to Mike. As she licked the envelope flap, a wanted poster on the bulletin board in front of her caught her eye.

While the man depicted looked very young, had long hair, a heavy beard and mustache, Jennifer's gut said this was Anton. *I'd better take this with me and go over it more thoroughly.* She glanced around to make sure no one noticed her, removed the poster from the wall, and stuffed it inside her purse. She dropped her letter to Mike into the mail slot in the lobby, and returned to the van.

While Elyssa and Brianna chatted with each other in the back seat, Jennifer viewed the wanted poster, careful that Nathan couldn't see it. She didn't want to alarm anyone unnecessarily.

WANTED BY THE FBI: Conspiracy to destroy a vehicle used in foreign commerce by means of an explosive; destroying a civil aircraft; destroying a vehicle used in foreign commerce by means of an explosive; killing nationals of the United States. Demas Antonio Centari is an Italian national with Sicilian Mafia ties. He is being sought for his participation in the 8/17/97 bombing of Alitalia Flight 569, which exploded on takeoff from the Milan Airport. A total of 124 passengers, crew members, and airport personnel were killed. Consider armed and extremely dangerous.

Jennifer's hands trembled. Anton was an international terrorist and now he had tracked her to Misha's house. *I'm not going to panic. This could all be a mistake. I'd better double-check this before sounding the alarm.* But, deep inside, she knew she hadn't escaped him...not yet.

Once they got home, Jennifer and Brianna helped Elyssa get settled in her room, then let her take a nap. The toddler headed for her bedroom, eager to play with her toys.

Jennifer went to her own room, grabbed her sketchbook and began to draw Anton's face. Once satisfied with the first drawing, she copied it, lengthened his hair and added a bushy beard and mustache. She compared this last drawing to the wanted poster—a perfect match. Demas Centari and Anton Carducci were the same man. *I'd better call Mike right away.*

She checked in on Brianna and headed for the kitchen. Nathan was nowhere in sight. Jennifer heard loud sounds outside. She looked out the window and saw Nathan splitting wood. Well, at least she'd have some privacy while she talked. She dialed Mike's office. As soon as she reached him, she told him Elyssa had arrived, then filled him in on what she had discovered about Anton's true identity.

Mike whistled. "If you're right about this, we're going to have to change tactics. I'll contact the FBI agent and fill him in. Don't be surprised if you're assigned someone. You'd better let Rob, Nathan and Elyssa in on this. They're in as much danger as you are. Can you have either Rob or Nathan get somewhere and fax those pictures to me, Jen? It will save a lot of time and speed up things a bit. Also, I need you to fax the information to the FBI agent in Portland. Put 'Attention Charles Bolton' on the cover letter."

He gave Jennifer the two fax numbers. "I was also able to follow up on some of the earlier leads you gave me. I may have located Anton's place. I'm heading over there to check things out. As soon as I know anything, I'll give you a call." After instructing her to stay out of sight as much as possible, Mike hung up.

Jennifer replaced the receiver. She felt nauseated as she took the sketches and poster downstairs. As much as she hated letting Nathan in on her discovery, she had little choice. *Mike's right. He needs to know about the danger he's in. Maybe Elyssa, Brianna, and I will have to hide out somewhere else.*

Nathan, however, had no intention of letting them out of his sight. "You'll stay here as planned. I don't care if I have to take a leave of absence to protect you."

Jennifer shook her head. "I can't let you do that."

"I don't remember giving you a choice. Here's Rob, so let's sit down and map out our strategy."

Rob pulled into the driveway and parked his Chevy. "Did Elyssa make it all right?" He opened the trunk and took some packages out.

"She's upstairs taking a nap," Jennifer told him.

Nathan helped Rob unload his drafting supplies. "Rob, we need to have a serious meeting as soon as we get inside."

"Is something wrong?" Rob closed the trunk.

"I'm afraid so, roomie, but it's best discussed in the house."

A calliope of anguish churned inside Jennifer's mind. If only she could turn back the hands of time and erase this nightmare she found herself in. Nathan held the door open for her. She stepped into the house and led the way upstairs to the kitchen.

Elyssa and Brianna sat in the living room reading a book. Jennifer felt guilty for leaving Brianna alone for so long. "Oh, I hope she didn't wake you up, Mom."

"Not at all. I busted in on her. I brought some gifts for my darling granddaughter and couldn't wait any longer to give them to her."

Nathan touched Jennifer's shoulder and spoke into her ear. "Why don't I take over with Brianna for a few minutes while you fill Rob and Elyssa in on what you found out. That way Brianna won't be frightened. Then, I'll switch places with Elyssa so we can figure out the best way to protect this family."

Jennifer valued his sensitivity. "Thanks, I appreciate that."

Elyssa and Rob each took a seat at the breakfast bar. Jennifer nervously sat between them. "I had hoped that once Elyssa got up here, we could put Anton behind us and get on with our lives. Unfortunately, that isn't the case at this time." She laid the wanted poster on the countertop. "You'd better take a look at this."

Elyssa looked at the poster. "What does this have to do with us?"

"Look closely at the face, Mom. Imagine him without all that hair."

Her friend shook her head. "I don't have the eyes you do, Jen."

"Let me help you out a bit." She laid the first sketch of Anton beside the poster. "Do you recognize him?"

"How could I possibly forget? That's that louse, Anton." She tapped the poster. "I don't understand. What does that have to do with this."

Jennifer set down the second sketch. "What about this one?"

Rob picked it up. "That's the man in the wanted poster."

"All I did was add hair to Anton's sketch. We've been dealing with an international terrorist capable of anything. His name is Demas Antonio Centari. He's eluded capture for the last ten years."

Elyssa placed the papers side by side as if to comprehend the significance of Jennifer's words. Silence blanketed the kitchen. Finally, she spoke. "Have you notified Mike?"

Jennifer nodded. "He wants these sketches faxed to him and to an FBI agent named Charles Bolton." She looked at her brother. "Do you know where we can use a fax machine?"

He gathered the papers. "Actually, I have one in my office upstairs."

"That's a relief. I thought you might have to venture out to town." Jennifer handed him her notes. "Here are the numbers. Could you send them out right away?"

"It's as good as done." Rob headed upstairs.

Jennifer quietly told Elyssa about Anton's call to Misha. "She put him off for a while, but I don't know how long that will last. I won't feel safe until he's behind bars. Anyhow, you and I are to screen all phone calls through the answering machine. This number is unlisted. However Nathan and Rob insist we are not to take any chances. On top of that, Mike says we are to stay out of sight as well."

Elyssa tapped her slender fingers on the countertop. "Ironic that we're the ones imprisoned, so to speak, while that snake-in-the-grass is still free." She drew a heavy breath. "I have no intention of spitting into the wind, so I'll go along with whatever plan will keep us safe."

An hour later, Rob took his turn to watch Brianna. When Nathan submitted his and Rob's final proposal for keeping the fugitives out of harm's reach, Jennifer and Elyssa balked slightly.

"Nathan, we still have to get boots and warm clothes for winter," Jennifer said. "Just how are we to accomplish that task from inside these four walls?"

He held up his hand to silence her argument. "I already came up with a solution." He left momentarily and returned with some mail order catalogs. "I'm sure you can find all you need in these. Give me a list of what you want to order and I'll handle it from there. You'll want the fur-lined mukluks. It gets *extremely* cold up here in the winter."

Nathan placed the catalogs in front of Jennifer. "Also, I want to remind you that you're not confined to the house. You are more than welcome to visit Aunt Maggie and Uncle Franz anytime. Just take the back path and stay away from the main road. I'm also going to train each of you how to use Spirit for protection. Follow me downstairs."

Jennifer suppressed her irritation. *I can't stand people with all the answers.* Still, she had to admit to herself that she couldn't come up with any viable alternative to Nathan's plan. She and Elyssa followed him to the barn.

For the next hour, Nathan taught them how to run Spirit through his paces. "Protect is the word you want to use if you want him to keep someone safe. Say 'protect' and point to the person or people you want him to take care of. I'll assign him to Jennifer, and then come back to show you how he works."

Dr. Pellitier turned toward Spirit. "Trial run," he said. He then pointed to Jennifer. "Protect," he commanded the dog. "Jen, walk around and keep him busy." Nathan left the barn.

Spirit followed Jennifer's every move. She tried, but couldn't shake him. "He should have been named Shadow," Jennifer joked with Elyssa.

Nathan returned, wearing what looked like an over-stuffed snow suit He pulled a ski cap over his head and face, and then pretended to sneak up on Jennifer. Spirit crouched down and growled at the masked man. The "intruder" tried to circle the dog, but Spirit matched his every movement. Finally, Nathan took the cue and backed off to the barn door. Spirit seemed frozen in his attack stance. Only his eyes moved—tracking the threat.

"Trial off," Nathan called out. He removed the ski cap, but remained by the barn door. "When the protection is no longer needed, you must tell him 'protection off.' Otherwise Spirit will remain on duty." The doctor gave the command. Spirit glanced at Jennifer and Elyssa as if to assure himself of their safety. Then he trotted over to his master.

Nathan knelt down, thoroughly petted the dog and told him what a good job he had done. "This is Spirit's favorite reward," he explained.

The lessons continued. "Now, let's say someone has broken in the house, or if someone is making life-threatening gestures toward you," Nathan said. "If your life is in danger, use the command 'fight' and point to the intruder. Spirit will attack and pin the intruder to the ground. If necessary, Spirit will kill. He hasn't done it yet, but from what Tom told me, he came close once. Don't use 'fight' unless you know you're in clear and present danger. Spirit is a lethal weapon and carelessness can lead to unnecessary injuries and lawsuits."

Jennifer jotted the commands on an index card so she could memorize them.

"Once help arrives," Nathan continued, "you must release Spirit from his duty. Otherwise, the police will not be able to get near the intruder. To get Spirit to release his hold, you must say, 'easy.' If there is some question whether the intruder will get away again, command Spirit to 'guard.' In order to release him from his duty, you must say 'guard off.' Just so you know, in a life or death situation, if you're not able to give orders, or not sure what to do, Spirit can and most probably will act on his own."

Nathan donned the ski mask again. "Trial run," he told Spirit. He had both women practice the commands he had explained. Spirit's prompt reactions to Nathan's every movement surprised Jennifer. *Protection doesn't get better than this.*

Once Nathan had become satisfied that Jennifer and Elyssa knew the various commands, he took time to stroke and praise Spirit as before. "Again, once the danger is over," he told the women, "make sure you fuss over him a lot. Like I'm doing now."

Jennifer and Elyssa fussed over Spirit until Nathan put an end to the session. "I think we can call it a night. Go inside and I'll put Spirit on guard duty outside the house."

The women didn't have their promised heart-to-heart chat until after Brianna had gone down for the night. Jennifer sat on Elyssa's bed while her friend emptied her suitcases.

"I'm so glad you are here, Mom. I couldn't help but worry whether Anton would track you down."

"To tell the truth, I had the same worries about you."

"What happened after we left?"

"The police finally let me go back to the apartment to see if I could possibly salvage something." Elyssa sat beside Jennifer. "Mike and an FBI agent helped me sift through the rubble. Mike's the one who found my old photo album. I should have put all those photos into the safe deposit box, too, but I looked at them so often, I just couldn't do it. Now, I'll have to pay the price."

Elyssa took a manila envelope out of her overnight bag and handed it to Jennifer. "Anyhow, these two were the only ones that survived. They're really fragile, so be careful taking them out. Do you think, maybe, that you could paint their pictures for me—so that I can put them on my bedroom wall?"

Jennifer opened the envelope and gingerly pulled out two charred photographs, each in cellophane. "The portraits of your husband and son. Of course, I'll get started on them right away. It's the least I can do after what happened. I'll never be able to forgive myself for your loss."

"Nonsense. I'm the one who told you to give Anton his marching orders," Elyssa assured her. "I don't blame you in the least, so neither should you. Let's put this behind us and go on. I have some amazing news to tell you."

Elyssa took a smaller envelope out of her bag and hugged it to her chest. "One of my greatest dreams has come true." Her brown eyes brightened. "On the way up here, my escort insisted I stop in Washington D.C. to see the Wall. He helped me find my son's name and even gave me some paper and a pencil so that I could do a rubbing." She slid some sheets of paper from the envelope.

Jennifer viewed them with great interest. A cluster of names stood out in the midst of the graphite rubbing. In the center of the paper, she found Elyssa's son's name—Lt. Roy Baker, USAF. Jennifer felt happy for her friend.

Elyssa spoke again. "I did two rubbings; one I will put in a fire safe. She placed the pages back in the envelope.

"The news gets better, Jen. While I was at the Wall, I saw a man place a framed photo of my Roy and an Air Force major below Roy's column. I asked him how well he knew my son. He said that my boy had kept him alive after they had been shot down."

Her voice choked, and she wiped tears from her eyes. "He told me he had the opportunity to lead Roy to the Lord just before his last mission. Can you imagine it? I will actually see my son in heaven."

Tears of happiness welled up in Jennifer's eyes. "That is the best news one could hope for, isn't it? I am so heart-glad for you, Mom."

Rob tapped at the partially open door. "Jen, Mike just called and asked me to give you a message. He said you'd understand it."

She faced her brother. "What is it?"

"Bingo. The net is set and waiting. We should have our fish fry soon." Rob looked at her curiously. "What does he mean?"

Jennifer smiled and clasped her hands together. "It means this nightmare is almost over."

Chapter 18

The days passed with no word from Mike. The newspapers announced the nationwide hunt for international terrorist Demas Centauri. Elyssa settled in and, as Jennifer had hoped, had become fast friends with Maggie. Each afternoon, after finishing their own chores and Bible study, Jennifer, Elyssa, and Brianna spent a few hours visiting the farm or exploring the fields and woods. Spirit, as ordered by Nathan, accompanied them on their excursions.

Going into town for church or any other reason was forbidden. Rob and Nathan took care of the shopping. The fugitives held worship services together at home. Jennifer missed being part of a congregation, but she knew this would only be temporary. Pastor Kevin West, aware of the difficulties faced by the family, discreetly provided tapes of the church services, and also came by to administer communion.

Jennifer forced herself to find the positive things in her situation. She turned her energies into her artwork and filled her sketchpad with drawings of her new surroundings. In the evenings, after Brianna was in bed, she worked on the portrait of Elyssa's husband, Roger Baker.

She missed spending time with Nathan, but between his varying schedule and her nights spent painting, their paths crossed mostly at suppertime, if then. *It's all for the best*, Jennifer told herself. *Anyway, I doubt it's really possible to start over after what's happened between us.*

Two weeks slipped by without any communication from Mike. Jennifer's apprehension grew. What if his trap didn't work? These things took time. Mike would call when he had news.

Her anxiety surged when Rob headed off to Portland to confront their father, unannounced, despite Jennifer's misgivings. "Don't worry," Rob told her, getting into his car. "I won't let Dad hurt us again. I just have some questions I need him to answer."

Jennifer watched him drive off, and then returned to the house where Elyssa waited to start their Bible study. "I'm so frustrated I could just scream!" She dropped into her chair at the breakfast bar. "Mike hasn't called for weeks, and now Rob's determined to dig up the past. Why can't things be—"

"The way you want them to be," Elyssa interjected.

"Precisely." Jennifer shrugged. "That's not so bad, is it?"

Elyssa shoved a cup and saucer across the counter. "Here, have a cup of tea. It's good for what ails you."

Jennifer took the offered drink and stirred in some honey. "Everything seems to bother me today."

"So I noticed. What'd you do, eat ugly pills this morning?"

She waved Elyssa off. "No, it's more like I read something that didn't agree with me. Last night I stumbled on some verses that irritated me to no end. I'm hoping you'll help me make some sense of them."

"I'll try my best. What are they?"

Jennifer opened her Bible to the first chapter of James. "'Consider it pure joy, my brothers, whenever you face trials of many kinds, because you know that the testing of your faith produces perseverance. Perseverance must finish its work so that you may be mature and complete, not lacking anything.'"

Elyssa set down her cup. "What is it that you don't understand?"

Jennifer scowled. "I'm supposed to be thrilled because my father abandoned me, my husband was murdered, and our home was blown up? That seems a bit absurd."

"A *bit*? I'd say absolutely absurd. Child, God certainly doesn't expect us to be thrilled about bad circumstances. What James is saying here is that we must see trials as opportunities to grow in the Lord." Elyssa slid her finger down the page "If you look at verse twelve, it gives you another part of the equation, 'Blessed is the man who perseveres under trial, because when he has stood the test, he will receive the crown of life that God has promised to those who love him.'"

Elyssa turned the pages of her own Bible. "Listen to what Peter wrote in his first letter, 'In all this you greatly rejoice, though now for a little while you may have had to suffer grief in all kinds of trials. These have come so that your faith—of greater worth than gold, which perishes even though refined by fire—may result in praise, glory and honor when Jesus Christ is revealed.'"

She looked at Jennifer, her brown eyes warm with compassion. "Humans learn through experience. Our faith is small when we first come to the Lord, but as we learn to apply the principles of God's word to our lives in the midst of trials and temptations, our faith grows."

Jennifer leaned forward. "So basically, what you are saying is that trials and temptations are necessary parts of the Christian life?"

"Exactly. In his second letter, Peter also said. '...make every effort to add to your faith goodness; and to goodness, knowledge; and to knowledge, self-control; and to self-control, perseverance; and to perseverance, godliness; and to godliness, brotherly kindness; and to brotherly kindness, love. For if you possess these qualities in increasing measure, they will keep you from being ineffective and unproductive in your knowledge of our Lord Jesus Christ.'"

Jennifer located 2 Peter 1:5-8 in her Bible, and then underlined each of the verses.

"When we first became Christians," Elyssa continued, "we didn't automatically inherit these qualities any more than Brianna knew how to walk and talk when she was born. Growing up in the Lord takes work, and it doesn't come easy. That's why we have to rely on the Lord's strength to help us through."

"So, difficulties are supposed to make me grow?" Jennifer felt a bit uncomfortable in that knowledge.

"It's how we deal with the difficulties God allows in our lives that makes all the difference. Trials should draw Christians closer to their Father. Unfortunately, too many avoid that opportunity, causing them to miss out on the blessings of maturing in the Lord."

Jennifer looked again at the verses in James. She remained quiet for a few moments contemplating Elyssa's words. Slowly, the verses began to make sense. "I think I understand now. Those who want to grow up in the Lord gladly accept the challenges that trials and temptations bring because it gives them the chance to grow."

The events of the past months took on new meaning—God was taking special pains to help her mature in Him. Despite the pain, her heart rejoiced to know that He was working with her personally. Now, it had become essential for her to understand the lessons He was trying to teach her.

Later the next evening Jennifer worked on the acrylic portrait of Roger Baker. "There, I'm finished." She daubed the last bit of paint onto the canvas. Jennifer stepped back and viewed her work. Pleased with the results, she cleaned her brushes and put away her paint. "Tomorrow I'll start on her son's."

The headlights from Rob's Chevy Impala flashed in the studio windows, catching her attention. *I wonder how things went for him.* Jennifer opened the side door.

Rob looked thoroughly drained. He greeted Jennifer with a terse smile and handed her a shoebox. "I can't talk right now—I have too much to think over. Any questions you have should be answered by what's in this box. When you've finished going through them, let me know and I'll sit down with you then." He turned and walked upstairs with his briefcase in hand.

Jennifer weighed the box in her hands. It felt very light. What could it contain? *Well, there's only one way to find out.* She sat on her stool and gingerly opened the lid. Inside lay a stack of sealed, yellowed envelopes. Her throat suddenly felt dry and her hands trembled as she sorted through them. She noticed that the envelopes bore her name and various dates starting from the first year her father had disappeared. At closer inspection, Jennifer realized that most of the dates coincided with her birthday.

Fearful she might be disturbed while she felt so vulnerable, Jennifer replaced the lid, turned off the studio lights, and carried the box upstairs. She peeked in on her sleeping daughter, and then slipped into her own room. Jennifer sat on the edge of her bed, opened the box, and flipped through the envelopes until she found one dated the day her father had left.

She chewed her lower lip, searching for the courage to look inside. Taking a deep breath, she ripped open the envelope and took out the folded papers, also yellowed with age.

My Dearest Jenny:

I'm hoping someday you'll be able to read this letter and understand why I had to disappear from your life. The hardest thing I've ever done is walk away from the house today without telling you and your brother goodbye. I saw you in the window and it was all I could do not to break past your mother and Grandpére Shelton to get to you. But, if I had, your grandpére would have harmed Uncle Peter and his family.

I wish I could hold you in my arms once more and tell you that I love you. I wish I could explain why I have to leave, why I have to hurt you and Robby—the last thing in the world that I want to do—but I don't know myself. I'm not even allowed to say goodbye.

I wish I could take you and Robby with me, Princess, but I have to leave; your mother and grandpére have seen to that. They won't even let me write or call you and Robby. I just wish I knew why your mother is doing this.

The divorce papers state I abandoned you and your mom. I know that I was away at sea for months at a time, but I always wrote you and always provided for your care until I could come home. Your mother's decision is rather odd since I had previously told her in a letter that I wouldn't be going out to sea again after this last voyage.

Do you still have the letters I wrote you when I went out to sea, or did your mother take those away, too? How I wish I could change this horrible mess.

I know you won't be able to understand why I have to leave honey, but I hope I can explain someday and that you'll forgive me. Oh, Jenny, you are so precious to me. You'll always be my little princess no matter how old you grow to be. I'll always love you and I hope someday I'll be able to show you how much.

I'm sorry I couldn't fix the boo-boo this time; so sorry that I couldn't find a way to stay with you and Robby. I can't even go to court on this matter. I'm certain Grandpére Shelton paid off the judge; otherwise none of this would have happened.

I'm sorry, honey. Please forgive me. I love you always and forever, Princess. Remember, honey. Remember.

Love, Daddy

Fresh tears washed Jennifer's face. Her father hadn't left her willingly. With trembling lips she read the rest of the aged letters to herself aloud. Each expressed the anguish of a doting father separated from his precious children. Each told of his love for his daughter and the agony of not being able to be with her on her birthday and the special holiday celebrations they had shared.

Princess, do you remember our last Christmas together? I took you and Robby to the forest to find our tree. Snow hadn't fallen yet, so we were able to dig up the little spruce and load it into the back of the pickup truck. It looked so small out there in the forest, but when we got it home, it wouldn't fit through the door. What a time we had. Finally, we tied the bottom branches against the trunk with twine and got it in the door. I'll never forget the look of sheer rapture on your face when we put the last of the strung popcorn and cranberries on the tree and I lifted you up to place the angel at the very top. My favorite memory, though, is of you dancing on the front lawn in your nightgown and robe. Snowflakes fell like a garland in your hair. I'm so glad I captured that day's adventures on camera.

Jennifer smiled at the memories. Laughter from that long ago Christmas reached through time to ring in her ears. She could see her father, Robby and herself sitting around the tree sipping hot chocolate and munching popcorn. Then the magical moment came when the snow began to fall. The trio rushed outside to catch the first snowflakes on their tongues. Jennifer had danced and twirled across the lawn.

These and the many other photographs and memories I have of you and Robby have gotten me through these lonely years. I hope someday I will have the chance to give you both these letters in person. Most of all, I pray that I will one day be able to hold you in my arms again. In the next envelope, you will find some of the pictures from this last Christmas celebration. I know it won't make up for my absence, but at least you'll know I haven't forgotten and that I desperately long to be with you both.

Jennifer eagerly opened the next envelope and looked at the photos. How she longed to bridge the gap of time and step into the pictures. Funny, though, she couldn't remember her mother taking part in any of the festivities. *I wonder why.*

When Jennifer finished reading the last letter and had composed herself, she went in search of Rob. She found him bent over a drafting table in his attic office. "Rob, why didn't Uncle Peter tell us anything about what happened?"

Rob looked up from his work. "He didn't know the complete details until recently. Dad apparently wanted to get solid proof of the payoff before he spoke up."

"Did he?"

Rob set down his pencil. "Yes. In fact, the judge was removed from the bench just a few months ago. I have the newspaper articles right here." He reached into his briefcase, picked up the clippings, and handed them to her.

Jennifer sat on a nearby chair and read the news stories in disbelief. How could someone so easily get a judge to twist the law and destroy a family's happiness? Worse yet, how could her mother and grandfather justify their actions? Perhaps she could talk to Grandpére and make sense of this insanity. She had only a vague recollection of the man—sometime before her father disappeared. "Where are Grandpére and Grandmére Shelton, now?"

Rob swiveled his chair around to face his sister. His eyes seemed troubled. "Apparently they died in a car accident just a couple hours before Corrine handed us over to Uncle Peter. The police said a wheel came off their car. The detectives figured Corrine loosened the lug nuts to get her hands on our trust funds, but never could come up with the evidence."

"I don't understand. Why didn't Dad contact us once Corrine had given Uncle Peter full custody?"

"He wanted to, but Corrine had made the stipulation in writing that Dad was never to contact us. If he did, Uncle Peter, Aunt Sarah and he would all be thrown in prison for contempt of court."

Jennifer shuddered. *What a nightmarish dilemma. Still, he might have found a way, somehow.* "But he could have contacted us once we were of age, right?"

Rob shook his head. "He realized too much time had passed and that he wouldn't be able to prove his claims. We wouldn't have believed him, Jen. That's why he had to expose the judge. It was the only way he could possibly clear himself in our eyes."

"He had those letters he wrote us," Jennifer insisted.

"They weren't enough to prove his innocence. He didn't want to risk losing his chance to be a part of our lives again."

As much as she hated to admit it, he was right. Over the years she had harbored so much bitterness toward her father that she wouldn't have listened to him. The events of the past seemed so ludicrous. Even with the newspaper clippings backing up his story, many unanswered questions remained. What would drive her mother to the extremes of banishing her husband and murdering her own parents?

Why, indeed! Jennifer recalled how Corrine dumped them on Uncle Peter's doorstep and disappeared, taking every last cent of their trust funds with her. At last report she had remarried and moved to Europe. *She probably suckered in some rich fool,* Jennifer told herself as she looked over the newspaper articles again. Yes, Corrine Shelton seemed capable of anything to get her way.

An overwhelming sense of grief hit Jennifer. She thought of the lonely years her father must have spent. How could she ever make up for it all? "Rob, I feel horrible about this whole thing. Do you think we could have him come up for a visit or something?"

Her brother nodded. "I think that would be a good start. He's going to be busy for the next month—moving from his place in Texas to Uncle Peter's. I'll call him when he returns."

Heavy footsteps bounded up the attic stairs. "Rob, Jen," Nathan called. "Mike Scavone just phoned. He said to tell you the waiting's over. Anton's behind bars."

"Praise God," Jennifer breathed. Her heart leapt with joy. "It's over. I can finally live my life in peace."

Chapter 19

Jennifer wasn't sure what to do first with her newfound freedom. She lay awake a good part of the night thinking about the gallery owner who wanted to view her work. *This is such a golden opportunity. Trouble is, I have nothing to show him. All of my new paintings went up in flames.* She should have sent them on to Uncle Peter in June like she had planned.

She thought of the box she had stored in her closet back in Long Beach and groaned. Shortly after Anton entered her life, he had impressed her with his knowledge and appreciation of the masters. She had even contemplated sharing her work with him. But, when he openly scorned what he deemed "meager attempts" of modern artists, she had nixed that plan.

Intimidated and insecure, she put her art away and hadn't touched it for months. Now her only recent creative paintings that remained were the self-portrait of herself and Brianna that she gave Rob for Christmas, and the seascape adorning the wall at the hospital.

She considered her newly-filled book of sketches. Maybe if she got these worked into paintings in the next few weeks she could invite Mr. Loring over then. She sighed. *I don't know. There's not enough variety to suit me at this point.* Perhaps she could drive around and find some good subjects.

The next day, the national news media prominently featured Demas Centauri's arrest on the radio, television, and in the local papers.

Jennifer settled into the couch with a copy of *The Bangor Daily News* and read the details of the raid and the capture of the man she had known as Anton Carducci.

Interpol revealed details about Demas's activities in Europe, including the murder of his mafia boss and everyone else aboard that same ill-fated aircraft. It surprised Jen to read that law enforcement had located many missing masterpieces from European art museums in Centauri's Long Beach warehouse. *It's no wonder he seemed so knowledgeable about the old masters.*

The reports also stated that at the time of his arrest, Demas Centauri possessed several priceless documents stolen from the United States Library of Congress. The jewels from the recent heist in California, however, remained missing. Jennifer grimly shook her head and set the paper down. Well, at least he was out of commission, now.

After breakfast, Rob took Jennifer, Elyssa, and Brianna to Presque Isle on a major shopping spree. The women stocked up on various clothing necessities for the upcoming winter while they waited for the catalog purchases.

While Elyssa, Rob, and Brianna browsed through the Service Merchandise store for toys, Jennifer went to the art store down the street to replenish her painting supplies and get a new sketchbook. Once they finished shopping, the foursome stopped for lunch and played for a few hours at Funland.

After Brianna went to bed that night, Jennifer told Rob, Nathan, and Elyssa her plans to do more sketching, and maybe some paintings. "I'm not sure I can come up with something your friend will like, but I'll give it my best shot."

"Of course you can," Elyssa assured her. "You'll have all the time you need. I can watch Brianna for you, so take that worry off your shoulders."

Jennifer smiled. "I really appreciate the offer, Mom, but I will not take advantage of you. I have to do my sketching during the day, but when I start the painting, I'll do it after Brianna is in bed."

During daylight hours for the next several days, Jennifer left Brianna with Elyssa and roamed the countryside, sketching anything that struck her creative fancy. Each evening she made steady progress on Roy Baker's portrait, and in fleshing out some of her more promising vignettes of northern Maine life.

Her brush and paints seemed to take on a life of their own, capturing the essence and spirit of the season and the local people. Two teenage potato pickers seemed momentarily frozen in time on one canvas. On another, a weather-beaten farmer wiped perspiration from his dirty brow while eyeing gathering clouds with concern.

A third painting made viewers feel that if they could put their noses close enough to the canvas, fragrance would waft from the fresh fruit and vegetables in the roadside stand. And, in yet another painting, the blaze of autumn color spilling over several hills gave the impression of a gigantic patchwork quilt.

The next Saturday morning, Jennifer led Elyssa into the studio to view the portraits restored from the charred pictures.

The older woman gasped in delight, and then dissolved into tears. "They're so life-like," Elyssa sobbed. "You don't know how much this means to me. It's almost as if I have them back."

Once Elyssa had recovered sufficiently, she allowed Rob and Nathan to hang the two paintings in her bedroom.

Her friend's response to the portraits gave Jennifer enough courage to let Glenn Loring come evaluate her work. She asked Nathan to invite the artist to dinner on the following Tuesday evening.

By that Tuesday afternoon, Jennifer and Elyssa put the final touches on the art studio as Brianna played with her uncle outside. Rob and Nathan had completed the heaviest work in the studio a few days before by moving the boxes to the loft in the large shed connected to the house. Since the walls had been freshly painted a few months before, Jennifer only had to arrange her canvases, brushes, and paint where she wanted them.

"It's so good to be painting again," she told Elyssa as they set various arrangements of dried flowers in the studio. "The magnificent scenery up here does wonders for my inspiration."

Elyssa gazed at her. "I'm glad you're using your talent again. Why did you ever stop?"

Jennifer shrugged. "Insecurity, I guess. Anton seemed to be such a connoisseur of art that I didn't dare let him see mine. I was afraid he'd sneer at me for even thinking I had any talent at all. So, I hid them from him." She left her open sketchbook on the easel where she had worked earlier in the day.

"Scum like that could taint something just by looking at it." Elyssa examined a painting depicting herself and Brianna at a recent picnic in a field of wildflowers. "You're amazing, Jen. If I hold still long enough, I might even hear the buzz of that bumblebee."

Jennifer gave a nervous laugh. "You're biased, Mom. But I'd be a little disappointed if you weren't. After all, what are mothers for?"

A florist delivery truck arrived with a dozen pink roses for Jennifer. The card bore Nathan's name.

"An admirer, huh?" Elyssa teased as she helped arrange the flowers in vases. "He must be taken with you to have sent such lovely flowers."

Jennifer rolled her eyes. When would Elyssa give up? "It's just Nathan's way of bolstering my spirits. He knows I'm extremely nervous about tonight."

"Is there something between the two of you?" Though she tried to hide it, Elyssa's face bore a hopeful expression.

Jennifer blushed and turned to watch Rob and Brianna play catch outside. The older woman touched her arm. "I don't mean to seem nosy. It's just that you're like my own daughter. I so want to see you happy. You've waited so long."

"I understand, Mom." Jennifer took a vase from the floor and placed it on a stand. "There's nothing between us. He hinted at it at one time, but I know it wouldn't work. Besides, I don't need a man to be happy."

Elyssa arched her eyebrows in amusement. "But they *do* make life a lot more interesting."

Jennifer shuddered. "After everything that has happened, I'm just not capable of loving a man again."

"You have no feelings for Nathan? Are you sure?"

She felt no resentment toward Elyssa's inquiries. Jennifer was flattered that her friend was concerned, but she wished she'd stop playing the matchmaker. "I'm physically attracted to him. What woman wouldn't be? But that's not enough to build a relationship on."

"True. I think, though, if you look deep inside yourself, you'll find you have more love than you thought you did."

"No, Mom. My ability to love died with Danny."

Elyssa put a hand on Jennifer's shoulder. "Give yourself time, Jen. Time heals much."

Jennifer shook her head. "How much time? When Danny died, part of me died with him and I haven't been able to resurrect it."

"I know what you are trying to say. I felt that way when Roger died."

"You haven't remarried."

Elyssa shrugged. "Not yet, but I haven't ruled it out altogether, either. The right one just hasn't appeared, yet."

The phone rang just then. Jennifer ran upstairs and answered it.

Nathan's voice sounded over the line. "Jen, Glenn will be over at six-thirty," he told her. "Do I need to pick up anything for you? The freezer is full of meat, fish, chicken and veggies, but I don't think we have any more lettuce for salad."

"I guess you can pick some up," Jennifer agreed. "You might also get some tomatoes, cucumbers, green peppers, and sweet onions if we don't have any. Make sure the onions are flat, as opposed to round. They'll be sweeter that way."

"What about dessert? We have about a ton of apples."

"I'll take the hint. Apples it is."

"Could you possibly make some cobbler?"

"All right, I'll make cobbler if I find a recipe for it. You'll need to pick up some whipping cream, then."

"No problem! Maggie's got the recipe." He repeated the grocery list, and then added, "Oh, before I forget, Glenn doesn't eat red meat." He hung up.

Jennifer's spirits sagged. *With my luck, I'd make a meal he detested.* She called Maggie for the cobbler recipe, and then returned to the studio. She had liked the way everything had been organized, but now, with the artist's arrival drawing near, Jennifer's nerves began to flutter in anticipation. She rearranged her canvases several times.

Elyssa finally grabbed her hands. "Give it a rest, Jen. Moving them around won't change their style. They're fine paintings and nothing you should be ashamed of. Now, what time is Glenn coming over and what have you planned for the menu? We should probably get started on the meal preparations."

Jennifer relayed Nathan's messages, and then threw her hands in the air. "I don't know where to even start. Oh, what if I make a horrible impression?"

Elyssa grabbed her by the shoulders. "Jen, calm down. Glenn Loring is merely another human being. He has no extraordinary powers and is no better a person than you. Just be yourself. What will be, will be. Now, let's go upstairs and set our menu."

The women went to the kitchen. Elyssa pulled several cookbooks from the shelf above the sink. "My motto is keep it simple," she told Jennifer. "It's when you try fancy stuff to impress that things fall flat. Let's find some easy recipes."

After a few minutes of silent browsing, Elyssa tapped her finger on a page. "Since Mr. Loring doesn't eat red meat," she told Jennifer, "here's a recipe for honey-glazed chicken that you can cook in less than two hours. Below it is a menu for a complete dinner. You already have a salad planned. We'll just use the apple cobbler for dessert." She handed the book to Jennifer. "I'll help in any way you need. First, let's get that chicken thawed."

Jennifer followed Elyssa downstairs to the converted barn. She wished she could just call the whole thing off. *Unfortunately, that's impossible.*

Sunlight filtered through a dust-coated window. Jennifer recognized the shapes of two snowmobiles off to one side. Maybe Elyssa and Brianna would enjoy a ride this winter.

Elyssa opened the chest freezer, balanced her stomach on the rim, and rummaged around inside. "I don't like this kind of freezer," she complained, her feet slightly lifted from the floor. "One of these days I'm going to land head first in it."

Her friend's words conjured up a vision of the older woman hanging upside-down in the freezer. Jennifer laughed. "I can hold onto your feet if you need me to.

"Never mind that, grab these packages."

Jennifer caught the various frozen bags that Elyssa tossed up to her.

"There, that should do it." Holding a package of chicken in one hand, Elyssa slid her body down the outside of the freezer, and then shut the freezer door.

They returned to the kitchen laden with the fowl, vegetables, a basket of apples, and several large potatoes. Jennifer placed the frozen chicken breasts into the microwave to thaw, and then began to peel the apples for cobbler. Elyssa peeled the potatoes and put them in water.

Nathan dropped off a bag of groceries at five, and then left again. Elyssa, noticing Jennifer's nervousness, offered to take over the dinner preparations. "I know you're feeling quite anxious over this, so leave it all to me. Get dressed. I'll put place cards at the settings so you'll know who sits where."

At six-thirty the food was ready for the table. Jennifer quickly peeked out of the dining room window when she heard Nathan's truck. Butterflies formed in her stomach as Nathan and Glenn started up the stairs. She envied Elyssa's self-assurance.

Glenn Loring walked with a quiet dignity that reminded Jennifer of some old Gene Kelly movies she had seen. The jaunty tilt of the artist's gray fedora brought a smile to her lips. *He won't be stuffy, that's for sure.* She just might enjoy herself this evening, after all.

The older gentleman hung his hat and gray woolen jacket on the coat tree just outside the kitchen and then turned so Nathan could introduce him.

As she shook his hand, Jennifer confirmed Glenn's solemnness was merely a front. Mischief lurked behind those quiet brown eyes. His thinning white hair had a tendency to curl—giving him a rakish appearance. The soft lines around his generous mouth betrayed his tendency for laughter, and even his debonair mustache seemed to confirm her suspicions.

"I appreciate you coming, Mr. Loring." The artist still awed her.

His friendly face broke into a hearty smile. "Please, call me Glenn. The pleasure's all mine. It's not often I get invited out to dinner these days." Glenn's eyes warmed up considerably. "I'm also looking forward to seeing more of your work. I'm quite impressed with that painting at the hospital."

She relaxed considerably, although some doubts remained. *I just hope he's not too disappointed.*

As Jennifer turned to go into the kitchen, Nathan introduced Glenn to Elyssa. The artist raised her outstretched hand to his lips and kissed it tenderly. Jennifer watched her friend out of the corner of her eye. *I could swear she looks like she's going to faint. Well, well, what happened to her "Glenn Loring is merely another human being" speech? This could get quite interesting.*

One thing was for sure; the older woman had lost her composure. Elyssa excused herself and headed for the dining room. Fluttery movements replaced her usual no-nonsense approach as she bustled aimlessly around the table, switching place cards.

Jennifer stifled a giggle. She felt a little sorry for Elyssa, but not too much. The older woman hadn't ceased her matchmaking attempts. Now came the golden opportunity to turn the tables on her friend.

She set the platter of chicken on the table. Noticing that Elyssa was busy with the salad fixings, she deftly switched the place cards around again, seating her friend next to Glenn Loring. She finished bringing the rest of the hot food items to the dining table, and then had Brianna ring the small dinner bell that Nathan had recently purchased.

Elyssa seemed shocked when she realized what Jennifer had done. "I'll get you for this," she hissed in her ear.

"What's wrong, Mom," she feigned. "Don't you feel well?" *At least I put Brianna on the other side of her, so she'll have an escape, anyway.* Jennifer settled herself directly across from Glenn so she could see his reactions to Elyssa, and vice versa.

Her friend resigned herself to the new seating arrangements. Sure enough, she took the opportunity to fuss over Brianna—cutting her meat and tending to any possible need. Her usual calm and composed front was replaced with shy silence.

Jennifer found the dinner conversation stimulating and enjoyed herself immensely. Better yet, she had a front row seat to the glances that flew between Glenn and Elyssa all through the meal. She was sure to enthusiastically praise Elyssa's cooking often, and noticed her friend blushed all too easily.

Finally, Elyssa subtly kicked her ankle under the table, prompting Jennifer to leave well enough alone, for now.

After dinner the older woman excused herself and escaped with Brianna to the child's room to get her ready for bed. Nathan and Rob offered to clean the kitchen, so Jennifer would be free to talk to Glenn in her studio.

Glenn moved unhurriedly from canvas to canvas. "Where did you study?" he asked Jennifer as he appraised her work.

"I've never had formal lessons," Jennifer replied, a little self-consciously. Maybe she should have asked Nathan or Rob to accompany them.

He lifted a whitened eyebrow. "You're not serious." His face held a great deal of wonderment as he faced her. "Surely, you must have studied somewhere?"

Jennifer shrugged. "No. When I was young, my mother forbade such classes. Later, I couldn't afford them. I just try to capture what I see in the best way I can."

"Amazing." Glenn turned back to the paintings, carefully viewing the portrait of Jennifer and Brianna. "Did you do this from a picture?"

Jennifer's hands turned cold. Maybe he didn't like her work after all. "No. I sketched my daughter first, then, I used a mirror to sketch myself." She swallowed a lump that had formed in her throat. "Is... something...wrong with my technique?"

Glenn shook his head, slowly. "Wrong? I should say not," he replied, rubbing his chin. "I've never met anyone with as much natural talent as you show." Light reflected on his white hair as he bent to pick up her latest sketch. "Your technique is exquisite. God has indeed endowed you with a great gift."

Jennifer couldn't believe her ears. "You...like my work?" she stammered.

"Like it? I love it! Why do you keep such fine work shut up away from those who should be privileged to enjoy it?" Glenn looked her in the eyes. "I want you to do a show at my gallery for the winter festival in February. That should give you some time to get your paintings together. Nathan said you have quite a few in storage?"

Jennifer swallowed hard. "Umm...those are from several years ago. I don't know if they'd be what you were looking for."

"Nonsense. I know artistic styles change, but I cannot believe that you could ever do a horrible painting." He waved his arm around the room. "These here are almost like photographs. I'm most interested in seeing how your technique has developed over the years."

He picked up a pencil sketch of Maggie and Franz dancing a Scottish jig at the harvest bonfire. "When did you do this?"

Jennifer cleared the anxiety from her throat. "This afternoon." She hoped it wasn't too rough.

"How long would it take you to work it into a painting?"

She quickly made some calculations. "About three days, if I work on it every evening."

"Good. Start on it tomorrow. I'll be back in a week. Now, if you'll allow me, I'd like to say goodbye to the rest of the lovely folk upstairs." As they turned to leave he suddenly stopped her. "Tell me, is Elyssa... spoken for?

Jennifer kept herself from laughing. "Not that I'm aware of."

Glenn smiled thoughtfully and nodded. A few minutes later he bade his hosts goodbye. He removed his jacket from the coat tree. "The dinner was delicious, ladies." His gaze stayed on Elyssa as he spoke.

"Nathan and Rob are very lucky men." He slid his arms into the gray woolen jacket. "Jennifer, work hard on that painting. I'll see you next Tuesday, about four?"

"That would be fine." Jennifer added recklessly, "Be sure to count on staying for dinner."

"A pleasure I will look forward to." He pushed his fedora onto his head and disappeared down the stairs with Nathan following behind.

"Well?" Rob demanded when the two men were out of sight. "What's the big verdict?"

"He wants me to do a show for the winter festival in February."

"That's wonderful!" Elyssa clapped. "You'll do it, of course?"

Jennifer wasn't sure how to answer. "I've never done a show before, so I don't know what to expect or where to even start." The enormity of the situation overwhelmed her. "Do you think it would be safe for me, now that Anton has been arrested? Or should I wait?"

Elyssa considered the question. "I don't see why not, but perhaps we should check with Mike, first."

"I'll talk to Mike," Rob said. "Whether you have to wait for the show or not, Jen, we can get your other paintings out of storage." Rob added. "I'll call Uncle Peter tomorrow and ask him to get them out of the attic." He went into the kitchen to use the phone.

Elyssa and Jennifer retired into the living room to wait until Rob gave them Mike's answer.

"What else did Glenn tell you?" Elyssa laid a log on the fire.

"I'm supposed to have a painting completed by next week."

Her friend looked up. "Do you have something in mind?"

"Actually, he liked the sketch I did of Maggie and Franz dancing. He asked me to put it into a painting."

"Well, you just rest your mind. I'll be more than happy to keep Brianna occupied while you work." Elyssa clapped her hands enthusiastically. "My daughter is going to be famous."

Jennifer laughed. "Don't hold your breath, Mom."

Chapter 20

Mike had given his assurance that the danger was over, now, and Jennifer could pursue her own dreams again. By Friday afternoon, she had finished the painting. She had worked steadily in the evenings and all this morning to make her deadline. Elyssa and Brianna had their own agenda today and, once the housework was done, had taken off with Rob for Funland and parts unknown. "We'll be back by supper time," Elyssa called gaily as they climbed into the gold Impala.

Jennifer breathed a sigh of relief when they drove off. Since she had teased her friend unmercifully the last few days about Glenn Loring, she didn't want Elyssa to know that she had accepted an invitation to fly kites with Nathan. The older woman would never let her hear the end of it. Of course, the outing merely served as a chance for them to develop an honest friendship, she told herself, but ever-hopeful Elyssa wouldn't see it that way.

Nathan came home just before two, carrying two kites and two spools of kite string.

"Ready to go, Jen?" he hollered up the stairs.

"All ready," she answered, coming down to join him. She wore a soft green sweater and a new pair of blue jeans. "Elyssa and Brianna are on a little excursion with Rob, so I guess it's our turn."

They crossed over Maggie and Franz's back field and headed into the woods. Autumn-clad bushes peeked through the filtered sunlight. Jennifer enjoyed the musky smell of the forest. Occasionally a squirrel darted across their path, then chattered at them from the safety of a tree branch.

Soon, Nathan and Jennifer tramped across an unkempt field of tall grass and wild flowers.

"There's the house," Nathan told her, pointing to a large wooden structure on the other side of the field. Boards covered the windows and barred the doors.

"Why is the barn attached to the house like that?" Jennifer hadn't seen anything like this before.

"Basically so the farmer wouldn't have to tramp through the snow to take care of the stock," Nathan explained. "Those mounds of dirt against the walls insulated the barn, keeping the animals warm in winter and cool in summer. As you can see, it hasn't been used in quite a while and it needs repairs."

"There's a door directly from the house into the barn?"

"Yes. As a matter of fact, it has a rather unusual entrance. Let's go inside and I'll give you the grand tour."

"Sounds intriguing."

Nathan laid the kites and string beside the front steps, and then pulled a set of keys from his pocket. "Since I'm the trustee of the estate, we can explore to our heart's content." He opened the great oak door and ushered Jennifer inside.

"Hold on a minute and I'll get us some light." He disappeared into the darkness, and then returned a moment later with an oil lantern and a box of matches. Nathan set the lamp on the floor and raised the glass top. He struck a match, and then nursed the wick until the flame shone strong. After replacing the glass, he picked up the lantern by its handle, then took Jennifer's hand and started through the room.

Jennifer felt strangely happy as Nathan grasped her hand. What was it about this man that disturbed her so? Her happiness tasted bittersweet—dare she step out only to be hurt once again?

She turned her attention to the house. Large white sheets covered the furniture in the expansive living room. Huge shadows flickered across the brick fireplace and along the bare walls.

As Nathan took her through the house, he explained how Mark Westley had built it for his new bride nearly a hundred years before. "This kitchen is really unique," he told her.

Jennifer looked at the huge pantry, the many cupboards and appliances. "It looks rather ordinary to me."

"How many kitchens have you been in that have a secret exit?" Nathan showed her the hidden door behind a large cupboard. "Tom's great-grandmother, Rose, was afraid that the animal smells would come into the house if her husband had a door directly from the kitchen to the barn, so Mark fixed a corridor between the two doors and hid this one behind the tallest cupboard."

He showed her the small corridor. Dust lay heavily on the wooden floor. A mouse scurried in front of them and disappeared into a hole. Jennifer stifled a scream and clung tightly to Nathan's hand.

"It's gone, Jen," Nathan told her gently.

Jennifer relaxed her grip. "I'm so sorry. I didn't mean to cut off your circulation."

He gently squeezed her hand. "Don't worry about it. I'll just have to put down some more mouse traps the next time I come."

They walked a few more feet, and then Nathan pushed on the wooden door at the end of the corridor. The hinges protested loudly as he widened the opening.

"There's the barn," he announced. "I'll need to oil these hinges, among other things." Nathan pulled the door shut. He led Jennifer back into the kitchen, closed the door behind them, and pushed the cupboard back into place.

"Next month I'll have to turn the electricity and heat on in here," he told her. "Tom Westley's son is supposed to come back sometime this winter, and he's asked me to get the place fixed up—painting and such. I might get Rob to help me find painters."

Jennifer sighed. "I wish I could offer my help, but I promised to get ready for the show."

"Thanks for the thought, but I might be contracting the job out. The hospital has been keeping me rather busy." They explored the upstairs. Jennifer was amazed at the many large rooms in the house, yet the atmosphere seemed sad.

"The house looks so lonely," Jennifer said. "It needs a family in it. Does Tom's son plan to live here?"

"He hasn't said. He and his family are missionaries in the Middle East. I know they will be on furlough for a while, but that's about it. If he plans to sell it, I hope to buy it."

They finished the tour and headed back to the front door. Nathan blew out the flame and carefully put the lantern back into its place.

Jennifer shielded her eyes against the sun as she stepped outside. "I can't believe how bright the sun seems. I should have brought sunglasses."

Nathan locked the door behind them. "It's amazing what our eyes put up with, isn't it?" He picked up the kites and string.

A gentle breeze stirred through the trees as they walked to a small hill just below the house. Nathan handed a yellow and blue kite to

Jennifer, showed her how to tie the string to the frame then guided her through the steps of letting out the string and reeling it in.

She faltered through several attempts before she finally got her kite airborne. Once hers was flying steadily, Nathan got his own orange and green kite in the air, then lay on the grass and watched it. Jennifer dropped down beside him.

Nathan let out a little more string. "This is so relaxing. I can feel the week's tension taking wing on my kite."

Jennifer agreed as she let out the rest of her string. She felt so comfortable lying on the grass, gazing into the bright blue sky. The last month's panic seemed a distant memory. Birds sailed by on open wing, lazily enjoying the Indian summer's day. The warm sunshine and sweet smell of grass lulled her to sleep.

"Jen, your kite!"

Nathan's warning jolted her from her nap, but too late. The spool had slipped from her fingers and the kite was gone. They watched it float with the clouds toward Canada.

Jennifer sat up and shook grass from her hair. "I'm so sorry, Nathan," she apologized. "I'll replace the kite for you."

"Don't worry about it, princess."

She looked at him. The doctor's face held a look of great tenderness that caused her heart to pound. Why did her life have to be so complicated? If only she could let her heart be as free as her kite.

Nathan's expression changed to one of vague sadness. For a moment he seemed a million miles away. He turned and released his kite to the wind. "It's time to go."

They walked home in silence. Sorrow weighed heavy on Jennifer's heart and she felt tears building. *I'll cherish today forever, but I can't*

spend time alone with Nathan anymore. It's only fair. I can't build his
hopes only to shatter them.

Besides, she felt Christ wouldn't want her to fall into a romantic relationship without love as its foundation. The only solution was to bury herself in church activities and the show preparations. Perhaps Nathan would grow tired of waiting.

During the following days Jennifer managed to minimize her contact with Nathan. When he was home, she spent most of her time in the studio or out sketching. She avoided Franz and Maggie's farm as well—afraid she might meet disapproval.

Nathan seemed a bit mystified about Jennifer's sudden distance, but said nothing. His eyes, however, spoke volumes, bringing fresh agony to her heart. He respected her decision and spent most of his spare time with Brianna and Elyssa. At meals, Nathan and Jennifer were polite to each other, but rarely spoke.

Jennifer missed him more than she cared to admit. Her heart ached when she would hear him and Brianna laugh together, but she fought the feeling by working on her paintings with a vengeance.

When that didn't work, she concentrated on her memory verses. Slips of paper covered the cupboards, refrigerator, bathroom mirror, and even the edges of her easel.

Rob and Elyssa teased her about the papers, but remained silent concerning the sudden distance between her and Nathan.

Tuesday evening rolled around again. Glenn Loring stopped by as promised and raved over the new painting. This was the beginning of many visits from the artist. Though he used Jennifer's ongoing work as an excuse for his weekly visits, she knew he really came to see Elyssa.

As the weeks rolled by, romance blossomed between the older couple. Elyssa appeared happier than Jennifer coulf ever remember. Her friend had even dared to try a shorter hairstyle that made her look years younger. While Jennifer rejoiced for them, she keenly felt the emptiness of her own heart.

Thanksgiving Day dawned, but to Jennifer the celebration seemed somewhat hollow. Glenn Loring came over for dinner, but Nathan had driven down to Pennsylvania to be with his family for the holiday. After that, he had to attend a medical conference in Boston. He promised Rob that he'd stop by Uncle Peter's to pick up Jennifer's paintings on the way back home.

Jennifer went through the motions of fixing the meal, trying to push her loneliness aside. Although she wore a mask of happiness, she harbored misery.

"I want Nafan," Brianna wailed, echoing her mother's silent yearning. "Why he go 'way?"

"Honey, he just went to see his mommy and daddy," Jennifer explained. "He'll be back before you know it."

She stepped into the kitchen to get the desserts. Jennifer bit her lower lip and stared out the kitchen window, lost in thought. What would she do if Nathan were to leave permanently? She wound a lock of hair around her finger. "God, I don't know what's wrong with me, but I can't go on like this," she whispered softly.

Elyssa placed the dirty dishes into the sink. "Give it up, Jen. You're already a goner."

Jennifer placed the teakettle on the stove, and then turned around. "What are you talking about, Mom?"

The older woman looked her in the eyes. "This game you're playing with yourself."

Jennifer's gaze faltered. She turned away. "This is no game."

"Anyone can see as plain is plain that you're in love with Nathan, but you keep pushing him away. You're making both of your lives miserable."

Jennifer opened her mouth to speak then shut it again. She had no defense. The older woman was right. She sat on a stool and buried her head in her hands. "What am I going to do?"

Elyssa sat beside her and slipped a comforting arm around her shoulders. "Nathan loves you, and he loves Brianna as if she were his own flesh and blood. He's not perfect by any means, but then, no one is. You should give the relationship a chance."

Jennifer lifted her head and shook it vigorously. "I can't do that. Don't you understand? The two men I loved the most took my love and left me behind."

"According to your father's letters, he didn't leave willingly. And Daniel certainly didn't choose to die."

"That's just it, Mom. I have no guarantees. My heart can't take any more pain."

"Life is full of risks, Jen. If you shield yourself from happiness because you're afraid of sorrow, you're just burying yourself alive." She patted her shoulder tenderly. "The choice is yours." Elyssa took the desserts into the dining room.

A tear stole down Jennifer's cheek, but she checked the flow and brushed the single betrayer away. As much as she respected Elyssa, she wasn't ready to give in on this issue. She did, however, tell Rob she would like to see her father.

Her brother relayed the information over the phone and set up a tentative reunion for just before Christmas.

The days crept by, and restlessness set in. Glenn Loring stopped by one Friday to see how Jennifer progressed on her other paintings.

"I can't bear to look at a paintbrush today, much less pick one up," she told him.

"When's the last time you took a day off, Jen?" he asked.

"Weeks ago," she admitted, remembering her day with Nathan. "I really need to take a break."

A light snow began to fall. Glenn rubbed his hands together. "It feels like the kind of day to pop corn over the fire, drink hot apple cider and listen to stories," he said. "I'll tell the stories if you fix the snacks."

"Sounds good to me," Jennifer replied. She led the way upstairs to the kitchen.

A slamming door and heavy footsteps on the stairs announced Rob's arrival. He burst into the kitchen waving a magazine in the air. "Jen, look at this. Your name is listed in this art magazine under 'Shows to See.'"

Jennifer scanned the page Rob held out to her. Sure enough, her name and an old photograph stared back in black and white. "How'd this get in here?"

"I hope you don't mind," Glenn explained, "I put it in to announce your upcoming show," he explained.

She blinked. "No, I don't mind. It was just a surprise to me."

"Good." He beamed at her. "I pulled some strings and made sure your show was announced in every prominent art magazine in the country. Now, what about that food?"

They decided to fix the snacks the old-fashioned way. Rob put a couple of logs on the fire and prepared the popcorn in an old metal popper over the coals. Jennifer poured the fragrant cider in an iron kettle and that, too, was placed over the fire. Elyssa and Brianna pulled the beanbag chairs in a semi-circle and settled in for the festivities.

Glenn proved himself a master of storytelling, as skillful in painting with words as he was in using a brush. Jennifer could almost see the early New England settlers as Glenn told of the strength and courage of these determined people.

While many of the stories brought laughter, others were colored with tragedy. Glenn told of a farmer whose sleigh broke down on his return home during a snowstorm.

"He unharnessed the horses, then started walking," Glenn said. "The animals got back to the barn safely that night, but there was no sign of the farmer. The search party found his body two days later, less than twenty feet from his sleigh. It seems he kept walking in circles. If he had mounted one of his horses, he would have lived."

Rob poked the fire. "It's hard to believe that such a beautiful place could be so deadly."

"The danger lies with those not equipped to face the harshness of this land," Glenn replied. "This is still mostly wilderness area. We share it with a lot of wildlife as well as the elements. Deer, moose, bear, wolves, coyotes, skunks, squirrels, beaver, and foxes are just a few of the animals making their homes in much of the wooded areas."

He then gave his audience detailed instructions of how to stay alive if caught in a snowstorm. Glenn explained how they must dress, as well as what type of equipment and food they needed to take if they should venture out into the woods or on the road during the winter.

Jennifer felt reluctant to let Glenn leave late that evening. The enjoyable day had helped to take her mind off of Nathan for a few hours at least. Now, in the dreadful silence of the night, loneliness returned and depression engulfed her.

"Father, help me," she pleaded as she cried herself to sleep.

Chapter 21

Two Sundays before Christmas, Michelle called to tell Jennifer that Nathan had picked up her paintings and was on his way home.

"That man is so gorgeous, Jen," her cousin's voice bubbled over the phone. "He's a real find for sure. We went out to dinner last night and I didn't know how to act, almost. I haven't been around a real gentleman in so long."

Her mouth felt dry as she struggled with her emotions. She hated how her voice shook when she spoke, so she cut the conversation short, using the time as an excuse to hang up. "We're just getting ready to leave for church, Misha. I'll have to talk to you later. Thanks for relaying Nathan's message."

Jennifer remembered little of what was said in Sunday school. Her thoughts drifted to memories of the times she had spent with Nathan. Would she lose him now to her cousin? She couldn't blame him, but if the past few weeks were any indication of what life would be like without him, she didn't know how she could bear it.

Once the worship service began, she became caught up in the spirit and warmth of the music as the congregation sang praises to God.

When the singing ended, Brianna skipped off with the other youngsters for children's church. Glenn sat beside Elyssa, and Jennifer felt the pangs of jealousy. How she wished she could step out of her fear and into life.

The pastor's wife sang, "Do I Trust You, Lord?" as an introduction to the sermon. Tears slipped down Jennifer's face as she battled the painful memories that still haunted her. How could God expect her to just let go of her past and trust her future completely to Him? Rob squeezed her hand and gave her his handkerchief.

When Pastor West began to speak, Jennifer tried to close her ears to the message. *I'd just put my heart on the line again,* she argued within. Her most recent memory verse rang in her head. *I can do all things through Christ who strengthens me.*

"Trust is the most important part of our relationship with the Lord. Without trust we cannot experience the blessings of God," the minister explained to the congregation.

"The Webster's New World Dictionary defines trust as the following: 'a firm belief in the honesty, reliability, et cetera of another; faith; confident expectation, hope.' Let's concentrate on two words in those definitions—faith and hope. We'll be going on a bit of a jaunt through both the Old and New Testaments, so bear with me. Turn first to the book of Hebrews, chapter eleven." The rustle of pages filled the room.

"'Now faith is being sure of what we hope for and certain of what we do not see. This is what the ancients were commended for.' Look over to verse thirty-one. 'By faith the prostitute Rahab, because she welcomed the spies, was not killed with those who were disobedient,'" he continued. "Let's reacquaint ourselves with this remarkable woman. We'll find her story in Joshua, chapter two."

He waited for the members of the congregation to find their place, then read the scripture passages aloud.

Pastor West made eye contact with the congregation. "Let's view things through the eyes of Rahab. Here she takes quite a risk in hiding these foreign spies, and then trusting them with not only her life, but also the lives of her family members. But, as we see in Joshua six, verses twenty-two through twenty-three, her actions paid off—her family was hustled out of Jericho and led to safety. Now, let's go to Matthew, chapter one."

Again he waited for the rustling of pages to stop. "Here we find the genealogy of Jesus Christ. If you will look at verse five, you might be surprised at the name mentioned here. 'Salmon the father of Boaz, whose mother was Rahab.' Now, I'd call that a real blessing! Rahab, a prostitute, took a huge risk to help the Israeli spies. Her actions saved her family from destruction. But she didn't remain a prostitute. She had the opportunity to embrace a new life and not only became the great-grandmother of King David, but a direct link to the birth of Jesus Christ, our Savior."

The information surprised Jennifer. *I really don't know my Bible very well.* She marked the verses for further study and returned her attention to the sermon.

"God loves us intensely," Pastor West explained, "and it is His intention to bring blessings and growth to our lives. He doesn't want us to remain as we are. Jeremiah twenty-nine, eleven says, '"For I know the plans I have for you," declares the Lord, "plans to prosper you and not to harm you, plans to give you hope and a future."'"

Jennifer turned the pages of her Bible and underlined the verses.

"God's plans, however, cannot be fulfilled if we do not trust Him," the minister continued. "Rahab knew in her heart that the spies were from God and that God had promised the land to the Jews. She was wise enough to realize it was futile to stand in the way of Almighty God. Instead she put her trust in Him and became His instrument in protecting the three men in her care. Rahab had no visible guarantees that the spies would keep their word, but she trusted God anyway. As a result, God gave her a new life, and gave her a place in the lineage of His son, Jesus Christ. If Rahab had embraced fear and turned in the spies, she would have been destroyed along with all of the rest of the inhabitants of Jericho. Thankfully, she did not let fear rule her life."

The words pierced Jennifer's heart as she realized that God was speaking directly to her through the pastor.

"Where are you, today? Are you at a crossroad? Can you trust God enough to obey Him? Can you allow Him to bring growth and blessings into your life? Or have you let fear take control of your life? God has told us He will never leave us, nor forsake us."

Jennifer listened, transfixed.

"Cleanse your heart of unbelief," Pastor West encouraged at the close of the service. "Give God His rightful place in your life. The altars are open. Come allow God to work in you. Rely on His strength and power rather than your own. Be willing to say, 'Lord, I believe; help me overcome my unbelief.'"

With shaky legs, Jennifer made her way to the front of the church and knelt before the Lord. When she finally left the altar, she felt a sweet release. The bitterness and fear of the past was gone. God had broken through Jennifer's prison of emotions and had replaced her terror of abandonment with trust of God's steadfastness. For the first time that she could remember, Jennifer was free to take the risk to love —love her father, herself, and now to even love Nathan.

But was she too late? Her joy of release now mixed with the sorrow of uncertainty. *If it's Your will for us to be together, Father, please work it out. If this is not Your will, then take away my feelings for him.*

On the way home from church, Rob shared his ideas for the upcoming holiday celebration. "Let's call Dad and have him come up Christmas Eve. In fact, let's have the whole family come up. I have someone for Misha to meet."

Rob's last few words hurt, but Jennifer smiled in spite of them. After all, she had left the doctor in God's hands.

Nathan called Rob in the early afternoon to say he would be delayed. The water pump in his truck had broken and he was waiting for repairs in Bangor.

"I guess we won't see him until probably tomorrow," Rob said when he finished explaining their housemate's mishap. "I told him to let me know if he needed any help."

Jennifer wrestled with frustration. She needed to talk to Nathan, but it would have to wait. Her heart weighed a ton as she lifted her pain to God. "I guess this is where trust is put to the test," she whispered. "Father, please give me the strength to hold on to You."

The house was empty the next morning as Jennifer drove the van into Caribou to meet with Glenn at his gallery. Rob was on his way to Edmundston, and Elyssa and Brianna had taken off for the farm. Nathan had called to say he was on his way back. He'd drop off the paintings, and then he needed to check on things at the hospital.

Jennifer had little trouble in locating the gallery. She parked on the street and braved the icy wind. *I should have worn pants today,* she told herself as she crossed the street. Her legs felt cold below her green skirt and long, black woolen coat. She hurried inside the gallery door. Soon, she and Glenn were finalizing the plans for the show.

"I'm greatly impressed with what I've seen of your work, Jen," Glenn said as he poured another cup of coffee, "and I'm sure the public will be equally thrilled. You need to set prices for your paintings so there'll be no confusion regarding sales."

Jennifer felt reluctant to part with her paintings, but Glenn set her mind at ease. "Think of this as a sort of ministry that God has given you. Perhaps you can find a way to use this as an opportunity to tell people about Christ."

She agreed to pray about what God would have her do. At noon Glenn took her to Yusef's for lunch. While they were seated at the restaurant, one of Glenn's friends stopped by their table for a chat.

"Some foreigner stopped by to see us at the real estate office yesterday," the wispy old man said, rolling a half-chewed toothpick from one corner of his mouth to the other. "Asked to buy the old Westley place—even offered to pay cash on the spot. Said he needed it for a movie he was setting up. Got real upset when we told him it weren't for sale. He said he'd give ten thousand dollars a week if we'd rent it to him until the movie was done."

Jennifer, remembering all that Nathan had told her about the property, listened intently to the conversation. "What do you mean, a foreigner?" she asked, unable to keep silent any longer. Perhaps the Westley family might be able to use the money. She could talk to Nathan and let him take it from there.

"What I already said. Some Latin fella wants the Westley place. Said he'd only need it for a little while. Lost his temper when we told him he couldn't even rent it. Offered to take him around to some other houses, but he left in a real huff."

Glenn didn't seem too bothered. "Well, that's his problem," he replied. "We've got enough worries of our own without taking on someone else's."

The old man shrugged. "By the way, Glenn. Radio says there's a nor'easter heading our way. Dumped several feet over Connecticut already. Should be here by late this afternoon." He waved goodbye and headed toward the door.

Glenn frowned at this news. "You'd better get home right away, Jen," he told her. "I hope your brother has enough sense to stay in Edmundston tonight."

Fear pricked at Jennifer's mind. Storms terrified her. She agreed that it would be best if she went home.

"Remember what I told you about these storms," her artist sponsor said. "You've got to be prepared. Did you make up that survival kit I told you to put in your car?"

"Sure did," she assured him. "I even have a smaller one for when I go for long walks."

Glenn paid the check and drove Jennifer back to the gallery where she picked up the van and headed home.

Jennifer stopped by Franz and Maggie's to tell Elyssa the news, but found no one home. Their car was missing from its usual spot. She thought she heard a noise near the front shed, but dismissed it after listening for a few moments.

She glanced at her watch. *One o'clock.* "Maybe Elyssa and Brianna went back to the house." Yet she found no one there, either. Not even Spirit seemed evident. Nathan had been there briefly, she surmised from the boxes now lying on her studio floor. She doubted, however, that he would have taken Elyssa and Brianna with him.

Jennifer kicked off her shoes and headed upstairs to search for a note. Where could they have gone? After changing out her skirt and top for woolen pants and a sweater, she absently wandered into

Brianna's room. The wood felt cool beneath her feet. She looked out her window toward the backfields. Perhaps the pair was exploring the woods nearby. *I'd better check. They won't know about the storm and I won't rest until they're safely home.*

She turned and headed for the door, but stopped short as she stepped on something hard and sharp. Jennifer reached down and pick up the offending object. Cradling it in her hand she stared at what looked like a small glass diamond. *What's this doing in here?* Brianna was too young for pretend jewelry, and none of their family or friends would have given her something like this.

Jennifer started for the door again, but stepped on a few more gems. Where in the world were these coming from?

She got down on her knees and ran her hands across the polished wood floor. Her search netted three more. Puzzled, she pushed Bear-Bear aside and sat on Brianna's bed. Sharp points bit through her pants. Jennifer jumped up and turned around. On the child's bed was a small mound of various sized unmounted jewels.

Her mind started spinning. *Could this be...?* In a daze, she took one of the "diamonds" and walked back to the window. Deliberately, she ran the point of the jewel across the corner of the glass window and etched a fine line in the pane. *Oh, Lord, it's real.* Her thoughts raced. How did Brianna get the jewels missing from the heist?

She looked around the room. Her gaze fell on Bear-Bear. *We never did find out where that bear came from.* Jennifer snatched up the stuffed animal and probed its seams. Her efforts were rewarded when jewels cascaded from a hole in the bottom of the bear. She picked up several and turned them over in her hands. Police had stated that over five million dollars worth of jewels were still missing. Were the rest of them in here?

Wanting to preserve any possible fingerprints, Jennifer grabbed the first aid kit from the bathroom, selected a pair of latex gloves, and pulled them on. She returned to Brianna's room with a seam ripper in her hand. As she pulled out a handful of stuffing, the edge of a white plastic bag came in view. With a few tugs, she pulled it out of the bear, scattering a few more gems.

Jennifer noticed a hole in the side of the small, sealed bag. *That's where the jewels are coming from.* She opened the bag and gazed at its contents. Diamonds, emeralds, rubies and sapphires glistened in the light. No wonder all of Brianna's animals were slashed open at their Long Beach apartment. *Strombolli was looking for these. When he couldn't find them, he came after us.*

She opened the bear's back, put her hand inside the opening, and pulled out ten more bags of various sizes. Convinced Bear-Bear held more secrets she opened the top of the bear's head and found three bags of rolled cash.

Once she had emptied the bear, Jennifer carefully took inventory of everything. Ten bags of jewels, rolls of hundred-dollar bills; a set of keys, and several passports—different names, but all with Anton's photo. She needed to let Mike know.

Jennifer took off the latex gloves and headed for the phone. She noticed the message light blinking on the answering machine. *Elyssa probably called to say where they were heading.* Ever since the news of Anton's capture, she had embraced her hatred of these types of gadgets and ignored the device. Now, she'd have to retrain herself. She hit the message retrieval button.

"Mrs. Warner, this is Special Agent Charles Bolton with the FBI. I must speak to you immediately. Please call me at..."

She grabbed a pencil, rewound the message, and jotted down the phone number. Mike had mentioned that an FBI agent might be assigned to her, but that was before Anton had been captured. *Why does he want to talk to me?* She quickly called him back. "Mr. Bolton? This is Jennifer Warner, returning your call."

"Mrs. Warner, I've got some bad news. Demas Centauri escaped from custody in California a few days ago. We've had reports that he was headed for the East Coast."

Horror gripped Jennifer's throat. *How could this happen?* She found her voice. "Why didn't you call sooner?"

"We needed confirmation," the agent explained "Without going into the gory details, Centauri was being transported between jails. However he and the U.S. Marshals never arrived. Police found the vehicle's burned-out hull the next day. It took a few days to identify the human remains. That's when we knew that Centauri had escaped."

Jennifer wanted to run to safety, but where could she go? "What am I going to do?"

"I'm on my way to New Sweden, now, and I will stay with you until his recapture. Just tell me how to find your house."

She quickly gave Agent Bolton directions. "You also need to know that I've just located the jewels from the California heist," she told him. "He'll no doubt be looking for them."

"I'll get the evidence and information from you when I get there about three o'clock," the FBI agent said. "Stay inside and keep your doors locked in the meanwhile."

Jennifer hung up the phone and paced the floor. Fifteen minutes slipped by. Where could Brianna and Elyssa be? She dialed Maggie's number, just in case she and Franz had returned home.

The phone rang into emptiness. Jennifer replaced the receiver. This was too weird. The couple rarely left the farm for long on a weekday—unless there'd been an emergency.

Maybe Brianna got hurt. She quickly looked up the number to the emergency room and placed the call. No. They hadn't seen anyone she just described. She hung up.

Another ten minutes passed. Jennifer decided to check the backfield after all. She donned her parka, and mukluks. The phone rang. She grabbed it, hoping it was Elyssa. "Hello?"

"Jennifer, *mi cara,*" a familiar voice taunted. "It's been a such long time since I've talked to you."

She froze. "Anton? How did you find me?" Her hand tightened around the receiver.

"It's not hard when every art magazine in the nation is advertising your art show. I have to say, your picture doesn't do you justice."

Her anger boiled to the surface. "What do you want?"

He chortled. "Actually, I have something, or should I say, someone you want," he taunted.

Jennifer could hear a child crying in the background. Her mouth fell open. Anton had taken Brianna!

"I said that you would pay if you left me." His laugh chilled Jennifer's blood. "I'm keeping my promise. After I've finished with her and the old bag, I'm coming for you."

"Don't—" Jennifer begged, but he had hung up.

The words of Glenn's friend echoed in her ears. "Latin fella... wants the Westley place...for a little while...lost his temper...."

Anton got what he wanted no matter what anyone told him. Memories of visiting the Westley farm flashed in Jennifer's mind. *Anton must have taken Brianna and Elyssa there.* She dialed the hospital again.

"Give me Dr. Nathan Pellitier. Tell him it's an emergency!" Jennifer's heart pounded wildly as she waited for what seemed an eternity. "Father, make Nathan hurry."

Finally the doctor picked up the phone.

"Nathan, I can't explain everything now, but Anton has Brianna and Elyssa. He just called—probably from a pay phone. Anyhow, I'm sure he's holding them at the Westley place. A friend of Glenn's told me that a Latin man was trying to buy or rent the place yesterday; said he needed it for a little while."

"Jen, I'm calling the police. Terry and I will be right home. Stay put until I get there."

"Sorry, Nathan. I'm going over there now. I won't stand by and let him kill them."

Alarm filled Nathan's voice. "No, Jen!"

Jennifer ignored his plea. "Anton's missing jewels and some other evidence are next to Bear-Bear on Brianna's bed. FBI Agent Bolton is on his way to our house, now. Make sure he gets the information. I love you, Nathan."

Jennifer hung up the receiver, grabbed her hiking boots, zipped her parka, and pulled on her thick gloves. She'd have to walk, so Anton didn't suspect anything. She slung a daypack across her shoulder and started out.

Chapter 22

Cold gray clouds descended as the wind tore at Jennifer's parka with icy fingers. She secured the hood around her head until the fur lining framed her face. Jennifer's breath formed a mist in the chilled air. She bent into the wind and hurried across the open field. *I have to reach the farmhouse.* If only there was enough snow on the ground so she could use one of the snowmobiles.

Leaves and twigs cracked beneath her boots. Small patches of snow dotted the ground. Snow began to fall, whipping mercilessly at her wind-burned face. Jennifer quickened her pace. If the storm broke in full fury now, she could die out here.

The temperature dropped. Jennifer trudged on. Fear clawed at her mind. What if she came too late? Jennifer battled horrific images that barraged her thoughts. She assaulted the visions with prayer. *Protect them, Father,* her heart screamed in silent desperation. *Don't let anything happen to Elyssa or my baby.*

Beyond a small hill, Jennifer could just make out the remote forms of the farm buildings. Their foreboding presence emerged in the deepening snow storm. A red sports car sat in the dirt driveway. It had to be Anton's, but why had he left it in plain view? Doubts assailed her. *What am I going to do? I'm no match for him, Father.*

"Do not fear, for I am with you," a still, small voice spoke in her heart. "Do not be dismayed, for I am your God. I will strengthen you and help you; I will uphold you with my righteous right hand."

"Give me wisdom and help, Lord," Jennifer prayed aloud. "I don't know what Your plan is, Father, but I choose to trust You."

Jennifer's path hugged the forest now. A stand of evergreen trees helped shield her from the snow. As she drew closer, she noticed that some of the boards had been taken from the windows. While Nathan had mentioned turning on the heat and electricity in the house to protect the water pipes and to make his maintenance easier, he hadn't said anything about the windows. At any rate, she had to be careful now. She must not be seen.

The trees sheltered her movements as she crept closer to the weathered structures.

When she was a few yards away, she paused. Jennifer perceived no sign of movement, and only the increasing wail of the wind provided any sound.

A light now flickered in one of the unboarded windows. How could she get in without being caught? Jennifer concentrated on the barn. If she could somehow manage to find the concealed door from this side, perhaps she could slip into the house unnoticed.

Jennifer took off her right glove and searched her pack until she found a flashlight. She placed it, a small box of matches and extra batteries into the deep right-hand pocket of her parka. she rummaged further into the recesses of her pack. Where was her knife?

She frantically plunged her hand into the front pocket of the pack and was relieved to feel the leather sheath. Jennifer pulled it out and removed the knife. Its broad, short, blade could come in handy in an emergency. She replaced the knife in its sheath, and then shoved it in the pocket alongside her flashlight.

Jennifer felt around the pack again, making a mental check of the rest of its contents—two emergency flares, a small New Testament, a first aid kit, extra socks and gloves, candles, lemon drops, soup mix, crackers, two candy bars, a tin cup and an extra sweater. Her survival lessons from Glenn would pay off—if she could keep a clear head.

Several deer darted across a nearby clearing. She watched them disappear into the swirling snow. Glenn had said there was plenty of wildlife in the area including bears, foxes and wolves.

An unexpected sound broke behind her. Jennifer whirled and choked back a scream as gray fur flashed from behind a bush several feet away. She dropped her pack and grabbed for her knife. Her glove fell as she struggled to free the blade.

The wolf's one blue and one brown eye regarded her cringing figure with interest. The animal's tail swished from side to side. As it drew closer, Jennifer got the glimpse of a tan collar and could see a long piece of thin rope trailing behind.

"Spirit, you!" Jennifer hissed. She held her hand to her heart. "Perfect timing. You nearly scared me to death!"

The husky mix rubbed against her legs. Jennifer stroked his head. "I'm really glad to see you, boy. I need the company." *Who tied him up?*

She retrieved her glove and slung her pack over her right shoulder. Jennifer decided to leave the knife sheath open. There might not be time to fumble with the snap if a real emergency presented itself.

The trick, now, was to get into that barn. The heavy snowflakes fell thicker. At any rate, the barn would provide shelter from the storm.

She slipped her glove back on, grasped Spirit's rope, and wound all but four feet of it around her left hand. "Let's make a run for it, Spirit. I just pray Anton doesn't see us. Come on."

They raced for the closest barn wall. Jennifer peered through a broken window. Satisfied that no one lurked there, she led Spirit to the door. She opened it slowly and the two of them slipped inside. The animal whined softly.

Jennifer turned on her flashlight and made a brief sweep of the barn interior with the beam of light. The wind and snow pushed through large cracks in the walls, ceiling, and through the broken windows. She cautiously made her way to the far wall. The empty hayloft above acted as an extra shield from the intruding elements.

Trembling, Jennifer crouched in the corner. Spirit lay next to her. The storm vented its full fury, buffeting the wooden walls with invisible blows. She fought the growing fear in her heart. *Why do storms have to affect me this way?* "I will not panic," she vowed quietly. "I won't."

She prayed for strength and wisdom to face the task ahead of her. Jennifer asked also for protection for Nathan and Terry as they drove in the storm. Finally, gathering courage, she searched for the door to the house, hoping she wouldn't have to jimmy it open.

The door opened easily, though the hinges screeched slightly. She hoped the howling wind would buffer the sound. Spirit followed her into the corridor. Jennifer closed the door behind them and turned on her flashlight again.

Nathan had kept his promise about laying mousetraps. Carcasses of the small pests filled several of those he had set. Jennifer swallowed back nausea and turned her gaze away.

When they reached the end of the short corridor, Jennifer found the latch to the kitchen door. She shut off the flashlight and listened. Cautiously she pushed the cupboard open a crack, bracing for noisy hinges. They moved freely. *Nathan must have oiled them.*

She peered into the house. The kitchen and back room were dark and quiet. With her hand still on Spirit's rope, Jennifer led the dog inside, closing the cupboard silently behind them. They reached the pantry and ducked within when footsteps sounded in the next room. She quickly shut the door.

Jennifer closed her eyes and tried to remember the layout of the house. A soft growl escaped Spirit. She placed her hand over his muzzle, silencing him.

Anton walked into the kitchen, swearing as he struck his foot on an old floor electrical outlet. His footsteps sounded heavy, as if he wore boots of some sort. Jennifer peered through the door crack and watched as he shone his flashlight around the room. In the glow of light, Jennifer could see the gun tucked into Anton's waistband. This definitely complicated her rescue plans. She chewed her lower lip. *I should have let Spirit jump him just now.*

She waited until he left the kitchen and headed up the stairs before she left her hiding place. Dim light filtered through the windows in the living room. She guessed Nathan took the boards off of them the last time he was here. Jennifer heard footsteps upstairs. Quickly, she and Spirit hid in the dark alcove beneath the staircase.

Jennifer laid her pack on the floor and contemplated her next move. Perhaps she could jump Anton when he came downstairs. Her fingers closed around the knife. She heard footsteps again and prepared to move, but had to abandon her plan when she heard voices.

"Let us go, Anton," Elyssa coaxed, her voice strained. "You have no need to do this."

"Shut up, you old bag. I'm tired of listening to you. I'm going to have a bit of fun at your expense before I kill both of you." Anton laughed.

"It's too bad Jennifer couldn't be here to witness this. I wouldn't have to kill her then. I'd have her under my control forever."

Brianna wailed. Jennifer cringed when Anton slapped the child.

"Stop your whining, brat," he shouted. "I'll torture you the most. If you hadn't been around, your mother would have been mine by now. You'll pay dearly for standing in my way."

Spirit tugged on his rope. Jennifer tightened her hold and silenced him. If they showed themselves too soon, there'd be shooting. She squatted down and untied the retired police dog while keeping a firm grip on the dog's collar. "Stay," she ordered. Jennifer quickly wound the freed rope and shoved it into her right pocket.

Tears burned her eyes as she watched Anton prod her friend and daughter into the living room. Their hands were tied behind their backs. In the dim light Jennifer watched Anton push his victims onto the floor near the fireplace, and then pull out his gun.

Fury rumbled in Spirit's throat.

"It isn't worth it, Anton," Elyssa told him. "You'll get the death penalty for this."

"I said shut up!" Anton kicked her in the stomach, silencing her. "By the time your bodies are found, I'll be long gone."

Jennifer spoke into Spirit's ear. "Fight!"

The dog sprang forward, growling savagely. Anton spotted the animal and fired at him. Brianna screamed.

The bullet grazed the angry animal's shoulder. He plowed into Anton, knocking him to the floor. The gun fired into the air. Spirit clamped his powerful jaws over the man's arm, forcing him to drop the weapon. Elyssa rolled to the side and kicked the gun across the floor toward Jennifer.

"Get him off of me!" Anton shrieked, his pain evident. He kicked at the dog, but Spirit dug his teeth in deeper.

Jennifer ran and grabbed the gun as Anton continued to fight Spirit. She pocketed the weapon and grabbed her knife. Taking advantage of the man's preoccupation, she cut her friend's bonds. Anton's screams continued to pierce the air.

"Are you and Brianna all right?" Jennifer pulled the rope free and dropped it on the floor.

"We're all right, now, child," Elyssa answered, rubbing life back into her numb hands. "Praise God, you two got here when you did."

"Mommy," Brianna wailed.

"I'm here, baby," Jennifer assured her. "It will be all right."

She handed Elyssa the knife. "Cut Brianna loose then take her to the barn and wait. Nathan and Terry are on their way."

"You think I'm gonna leave you alone with that fiend? We're staying," Elyssa retorted. "Easy," she commanded Spirit before he could kill Anton.

Jennifer took the gun from her pocket just as Anton tried to grab Elyssa, though blood soaked both of his sleeves. "Freeze, Anton. I'll shoot," Jennifer shouted, holding the gun with both hands and aiming it at him.

Elyssa quickly pushed Brianna to safety and rolled clear of Anton.

"Spirit, guard," Jennifer ordered as she kept the gun aimed at Anton's chest. The angry beast stood snarling over the man.

Realizing the odds had turned against him, Anton allowed Elyssa to hogtie him.

Out of the corner of her eye, Jennifer could see her daughter standing near the staircase, crying. She longed to hold her, but she'd have to wait until Anton was securely bound. As long as any of them were near that man, they were in danger.

"Brianna, hon, it's going to be all right," she said. "I need you to sit on the bottom step until I tell you to move. Do you understand?"

The little girl nodded and quickly obeyed her mother's instructions.

Jennifer smiled at her. "That's my girl. I'm so proud of you."

"We'd better dress his wounds." Elyssa tore a dust cover into strips. "I'd hate for him to miss his trial."

Anton sneered. "What trial? Mere females could never expect to conquer the great Demas Centauri." He spat at them in contempt, but froze when Spirit growled.

Jennifer kept the gun trained on him. "Hold still unless you'd like Spirit's teeth sinking into you again." She motioned with her head. "Elyssa, there's a first aid kit in my pack over by the staircase."

"These strips will do just fine for now," the older woman insisted. "I'll only stop the bleeding. The hospital can deal with the rest."

Minutes hung suspended in the frosty air as Elyssa wrapped their attacker's arms. The wind howled outside and shook the exposed windows with each violent breath.

Jennifer glanced over at Brianna, who huddled dejectedly against the railing on the bottom step. "Everything's going to be fine, pumpkin. Mommy will hold you just as soon as Grammy and I get finished here."

The growing blizzard must have made the roads impassable. Their rescuers could be a long time coming. Again, Jennifer offered a prayer for their safety then focused her attention back on Anton. She would have to remain vigilant.

Hatred seemed to ooze out of his very pores. How could anyone allow himself to become like that? Immediately Jennifer remembered the bitterness she had harbored against her parents for so long. *Forgive me, Lord. My attitude was no better than his. If it weren't for Your love, I could be in his shoes.*

How precious God's love had become to her these past few months. She could see how He had caused her to grow through the fire of trials. Besides providing her with opportunities to mature in her faith, the Lord had given her many gifts of love and friendship in her new home.

Anguish pierced her heart as she thought of Nathan. *Father, I'm such a fool. Why couldn't I see that Nathan was another one of Your precious gifts?* She wanted a chance to set things right.

"Well, that's the best I can do." Elyssa secured the last make-shift bandage. "The bleeding's stopped." She grabbed the first aid kit and checked Spirit's shoulder. "Our furry friend, here, looks pretty good," she told Jennifer. "His wound's already closed up." Elyssa patted the dog and scratched behind his ears. "Spirit, guard."

"Thanks, Mom." Jennifer ensured Anton posed no immediate threat then lowered the gun and placed it on a nearby end table.

She turned and held her arms out to Brianna. "Come on, baby."

The child fairly flew into her mother's embrace.

"Thank the Lord you're all right," Jennifer whispered, holding her daughter close. "Mommy's so sorry this happened, honey. Everything's going to be just fine, now."

"Jesus help us, Mommy," Brianna declared. "Grammy says He did."

Jennifer kissed Brianna's forehead. "Yes, He certainly has and we need to thank Him." She bowed her head and prayed aloud, thanking God for protecting them.

"Amen!" Elyssa said at the conclusion of the prayer. She rubbed her hands together and shivered. "It's awfully cold in here. Could we light a fire or something?"

Jennifer set Brianna on the couch and grabbed her flashlight from her pocket. "Let me check to see if Nathan turned on the lights and gas. He had mentioned something about it before."

She headed for the back room then located the breaker box and furnace switch. After turning them on, she went back to the living room and tried a lamp. Soon the living room was flooded with light. A slight rumble beneath the floor announced the furnace had kicked in. Elyssa explored the rooms on the first floor.

Jennifer sat beside Brianna on the couch and examined the bruises on her daughter's face. The child's tender skin bore the imprint of Anton's savage blow. She hugged her daughter and fought a surge of rage. *Father, help me not to give in to these feelings,* she prayed silently.

"Care for some tea?" Elyssa stood in the dining room doorway, proudly displaying a kettle and a handful of tea bags.

Jennifer caught her breath as she gazed on her friend's face. An ugly gash over Elyssa's left eye stood as a glaring testimony of Anton's savage brutality. The skin around the older woman's eye was swollen and beginning to turn black.

"Let me take care of your eye, first, Mom."

Elyssa shook her head. "That can wait, Jen. I've got my mouth set for a cup of tea. If only we had some biscuits or sandwiches to go with it."

"I have a package of crackers, instant soup, and some candy in my pack. Will they do?"

"Sounds fit for a king. Prepare the coffee table; we're going to have a tea party. I noticed some dishes in the cupboard. I'll be right back."

Brianna helped her mother remove the dust cover from the coffee table then pushed the magazines and books to one side. Jennifer opened her emergency pack, pulled out the crackers, candy, and soup mix, and set them on the table.

After instructing her toddler to stay on the couch, Jennifer tore off a piece of one of the dust covers. She opened the front door just a crack and gingerly reached outside to gather snow for a cold compress. The sharp wind whipped at her face. She quickly filled the cloth with the icy flakes then retreated inside.

When Elyssa returned with a tray of tea, cups, bowls and silverware, Jennifer took it from her and instructed her to sit down. "You can drink your tea while you hold this to your eye, Mom. Otherwise you'll look like you've been in a boxing match."

Her friend laughed, but complied with Jennifer's wishes. Once Elyssa had finished her tea, she set down her cup. "We'd better give Anton some tea, too. He's lost quite a bit of blood and we don't want him going into shock."

Jennifer picked up the gun and trained it on Anton. Elyssa fixed a cup of tea and walked across the room. She knelt beside him, helped him sit up, and held the cup to his lips. He took a long sip of the warm drink and promptly spit it into Elyssa's face. The older woman shrieked and fell back. Spirit snarled savagely and jumped between the older woman and Anton.

"Get away from him, Mom," she shouted. Elyssa once again moved out of Anton's reach.

Anton glared at Jennifer, malice gleaming in his eyes. "Why don't you go ahead and shoot me, *mi cara*? I know you want to. There's something so satisfying about taking someone else's life. I felt such a rush when I blew up that plane—imagining the panic and terror the people felt."

Jennifer hid her disgust. "Why did you have Lou Strombolli blow up my apartment?"

Anton laughed. "So he tracked the jewels to your place, did he? He's smarter than I thought. It's unfortunate you weren't home at the time. But don't worry, he'll kill you when he catches up with—" His voice broke off and his eyes narrowed. "Wait a minute. How did you know about Lou?"

Jennifer shrugged. "Your friend did try to kill me, but he ran his car off a bridge and didn't survive the fall. The police tied him to you." She watched various emotions play across Anton's face and found a sense of satisfaction in his discomfiture. "By the way, I found the jewels and passports you hid in the bear and turned them over to the FBI."

Anton cursed then fell silent. He glared at Jennifer for a moment, and then a slow, evil smile crept across his face. "You know, of all the crimes I've committed, nothing has given me more pleasure than killing your husband. I kept his wallet and gun as souvenirs. I should have made sure of his partner, then, too, but I figured he'd be dead before help arrived. Oh, well, live and learn."

Waves of nausea struck her. "You don't have an ounce of conscience, do you?"

Anton jeered. "A cop's life isn't worth a plug nickel, and as for females, they only have limited uses, if you know what I mean. Did you think I wanted to marry you because I loved you? I merely planned to claim the spoils from that filthy pig's death, and then use you until I tired of you."

Jennifer felt her trembling fingers begin to squeeze the trigger. *The lout deserves to die. He's nothing more than a deranged animal. The world would be better off without him.*

"What's wrong, Jen?" he taunted. "Oh, I see, the gun is a bit much for you, isn't it? Too bad. I'll manage to get away again, you know. You'll live your life in constant fear, wondering when I'll be back to finish what I started."

"I won't live my life in fear." *No one would blame me for killing him.* Jennifer glanced first at her daughter, and then at her friend.

Elyssa shook her head in warning. "Don't do it, Jen. Don't become like him."

Jennifer stared at Anton and battled the conflicting emotions raging inside her. Tender memories of her husband played in her mind like a favorite movie. Anton heartlessly shot Danny and watched him die. Why should he continue to live?

The moments crawled by. Jennifer could hear Anton's voice in the background, but she shut out his words. He'd get the death sentence anyway for all of the murders he committed. Maybe she should save everyone the time and effort of convicting him. Anton egged her on.

A recent memory verse sounded in her heart. "'Vengeance is mine,' says the Lord.'" Finally, Jennifer's senses took over. She wouldn't buy into Anton's game. instead, she took her finger off the trigger and lowered the gun. "You really want me to kill you. But you're not worth the scars. I'd much rather see you go to trial and have the entire world know that *mere females* and a dog brought you down."

Anton began a barrage of cursing. Jennifer twisted her face in disgust. "It's too bad we have to listen to garbage."

Elyssa stood up. "Oh, I can fix that." She tore off more pieces off the dust cover and stuffed it in Anton's mouth, securing it in place with another strip of cloth. "Shame on you for talking like that in front of ladies."

Chapter 23

When Elyssa had settled herself on the couch, Jennifer went to the front door to fill another piece of cloth with snow. She flipped on the porch light and peered out into the growing darkness. Huge snowflakes pelted her face and covered her hair. She quickly filled the second ice pack and shut the door. "The snow's coming down pretty hard. We must have gotten a foot or more already." She looked at her watch. "Almost five-thirty. I sure hope the storm ends soon."

The night passed slowly. The howling wind shook the windows and pulled at the shutters. Jennifer shuddered at the sounds, but felt surprisingly calm. Spirit continued to guard the prisoner. Brianna sat on her mother's lap and clung to her.

Once Elyssa finished eating, she relayed how Anton had kidnapped them at gunpoint that afternoon. "Apparently, he saw us go into the farmhouse for lunch. He knocked at the front door and when Maggie answered it, he pulled out his gun and ordered her back inside."

The battered woman took a sip of tea. "When Brianna spotted him, she screamed. I thought for sure he'd just shoot us all right then and there. Franz and Spirit must have heard Brianna because they both came running in. Anton held his gun to Maggie's head and made Franz tie Spirit to the porch."

Jennifer contemplated her friend's words. "Spirit must have chewed through the rope. What happened to Franz and Maggie and how did you get the gash on your head?"

Tears filled Elyssa's eyes. "I don't know. When Anton grabbed for Brianna, she bit him and he struck her. I tried to stop him, but he hit me with the gun. When I awoke, my hands were tied and I was in what I figured was the trunk of his car. Brianna lay crying next to me and I prayed desperately for her protection. We had stopped for a little while. I could feel the vibration of the engine, but we weren't going anywhere. A few minutes later, the car started moving. Next thing I knew, he brought us in here."

"That stop must been when he called me, though I don't know how he got our phone number." Jennifer thought about their missing friends. "I sure hope Maggie and Franz are all right. I went by the farm looking for you, but I didn't see or hear anyone. Spirit must have gotten loose before then."

Elyssa wiped her eyes. "How did you know to come here?"

Jennifer related what she heard in the restaurant and the agent's phone call. "When Anton called, I knew he had to be the man Glenn's friend spoke about." She hugged Brianna again and feasted her eyes on Elyssa. They were so precious to her. "Thank the Lord, Spirit and I got here when we did. I pray that Franz and Maggie are all right."

At the height of the blizzard, Jennifer felt panic rising. Elyssa noticed her discomfort and suggested they sing, to keep her mind off of the storm. Jennifer agreed and the women joined together in worship songs. Brianna snuggled close and drifted off to sleep.

Around ten, the storm tapered off, losing much of its punch. Elyssa checked outside the door. "The wind's off, but the snow's still pretty thick," she reported when she came back to the couch.

About midnight, Elyssa fell asleep. Jennifer tried to keep her awake to no avail. *Father, please send help,* she prayed as she watched her friend's sleeping form. Spirit helped continue their constant vigil throughout the night. Jennifer felt exhausted, but she dared not sleep. As long as Anton was anywhere near, she'd be on guard.

Just before three, Jennifer thought she heard a noise in the kitchen. She gently placed Brianna on the love seat, grabbed the gun, and carefully crept through the dining room.

Hiding next to the kitchen entryway, Jennifer scanned the kitchen. In the dim light she could see the large cupboard slowly begin to move. Moments later, two large figures emerged. One held a black satchel in his left hand; the other held a revolver.

Jennifer aimed the gun with both hands. "Hold it right there," she ordered. "Don't move."

The two figures froze. "Jen, it's Nathan," the one with the satchel said. "Agent Bolton's with me."

She lowered the gun, relieved. "I thought you'd never get here. Where's Terry?"

"Never mind that," Agent Bolton interrupted. "Is Centauri armed and is he alone?" Snowflakes melted on his black ski cap and gray parka. His sharp brown eyes looked past her and scanned the dining room and doorway beyond.

Jennifer noticed the gun in his hand. "Anton's disarmed and tied up on the living room floor." The agent didn't seem convinced, so she continued. "He got into a fight with Nathan's dog, Spirit, and lost. When we got them separated, Elyssa trussed Anton up like a Thanksgiving turkey."

Nathan swung the cupboard back in place. He and the agent walked over to the doorway where Jennifer stood. Lines of concern formed around his somber blue eyes. "Where are Elyssa and Brianna?"

"Asleep in the living room. Nathan, you've got to take a look at Elyssa. Anton clobbered her up side the head with his gun earlier, and she's got a huge gash. I tried to keep her awake, but it didn't work."

Nathan set down his medical bag so he could remove his gloves and gray-green parka. "What about Brianna, is she badly hurt?" He picked up the bag again.

Jennifer shook her head. "She's a bit worse for wear, but safe and sound. She has a bruise on her face where Anton hit her, but I didn't see any other injuries."

"Praise God you're all right. I've never prayed harder in my life than I have since you called."

"Save the reunion for later, folks," Agent Bolton interjected. "Is that Centauri's gun?"

Jennifer hadn't noticed that her right hand still tightly gripped the revolver. She stared at it; slowly realizing her ordeal was over.

It seemed as if ages had passed since Anton's call. She had faced and conquered a world of fears, and now it was nearly over. Jennifer willed her hand to relax. She surrendered the weapon. "Yes, this is the gun he used."

Agent Bolton took it from her, clicked on the safety, and pocketed the gun. "I'd better check on Centauri to make sure he's not going anywhere." He brushed past her, strode through into the living room, and returned almost immediately. "Can you call the dog off? He won't let me near the prisoner."

"Sorry, I forgot." Jennifer led them into the living room to where Anton lay. She didn't know if she'd ever get used to calling the criminal by his real name. Maybe it didn't really matter. "Easy," Jennifer told

Spirit. When the dog trotted over to her, she thoroughly fussed over him. "What a good boy, you are. Good job."

Nathan set down his bag and joined her in petting the fine animal. Agent Bolton took off his gloves and checked the prisoner's pulse.

Jennifer showed Nathan where the bullet had grazed Spirit's shoulder. "Anton shot at him, but he doesn't seem much hurt."

Agent Bolton rejoined them. "Centauri's pulse is on the weak side," he told Nathan. "Could I get you to look him over?"

"Sure." Nathan picked up his bag. Spirit returned to his post, as if to ensure Anton would not strike out again. Jennifer moved to the love seat, out of the men's way.

Brianna lay curled up on one cushion. Jennifer sat next to her and tenderly stroked the child's sleeping form. Another prayer of gratitude slipped from her heart.

Jennifer watched Nathan and Agent Bolton and reflected on the events that followed Anton's phone call. It amazed her that she hadn't fallen apart. A supernatural strength must have sustained her. *There's no way I could have faced this alone, Father*, she prayed silently. *You know what a nervous wreck I become. That power had to come from You. You heard my cry and helped me. How can I ever thank you?*

Nathan finished examining Anton. "He's unconscious and has lost quite a bit of blood," he told the agent. "He'll definitely need stitching, but his blood pressure appears stable." He put his gear back in the bag. "The ladies did a fine job of patching him up. We'll leave these bandages as they are until we get him to the hospital. It'll be a while before we can move him. The snowplows will have to shovel off the roads before the state police and the ambulance can get through."

The agent nodded. "How long will that be, do you think?"

Nathan unfolded his frame from its crouched position. "Give them another couple of hours or so. We've got about three feet of snow out there." Nathan gathered his supplies and started to cross the room.

Jennifer motioned to him to come talk to her. "How'd you get here?"

Nathan sat on the arm of the love seat. "Snowmobiles." His voice was low so as to not awaken Brianna.

"So, where's Terry? Outside in the barn?"

He cleared his throat. "He's at the hospital with Queenie and Uncle Franz, right now."

A sense of dread fell over Jennifer. "Where did you find them? Are they all right? Elyssa didn't know what happened to them after Anton knocked her out." How big a price had they all paid for her mistakes?

"From what we've pieced together, Anton pistol-whipped Queenie, and then shot Uncle Franz when he tried to defend her. Anton locked them into one of the sheds, apparently hoping they'd die from either their wounds or exposure." Nathan heaved a sigh. "He almost had his wish. Uncle Franz bled quite a bit. Aunt Maggie regained consciousness and was able to stop Franz's bleeding. However, the combination of blood loss and hypothermia...well, we need a miracle."

Guilt exploded in Jennifer's stomach. Tears pricked her eyes. "I feel horrid. I assumed that since their car was gone, no one was home. If I had checked out the noise that I heard coming from the shed, Franz and Maggie would have gotten help much earlier."

Nathan placed his hand on her shoulder. "You can't punish yourself for that, Jen. You didn't know that my uncle took the car to be serviced. Anton is the criminal—not you."

Jennifer's lips quivered. "That won't comfort Maggie if Franz...." Her voice trailed off.

"She doesn't blame you at all. In fact, she's worried you won't forgive her for not protecting Brianna better."

Jennifer gasped. "She nearly died for Brianna, and now she may lose Franz." A tear stole down her cheek. "There's nothing to forgive. I can never repay her, Franz, and Elyssa for their sacrifices."

Nathan made her look at him. "Don't you get it, Jen? They're not interested in payment. They just want the opportunity to continue loving you and Brianna. Just like I do."

When she opened her mouth to speak, he placed his finger on her lips. "Not yet. We'll have a heart-to-heart talk about it later. Right now, I need to check you three for injuries. Did he hurt you?"

Jennifer shook her head. "No, I'm fine. It's Brianna and Elyssa I'm worried about."

Nathan glanced down at Brianna's sleeping form. "It would be best to let her sleep as long as we can. She's been through quite an ordeal and her body needs the rest. As for Elyssa, I'd better start with her."

He moved to the couch. "Wake up, Elyssa," Nathan coaxed, kneeling beside her. "I need to examine you." He opened his medical kit.

Elyssa stirred and struggled to a sitting position. "Nathan?" She immediately grabbed at her temples. "Oh, I have a splitting headache!"

"I bet you do," Nathan said. "I have to check your eyes with this light. It may be uncomfortable for you, but it's absolutely necessary, so don't deck me."

Elyssa lay back and submitted to Nathan's examination.

Jennifer's mind whirled as she watched Nathan work. Had he really said what she heard? *Father, are you giving me another chance?*

Brianna whimpered in her sleep. Jennifer stroked her daughter's face and spoke softly. "You're all right, baby. Mommy's here and Anton can't hurt you anymore."

The child opened her eyes, flung her arms around her mother's neck and hung on with all her might. Jennifer rocked Brianna until her daughter relaxed.

Agent Bolton stepped over to the love seat. "I'm going to need a statement from you and the other woman," he told Jennifer. "Since we'll be here for a while, yet, why don't we get started? I'll get a chair for myself from the dining room and we'll begin."

When he returned, the agent set down the wooden chair, shed his parka, and pulled his ski cap off of his short, sandy brown hair. He sat down, took out his notepad and pen, and then began questioning Jennifer.

Over the course of the next couple of hours, both women gave their statements about this latest encounter with Demas Centauri. When both women had finished, Agent Bolton shook his head. "You don't know how lucky you are to be alive. Centauri's victims rarely survive direct attacks."

Jennifer shook her head. "Luck has nothing to do with it. We have a great and mighty God who watches over us. With Him, we can face anything that comes our way."

Chapter 24

Several days later, Jennifer stood on the back walkway of Franz and Maggie's house, resting against the handle of a snow shovel. Her arms and back ached from the hours spent tunneling through waist deep snow. Toward the barn, the steady roar of the snow blower marked yet another day of battle against the elements.

She studied the leaden sky hoping for a sign of reprieve. "Katie, am I imagining things, or are the snowflakes starting to taper off?"

Katie Pellitier dumped a shovel load of snow toward the middle of the yard. "Don't count on it. Every time I think the weather is going to break, we get several more feet of snow."

Nathan's cousin stretched her neck from side to side as if to relieve some of the tension she felt. "This is the worst winter I can ever remember. It's a good thing that Grandma and Elyssa got home when they did. Otherwise, Lord knows where they'd be stranded."

"Just how many blizzards can we get in one week?" Jennifer shook her head. "Never mind, forget I asked that. I don't want to know. I'm glad Maggie insisted we all bunk in together here. I'm not sure we could have survived at our house with the furnace out. Maybe Rob and Nathan will agree to install a few wood stoves after this."

Katie loosened her scarf, exposing a long black braid. "I know Grandma sure appreciates the company—even that crazy rabbit. Watching after Brianna and Bunny, and working on Christmas presents keeps her mind from dwelling constantly on Grandpa Franz."

The snow blower stopped. Jennifer watched Rob struggle with the machine. "Miss Brianna may be the reason we're still getting buried. Last night she asked God to keep the snow coming so we could have a Christmas like Maggie had when she was a little girl."

Katie's face brightened. "I have to admit, despite the horrendous inconvenience, an old-fashioned Christmas does sound a bit romantic. We have no guarantee that we'll be able to do any Christmas shopping, so, what say we try our hand at some homemade gifts of our own?"

Jennifer pushed a swath of auburn hair out of her eyes. "The only thing I know how to do is paint, and I'm afraid I only have enough supplies to finish the canvas I'm making for my father. Do you think you could teach me how to make some other type of crafts?"

"Sure." Katie leaned on the snow shovel. "If we're not too exhausted after the chores, I'll look up some simple projects in one of Aunt Maggie's craft books to get you started on."

Jennifer shook the snow off the hood of her parka. "If this snow keeps up, we don't stand a chance. No sooner than we get all the pathway cleared, then we're at it again."

Katie chuckled. "I'll take a blizzard over an ice storm any day. Nothing's worse than sheets of hard, slick ice."

Elyssa called to them from the porch stairs. "Why don't you three take a break for a bit? Nathan has his hands full with enough heart attack victims as it is, we don't need you added to the list."

A small bandage now replaced the large gauze wrap that had decorated her head for the past week. She gingerly balanced a tray of refreshments as she made her way down the steps. "I've got hot chocolate and cinnamon rolls."

"You won't need to ask me twice." Jennifer caught her brother's attention and waved him over. She stuffed her gloves into her pocket, accepted a mug of hot cocoa, and inhaled the heady aroma. "I've never seen so much snow at one time before." She reached for a roll. "Is there any hope for a respite? Perhaps, even a glimpse of sunlight?"

Elyssa shifted the tray in her hands. "The weather forecaster said this should clear off by early afternoon. Maybe the snowplows can finally get the roads open so we can head into town to choose our Christmas tree. Brianna's expecting a very special present and insists we must have just the right tree for this occasion."

"Not to worry," Katie laughed. "Nathan promised that as soon as the weather broke we'd take the snowmobiles and sled out to the back forty and harvest our own. Doesn't that sound adventurous?"

Elyssa shuddered. "Thanks, but I've had enough adventure to last me for quite a while. I'd be better off here baking Christmas cookies." She raised her voice. "Want to warm up a bit, Rob?"

Rob removed his hat and coat. "I'm right toasty, now, but I could never turn down hot chocolate." He took a sip. "Hey, where are the marshmallows?"

"Your niece ate the last of them," Elyssa explained. "Maybe you could take one of the snowmobiles into town later and get a bag of them as well as some other groceries."

Rob shook his head. "We'll be lucky if the store has anything at all. Deliveries haven't been made since last Monday. But, if the storm lets up, I'll see what I can find."

Elyssa smiled. "I'll make my wish list." She set the tray on the bottom step and headed back into the house.

Rob downed a cinnamon roll, followed by a few swigs of hot chocolate. "Jen, are you positive you don't mind spending Christmas here at the farm this year? It just seems like the best thing right now."

"I don't mind at all." Jennifer assured him. "After everything we've all been through, I think sharing the Christmas celebration is more than fitting."

Her brother looked relieved. "Thanks. I was worried about trying to shop for Christmas stuff at this late date."

"Gee, Rob, is that the least of your worries?" Katie pelted him with a few snowballs.

Rob looked a little uncomfortable. "What I meant was—"

Katie shook her finger. "Give it up, sweetie, before you stick the other foot in your mouth."

Jennifer rolled her eyes and joined in Katie's ringing laughter.

Her brother sipped at his hot chocolate for a few minutes. Finally, he spoke. "I think I'd better clear the barn doors."

"Praise God!" Katie kissed him on the cheek. "Those poor cows will be ecstatic to see the old milk pails." She and Rob finished off their drinks and slogged toward the barn.

Jennifer put her mug back on the tray and started shoveling again. Her thoughts wandered to Nathan. She had scarcely seen him since Elyssa and Brianna came home from the hospital. And even then, there had been no time for the doctor's promised talk. Would she ever get the chance to tell him how she felt?

Out of the corner of her eye, she glimpse a snowmobile and what seemed to be a miniature sleigh, glide to a stop just outside the front gate. She turned and watched as Nathan took off his helmet and climbed from his seat. Her heart danced at the sight of his face. He stooped to talk to a heavily bundled person seated in the sleigh.

I wonder who he's got with him? Jennifer trudged over to the fence. "Sorry we haven't finished clearing the walkway yet. I'll have this gate free in a jiffy."

"Let me help," Nathan insisted. He reached across the fence for the shovel. Once he cleared the front side, he swung the gate toward himself, and finished shoveling the remaining snow in his way.

Within fifteen minutes, Nathan helped his sled passenger down the walkway. As they neared the gate, Jennifer found herself face-to-face with a pale and fragile friend.

Jennifer's mouth fell open. "Franz! We didn't expect you for days." She gave him a warm hug. "I hope you didn't feel we had abandoned you. There was no way for us to get in to visit."

Franz did not return her hug and wouldn't even look up at her. Instead, his shoulders sagged and he kept his head down. He seemed to wear the air of a totally defeated man.

The awkward silence jabbed at Jennifer. Nausea swept over her. *He probably hates me for what happened. Father, God, what do I do now?*

Nathan seemed to read her thoughts. "Uncle Franz, it's best to clear the air now, before this gets any worse."

Franz looked at Jennifer with tortured gray eyes. "The boy's right." The farmer's voice shook. "I've got to get this off my chest. Nathan said you don't hold Maggie and me at fault for what happened. Well, I do."

Jennifer tried to interrupt him, but he silenced her.

"Let me say my piece while I've got the nerve." He took a deep breath. "When I saw that fella with the gun, I got scared and lost my head. With Elyssa laying on the floor and Brianna screaming, I didn't know what to do. I thought if I told him how to reach you, he'd leave us alone and I'd have enough time to call for help."

Franz's gaze dropped. "I did what he said. I tied Spirit outside. The next thing I knew, he herded Maggie and me into the shed, hit my wife with the gun, and then shot me. Now you know the truth. I'm nothing but a coward." He covered his face with his hands.

Jennifer put her arms around the old man's neck and kissed him on his grizzled cheek. "Franz Michaud, you are no coward. You are a warm-hearted, dear friend, whom I love dearly. Anton's the coward. He chose to kill and steal rather than face life with courage and honesty. He has a lot to answer for. I just hope he gets his life right with God before it is too late."

Nathan cleared his throat. "Jen, the FBI shot and killed him last night when he tried to escape from the hospital."

Jennifer expected to feel elated with the news that the man she had known as Anton Carducci was dead, yet the thought sobered her. He had entered eternity as an enemy of God. "It was his choice," she said softly. "I pray we will put all of his hatred behind us, now, and let God begin to heal our hearts."

"Amen, to that," Nathan agreed. "Now that we've got things in proper perspective, it's time for my patient to get some rest."

Nathan and Jennifer walked on either side of Franz and guided him into the kitchen where pure bedlam broke out. It took several minutes before the old man safely passed through the gauntlet of loved ones and settled into his favorite chair.

Maggie fussed over her husband until Nathan warned her she was in danger of spoiling him. "He's doing fine, Queenie. He needs to take it easy for a while, though. No farm chores for a few weeks or so."

Franz waved Nathan away. "Bah, I'll do my chores when I feel like it." But, when Maggie started scolding him, he added, "Right now, though, I think I'll have a bit of a vacation."

Early Christmas Eve morning, Jennifer sat in the Michaud's living room and finished working on her father's Christmas present. She carefully picked up the painting and inspected it for flaws.

Fairy-like snowflakes seemed to blow about the canvas. A small, red-haired girl, dressed in a white flannel nightgown and pink robe, danced barefooted in a ring of light on the newly fallen snow. Just on the fringe of the light, a dark-haired man laughed heartily.

Jennifer sighed and slid the painting into its frame. Would her father like it? Her hands shook slightly as she wrapped the gift in Christmas paper. In just a few hours he'd step back into her life. What should she say? How could she make up for the time lost between them? What would he think of her? Would he be disappointed in how she turned out?

A light wind tapped at the window as the gray dawn pushed its way through the winter darkness. She looked out as the headlights from the snowmobiles illuminated the front window.

Katie knocked on the door. "Come, on, Jen, we're going to be late. We don't want anyone else to get our tree." She and Brianna resembled well-padded bears—heavily cloaked in layers of sweaters, coats, hats, mittens and scarves. Both wore high-topped mukluks. "Rob and Nathan are waiting for us."

A horn sounded outside. Jennifer quickly put on her own mukluks, bundled up, and stepped into the bitter cold. "Oooh, Elyssa has better sense than any of us. She's sleeping in. Couldn't we wait until it warmed up a bit before heading out?" She climbed onto the sled behind Nathan's idling snowmobile.

Nathan shook his head. "No way. I've had this tree staked out for a year and I mean to get it. Besides, Maggie and Elyssa are expecting us for breakfast in little more than two hours." He lashed two backpacks and a long stick to the long, flat, open sled hooked to Rob and Katie's snowmobile while the couple strapped on their helmets.

Jennifer wrapped warm scarves about Brianna's head until only the youngster's eyes showed. "Mommy's going to wear hers like that, too," she told her daughter. Her breath hung in front of her. "We'll stay warmer this way." She swathed her own head in thick scarves, tucked Brianna tightly between her legs, and then held on to the wooden rails surrounding the top of the sled.

Nathan mounted his seat, buckled on his helmet, released the brake, and set the snowmobile into motion. The sled jerked slightly at first, and then settled into a smooth, yet breezy ride. The two snowmobiles caravanned into the woods for a few miles with Nathan in the lead. Within half-an-hour the group parked the snowmobiles on the edge of a small clearing near a line of evergreens.

"Stay here," Nathan told Jennifer and Brianna. His voice sounded strangely loud and crisp in the frigid morning air. He stepped off of his snowmobile and immediately plunged into powder just below the fur tops of his mukluks. With some effort, he waded through the snow to Rob's snowmobile. "We'll have to go on foot from here," Nathan told them. "I'll take the lead, but wait until I come back with the others."

Nathan unhooked the open sled from the other snowmobile and unstrapped the backpacks and stick. Using the stick to gauge the depth of the snow, he pulled the sled over to Jennifer and her daughter.

"Brianna, you'll need to ride on the sled until we know just how deep the snow is," Nathan told the child. "You don't want to get in over your head."

The toddler flashed him her biggest smile. "Okay, Nafan." She allowed him to transfer her to the other sled. Just as Nathan set her down, Brianna and he had a brief, whispered conference.

"What was that all about?" Jennifer took his hand and stepped into the deep snow.

Nathan shook his head. "Sorry. This is the time of year for secrets. No questions allowed. You'll find out soon enough. Now, I need you to follow directly in my footsteps."

The group found their first few steps difficult as they headed for the tree line. They walked in single file, allowing Nathan to plot the easiest course for them to follow. Once they reached the cover of the tree branches, the snow depth lessened. A small, half-frozen stream trickled across their path. Snow crunched beneath their boots as they dodged low tree branches until Nathan stopped before a relatively small, well-formed spruce tree in a sparse area of the forest.

"Well, what do you think?" Nathan asked Brianna as he lifted her from the sled and carried her to inspect the tree. "Does this fit your expectations, milady?" He set her down on the ground at the tree base.

Brianna's eyes seemed to grow as large as saucers. She caressed the branch nearest her then craned her neck to see the very top of the tree. "Ohhh! Me wants it! Me wants it," she squealed from beneath her layers of thick scarves.

"Then, we'll take it home." Nathan opened the backpacks and pulled out two axes, several lengths of rope, three thermoses of hot chocolate, and some metal mugs. "You ladies make yourselves comfortable while Rob and I fell the tree."

Jennifer sat on the sled and gazed at the spruce. It towered at least three feet higher than Nathan's head. She tried to recall the height of the farmhouse living room. "Are you sure that one's not too tall?"

The men waved her off and started chopping at the base of the trunk with their axes.

Jennifer and Brianna loosened the scarves from their faces while Katie poured the hot chocolate into cups.

"Give it up, Jen," Nathan's cousin advised. "They'll find out on their own when they get it home."

Within the hour, the group returned to the snowmobiles with the Christmas tree safely stowed on the long wooden sled. Brianna rode on Nathan's shoulders as he led the way, carefully stepping in his previous footprints. Rob pulled the sled while Jennifer and Katie walked behind.

When Jennifer and her companions arrived at the farm, the fragrance of breakfast met them at the door. Jennifer inhaled deeply, savoring the smell of freshly brewed coffee, browning home fries, and sizzling hunks of ham and sausages on the large wood-burning stove. Her mouth watered from hunger.

"There's nothing like a hearty breakfast to warm you up after a tramp in the woods." Maggie beamed as she grabbed a seasoned iron skillet from a hook beside the stove. "We're having muffins, blueberry pancakes, and scrambled eggs, plus what you see here. I hope you're hungry." She rinsed the skillet and placed it on the stove. "So, did you find the tree that Nathan has been bragging about?"

Nathan wrapped his arms around his aunt and hugged her. "Not only found it, but brought it home with us, Queenie. If you will tell us where you want it, Rob and I will set it up when we've finished eating."

After breakfast, Franz, Elyssa and Brianna supervised the rearrangement of furniture in the living room as a special place was made for the Christmas tree. Maggie and Katie brought down huge boxes of ornaments and Christmas decorations and set them on the floor near the amber, old-fashioned country couch.

Soon everyone gathered in the kitchen to watch Rob and Nathan bring in the spruce. First, Nathan trimmed the end of the trunk with a handsaw. Then, while Katie held the door open, Nathan and Rob lifted the tree and walked up the porch steps.

As soon as the men reached the door they realized the lower branches had no intention of cooperating. "We have to tie it off tighter at the bottom." Rob pulled on the rope.

"It's too tall" Elyssa complained.

Maggie agreed. "You'll have to cut off those branches."

"Queenie, they're the best part of the tree," Nathan argued.

The women cast knowing glances at each other, but wisely said nothing more.

After several failed attempts to tame the large branches, Nathan and Rob carried the Christmas tree back down the steps. The whine of a chainsaw marked the men's defeat. One by one, the prized branches fell to the ground.

Katie pointed out the back window. "We can use some of those to make wreaths," she told Jennifer. "I'll show you how."

Once the bulky spruce stood fully dressed in its corner, the men muttered something about the tree topper barely brushing the ceiling.

"Well, it doesn't belong *in* the ceiling," Katie playfully teased Rob.

Nathan pulled Jennifer aside from the festivities. "Now it's time we had our talk."

She nodded, put on her parka, and followed him onto the covered back porch.

He fumbled with something in his coat pocket for a few moments, and then cleared his throat. "Jen, I realize that you were under a lot of stress the other day, so I won't hold you to what you told me on the phone if it was said merely in the emotion of the moment. But I have to know. Do I have any hope of winning your heart?"

Jennifer caught her breath. *He still wants me!* She reached out with trembling fingers and touched his face. "You already have."

Nathan smiled at her tenderly. "Jen, the Lord knows I'd erase the evil that has touched your life if I could. But, I can't. I can't even promise to shield you completely from all sorrow and hard times. I'm merely an imperfect man. But, I can promise you that I will love you with all my heart until my last breath. I will stand beside you through good times and bad, and I will protect, love, and care for Brianna as my own daughter."

Jennifer lifted her face to gaze into his blue eyes. Nathan's declaration filled her with a deep sense of peace. "I couldn't ask for any more than that, Nathan." She stroked his beard. "I love you so much."

His left arm encircled her waist, drawing her near. Nathan claimed her mouth in a passionate, but gentle kiss. When he finally released her, he took a small box from the pocket of his parka. "Jennifer Lynn Warner, will you marry me and trust God to give us the strength and wisdom to face the future together?"

Tears of joy trickled down Jennifer's cheeks as she whispered, "Yes." She hardly noticed the opening of the back door as Nathan slipped the diamond ring on her hand.

As they sealed their commitment with another kiss, Rob goaded them from the doorway. "Well, it's about time! I just hope we don't have to wait forever for the wedding."

Brianna squealed with delight. "Nafan's gonna be my daddy!" She ran and hugged Dr. Pellitier's legs.

Jennifer scooped her daughter into her arms. "I take it from your reaction, you like this idea?"

The child's eyes sparkled as she grinned. "Nafan's my Cwistmas pwesent." She leaned over and kissed him on the cheek.

Jennifer looked at Nathan. "What is she talking about?"

He smiled and wiggled his eyebrows. "You, milady, are the victim of a conspiracy. We've been plotting this for months. Do you mind?"

Her heart overflowed. God's blessings were so good. "I wouldn't have it any other way."

A car's horn sounded out front. Rob cleared his throat. "I hate to break this up, folks but Dad's here."

Light butterflies danced in Jennifer's stomach. She took a deep breath and whispered a prayer.

Nathan gently squeezed her shoulder. "Will you be all right?"

She smiled at him. "Yes. Come on. It's time Dad got to meet his granddaughter and future son-in-law."

CPSIA information can be obtained
at www.ICGtesting.com
Printed in the USA
LVHW041140311019
635934LV00002B/237